I hate Walt

03/08/15

For Edward,

I hate Walt

Be careful what
you pray for!
Blessings,

Vicki Andree

Vicki Andree

Phil 4:6

aventine press

Published by Aventine Press
55 East Emerson St.
Chula Vista CA 91911
www.aventinepress.com

ISBN: 978-1-59330- 875-9

Printed in the United States of America

Dedication

To Scott and Craig

My sons, who have triumphed over life's trials and emerged as victorious men of God. You make me proud!

Table of Contents

Chapter Twenty-One

Chapter Twenty Two

Chapter Twenty-Three

Chapter Twenty-Four

Chapter One

Monday, December 24, 2012
Denver, Colorado

Mary Lou Stots tapped her fingers on the handle of the heaped shopping cart. She resisted the urge to scream and stood on her toes to check. Sixth in line from checkout. When she had stepped into line half an hour ago, she had counted twelve in front of her. The sounds of "White Christmas" blared through the intercom for the tenth time, making it hard for her to think. She leaned on the cart and sucked in a long breath. Once again, she mentally checked the list in her head. *Slippers for Mom, another tie for Dad, that beautiful scarf for Eileen... Oh, why do I always put this off until Christmas Eve?*

Shoppers squeezed in front of her to get through the line to the rest of the store. *Oh, please. You people are all procrastinators, just like me. Let's see now... A scarf for Eileen, a pair of gloves for Aunt Louise, a Thighmaster for Larry. Ha! That's my best gag gift. He will hate it, but that's what he gets for teasing me all the time about being so skinny, not to mention all the "short" jokes. It's the least a girl could do for her big brother.*

For crying out loud, it's Christmas Eve. I'm so not ready. Uncle Peter gets the Broncos key chain. She checked the cart for wrapping paper and ribbons. The line shrank until she could see the cash register. Only four to go. *Did I get the tape? Oh, there it is, under the Legos and darts for Larry's kids. My sweet nephews will love those, along with the drum set.*

Come on, people—get this line moving, it's almost four o'clock. I have gifts to wrap!

Mary Lou felt the phone in her pocket vibrate. She dug it out to find a text message from the scrooge who owned the company she worked for. *Get to the office. Meeting at 5:00. DO NOT BE LATE!*

Her heart dropped to her toes. *What could possibly be wrong? What am I going to do? It's an hour to the office on a good day. I can't possibly check out and get through the parking lot in less than half an hour. I have to leave now. I have to leave my cart.*

She stepped out of line.

Later the same day
Denver, Colorado

Mary Lou Stots steamed across the International Enterprises lobby. "I swear, I am going to kill Walt Pederson."

The two security guards gave her a look.

"Oh." Mary Lou reddened. "Did I say that out loud?"

Both men studied security screens in front of them.

She kept her pace and commented over her shoulder, "I'm sure you know what I mean. Merry Christmas."

Neither man responded.

Joe Gillespie caught up to her. "That was some text I got. Do you know what's up?"

She quickened her pace. "You're my boss. How would I know?"

"I haven't a clue. It looks like I'll be late for our traditional Christmas Eve fried fish feast. Problem is… I'm the cook. "

"I left my shopping cart full of gifts to get here on time. I don't how I'm going to get my Christmas shopping done. And I have a date with Bobby tonight."

They entered the glass-enclosed conference room.

Walt Pederson, owner and CEO of International Enterprises, sat at the head of a long conference table. He glanced up from reading what looked like a legal document. Six other employees sat on one side of the table.

He growled. "It's about time you got here."

Mary Lou bit her lip to keep from lashing out at him.

Joe pulled out a chair.

Walt stared daggers through Mary Lou. "Well, sit down. We have work to do."

Joe leaned forward. "I got here as soon as I could. What's the emergency?"

Walt shouted, "We're short. If we don't get this contract in here by the end of the year, our numbers will be less than the previous year. I can't allow that to happen."

Joe raised his hand to stop the drama. "Walt, I'm here to do whatever it takes. Just tell me what you want me to do. The sales team is here. We can figure it out. Now, what's the problem?"

Walt stood. "It's not what. It's who. It's Feldman. Feldman in Zedlav didn't close on his rotten contract. If he had signed the contract, I'd be sitting pretty. But he didn't, and now I'm not going to make the projected numbers. I need that contract, and I need it by the end of the year. One of you is flying out of here to Zedlav, Alaska, tomorrow morning. I've set up a meeting with Feldman on Wednesday morning, and you're going to get that contract signed. Now, who is it going to be?"

Joe held up his pencil. "Hold on, Walt. This is an emergency, but you didn't need to call the entire sales team in." He waved the pencil toward Mary Lou and the agents on the other side of the table. "You can go. Walt and I will take care of this."

The six men across from them scrambled out of the room.

Mary Lou didn't move. *Zedlav is Jackson's account. Jackson is in Florida with his parents for Christmas.* "I'm not leaving."

Walt shouted at her, "Get out of here, girlie! Your boss and I have arrangements to make."

Mary Lou felt heat rise from somewhere deep inside. She struggled to speak in a calming voice. "I am your top salesperson. I can handle it. Mr. Pederson, you do know it's Christmas Eve?"

Walt motioned to the door with his thumb. "Christmas doesn't pay your check, girlie."

She looked at Joe. "You have a family. Your wife and kids need you to be there on Christmas Day. I think it would be better if I go. I'm single, and my family will understand. But your kids..."

Joe smiled. "That's very generous of you, but I can't let you do it. I don't send my employees to Alaska on Christmas Day—"

Walt jumped in. "You two work it out. I don't care who goes. Just get that contract signed." With that, Walt Pederson turned on his heel and left.

Silence draped the room.

Mary Lou brushed a strand of blonde hair from her eyes. "If he calls me 'girlie' one more time...." She turned to Joe. "Please let me go. I've never been to Alaska in December. I'm sure Jackson won't mind, since he's in Florida."

Joe started to smile, and then they both broke out in laughter.

He wiped a tear from his eye. "Mary Lou, this is a very kind thing to do for me and my family."

Mary Lou shrugged. "Just so you know I'm not doing it for Walt Pederson."

She left the conference room and made her way down the hall to her office. She sighed. *It's six o'clock. I have all my Christmas shopping to do. My feet are killing me. I need to get gifts, get them wrapped and delivered. I need to let my parents know I won't be here for Mom's Christmas dinner. Remind me again why I wanted to get into the oil business?*

What do you wear to the office in Zedlav? Wait until I tell Eileen. Perhaps she can explain to our parents. I don't have an hour to listen to Mom tonight.

And Bobby asked me out tonight. I think he just might be ready to propose. We've only been dating for a few months, but I'm pretty sure I could marry him. He's the best-looking cop on the force. I'm such a sucker for a uniform. Her heart skipped a beat. *Now I have to break our date. Ugh! I hate you, Walt Pederson.*

I'm pretty sure Walt's trying to kill me. I'll probably freeze to death in Alaska in December.

Tuesday, December 25
Denver International Airport

Mary Lou boarded Alaska Airlines for her eight forty-five a.m. flight—which would take eleven hours, including layovers. The plane was as crowded as expected. She found her seat and struggled to reach the overhead bin. She was a few inches too short to reach. Finally, the man behind her took her bag and placed it in the bin for her.

She thanked him and took her aisle seat next to a young man returning to Zedlav to see his parents for Christmas. He said a few words and opened his book. Obviously he didn't want to talk.

She opened her laptop and looked through the contract for the sale of heavy equipment to the corporation in Zedlav. Heavy construction trucks, loaders, and diggers, adding up to more than a hundred million dollars, had been contracted. All she needed was the signed document.

The Alaska Airlines flight left on time. She yawned and put away her laptop. *At least I can sleep all the way to Seattle. Let's see…* She rechecked her itinerary. *I get into Seattle at a quarter to eleven, then have a two-hour layover there and in Anchorage before I finally get into Zedlav at seven fifty p.m., my time. At least I should get a good night's sleep when I get there.*

This is so Walt. Here I am on Christmas, flying to the most remote place on earth.

The flight to Seattle took forever. Instead of sleeping, she found herself rehearsing her pitch and her plea to get the contract signed immediately. *I just want to get home as soon as possible.*

The meeting starts at nine o'clock. With any luck at all, I could make my presentation and get the signature by lunch. After all, they already have the quotes and estimates. It's not like I'm going in cold. They fully expect to sign that contract tomorrow.

After two layovers and the switch to a smaller aircraft, her plane finally landed. She walked out of the terminal to board the freezing-cold hotel shuttle. *I thought this was the land of the midnight sun. It's pitch black out there.* She peered out the shuttle's frosted windows and hugged her purse to her chest. *It's so cold.*

Half an hour later, she checked into the Moose Run Hotel.

It was almost seven o'clock Alaska time, but it seemed like midnight. Traveling had drained her; three flights in one day were more than enough. She stopped at the hotel coffee shop to order hot chocolate and a bowl of clam chowder. The warm liquid chased the shivers away, but she kept her coat on.

Her mind raced from one corner to another. *I tell you, Walt Pederson hates me. He's trying to kill me.* She pictured Larry with his family, Eileen, and her parents enjoying a warm Christmas dinner in front of the fire back in Denver. She thought of Bobby being alone when they could have been together. *I hate Walt Pederson. Yet here I am trying to save his bacon for year-end numbers. Well, better me than Joe. I hope his wife and kids appreciate what I'm doing.*

She tilted the soup bowl to get the last spoonful of chowder. Then she wiped her mouth with the heavy cloth napkin. She gathered her purse and bag and took the stairs to her room.

The frigid room greeted her, and she immediately flopped on the bed. She was glad she'd remembered to pack her large heating pad. She quickly got ready for bed and got under the covers. Her body shivered on ice-cold sheets. *I am so glad I brought the heating pad.*

Mary Lou retrieved the heating pad from her suitcase. She searched the room for an outlet. She could unplug either the lamp or the clock. She was desperate to get some sleep, but she could not afford to oversleep. She pulled the plug for the lamp out of the socket. Then she struggled in the darkness to fit the plug from the heating pad. Her shoulder touched something, and she heard the lamp hit the floor.

She felt the plug go into the outlet. *I'll deal with the lamp in the morning. I can't do this now.* She fumbled with the switch on the heating pad and turned it on high. She slipped back into bed with the heating pad across her body.

Two hours later, she tripped over the lamp on her way to the bathroom. She fell, crushing the lampshade and hurting her knee. *That's going to bruise.* She rubbed the knee and then felt around the lamp for the light bulb. She whispered, "Thank Heaven the bulb didn't break," and placed the lamp back on the nightstand. *Will this night ever end?* She found the bathroom and felt her way along the wall for a light switch. Finally she felt the switch, and the white room lit up, blinding her at first. After she finished in the bathroom, she left the light on and cracked the door a little to let light into the bedroom.

Once she had stumbled back to bed and settled in, with the heating pad on her sore knee, she closed her eyes. It took a few minutes to get into a comfortable position. She took a deep breath and relaxed. Only then did she realize the thin shaft of light from the cracked bathroom door fell across her eyes. Not wanting to get back up into the cold room, she attempted to find another comfortable position. She fought the heating pad, the heavy blankets, and that bathroom light all night.

A shrill ring woke her the next morning, and she pulled herself toward the red flashing light on the nightstand and answered the phone. "Hullo?"

An automated voice returned, "This is your requested wake-up call. It is six o'clock."

Mary Lou dropped the receiver into its cradle. She groaned as the alarm went off.

Chapter Two

Wednesday, December 26
Zedlav, Alaska

"Mr. Feldman will see you now. Please follow me." The receptionist led Mary Lou down a short hall to an enormous office trimmed in deep brown wood. As the woman opened the door, an older man with gray hair and a friendly smile stood and motioned for Mary Lou to take a seat.

"You must be Mary Lou Stots from International Enterprises."

She sat in the leather chair across from his desk. "Yes, thank you for seeing me."

He smiled. "Can we get you something to drink? Coffee?"

Coffee sounded so good, but she had already had some with her breakfast that morning. She wanted to get on with the business at hand. "No, thank you for offering. Have you looked at the proposal we faxed to you?"

He sat. "Yes, of course. I told Walt I could fax the signed contract to him, but he insisted you come and formalize the deal in person."

"Walt is very thorough." She hoped her emotions weren't showing. *So Walt could have had the contract without me making this trip. This is just another of his grandiose schemes to try and impress someone. I hate that man.* She looked past Mr. Feldman, through the window behind him. It was solid black. The sun still had not made an appearance. *I could kill Walt for this.* She looked back at Mr. Feldman. "Would you like me to walk you through the proposal?"

Mr. Feldman smiled. "Between the legal staff and accounting, I believe we understand. But please, walk me through it, to make sure we haven't missed anything."

Mary Lou opened her file folder and pulled out the twenty pages of material. They began working through it and were almost finished before noon. Her heart began to beat a little faster. *I'm going to be on the next plane home.*

Mr. Feldman insisted they go to lunch and finish the meeting afterward. *He's the client. If he wants to go to lunch, fine. I am hungry.*

Mr. Feldman walked her to the company cafeteria, which was located in the building next to his office. The sun had finally risen.

Mary Lou ate a quick lunch while Mr. Feldman continued to talk about his company, his family, his grandkids, and living in Alaska. Mary Lou fought to be calm and respond politely. But she was thinking that the man had to be very lonely, pouring his heart out to a business contact.

After ninety minutes that seemed like hours, they walked back to the office and finished their work.

Mr. Feldman picked up the contract and looked her in the eye. "What's a nice woman like you doing, working for Walt Pederson?"

She was taken aback and felt her face redden. "Why, I guess I'm learning the business."

He smiled, "I think you're doing a great job. I believe you know more about the business than you realize. I'm impressed."

Her mouth went dry. "I—I'm flattered."

He smiled disarmingly. "Don't be. I'm being honest. I don't suppose you would entertain working here in Zedlav? I could use someone with your work ethic."

She swallowed. "My family is in Colorado."

Mr. Feldman shook his head slowly and ended their meeting by picking up his pen. "Let me sign this now." He made two quick, undecipherable swishes with the pen and handed the contracts to Mary Lou.

"Thank you, sir. It's been a pleasure."

He stood and walked her to the door. "Happy New Year."

She felt grateful that everything had gone well, and she thanked him again. Then she made her way back to the hotel. She wondered if Walt had put him up to asking her if she would move to Zedlav. *Walt would love that, me freezing all the time.*

She hurried up to her room and began throwing things into her bag. *I can't wait to get this contract to Walt. I can't wait to get home. I can't wait to see Bobby.* Less than ten minutes later, she dashed down the stairs to check out.

She stood at the counter, waiting for the manager. *Where is that man?* She tapped her fingers on the counter.

After a few minutes, the man who'd checked her in the day before appeared. "May I help you?"

She pushed the room key toward him. "I'd like to check out. Are there additional charges?"

"Are you sure you want to check out?"

She frowned. "Of course, I want to leave. My business is done here."

The man smiled. "Of course, you want to leave. But all flights have been cancelled today. There was an avalanche. The airport shuttle is buried under thirty feet of snow. Rescue crews are trying to retrieve the bodies. It will be a few days before they can clear the road."

Mary Lou stepped back from the counter. "I need a moment." She took a deep breath and rubbed her forehead. "I guess I am going to need my room." She turned around and dragged her bag up the stairs to the less-than-warm room that she had just left.

Once in her room again, she sat on the bed. *Oh, how I hate calling Walt, but the office is closed, and he has to get this contract.* She punched the number on her cell. *At least I have service here.*

Four rings later, Walt answered, "Mary Lou. What do you want? Did you get the contract? Why are you calling me on my cell?"

The hair on the back of her neck stiffened. She fought to keep defensiveness out of her voice. "The office is closed, and I called because I can't get back to deliver this signed contract to you. There's an avalanche, and the roads are closed. I'm stuck here, but I can fax you the contract. I wanted you to know that it will be at the office."

"When are you getting back?"

Mary Lou wrinkled her nose. *What? No, "Gee, thanks. Good job. You got the contract signed"?* "I don't know. It depends on how long it takes to clear the road. The hotel manager said it could take days."

"Days? You won't be in on Monday? I guess you could take a few days of vacation. It would finish out the year."

Vacation? I am going to kill this man! She kept her voice calm. "I am stuck here on company business. You sent me. This is not a vacation."

Walt cleared his throat. "I'll tell Joe to pick up the contract and process it. You can take the vacation business up with him." The call went dead.

He did not hang up on me! Walt, you are king of the jerks!

She fell back on the bed and looked at the ceiling. "God, what did I do to deserve this? Why are you punishing me?"

She stared at the ceiling for a few minutes. Silence enveloped her. Then she sighed deeply and sat up.

Mary Lou touched her sister's number on her cell phone.

Eileen's voice immediately calmed Mary Lou. "How exciting for you to be in Alaska. Everyone missed you yesterday. Mom and Dad said for you to take a lot of pictures. When will you be home?"

Mary Lou sighed. "It looks like it may be a while. I got everything done here and went to check out. That's when I found out about the avalanche. I could be here another few days. The sun is already going down. It is so cold here. Forget pictures. I'm just surviving."

Eileen laughed. "You are such a drama queen. It can't be that bad. 'Rejoice in the Lord always. I will say it again: Rejoice! Let your gentleness be evident to all. The Lord is near.' Philippians 4:4-5."

Mary Lou rolled her eyes. "I have to go. I have to find a fax machine so I can get this contract to the Denver office." *Fine. Drama queens don't have to talk to unsympathetic sisters.*

Thursday, December 27
Lakewood, Colorado

Beth Pederson started her day like any other day. She slept in, took her bath, came down to the kitchen, and fixed a cup of designer coffee. She added creamer and sugar, then took her seat at the kitchen table. She had been awake, pretending to sleep, when Walt left their bedroom. She heard him walk down the stairs and assumed that he had left. The offices were closed; he would have gone to the club.

She was used to him not saying good-bye. She took a minute to contently contemplate her day ahead.

She peered through her sliding glass doors to the patio. The edges of the covered patio retained a small amount of ice from the storm a few days before. The sky was a bright blue with bleached white clouds. It was going to be a nice day.

The phone rang, interrupting the peaceful moment.

She lifted the receiver.

The loud voice caused her to relax. "Hello, Beth. Is that you, Beth? Beth, it's Ralph. It's Uncle Ralph. Are you there? Can you hear me?"

Beth thought she heard a click on the line but raised her voice so her uncle could hear her. "Uncle Ralph, this is Beth. I can hear you."

"Beth, Beth—they've agreed to exhume the body, and soon we will finally know the truth!"

Beth thought she heard another click on the line. "Just a minute, Uncle Ralph." She put the phone down and headed towards the other phone. "Walt? Is that you, Walt?"

Walt met her in the foyer. "Well, who in blazes do you think it would be?" He went to the closet and pulled out his lined trench coat.

Beth took a step back. "I—I didn't know you were still here." She put her hands on her hips. "Were you listening in on my phone conversation?"

Walt ignored her and put his coat on.

She tilted her head. "Walt, were you listening to my phone conversation? How many times do I have to ask you?"

He pulled on his favorite hat. "Of course I wasn't listening to your phone conversation. Why would I care what you have to say to your old Uncle Ralph?"

Beth folded her arms and stood taller. "I knew it! Who said I was talking to Uncle Ralph?"

Walt turned and headed to the door.

She shouted after him, "Have you had breakfast?"

"I'll grab something at Starbucks." He slammed the door behind him.

She made her way back to the kitchen table and picked up the phone. "Uncle Ralph, tell me what you're so excited about."

"Well you know that doggone soap opera, *On the Horizon?* They finally made a move. I'll bet it's been two years we've been waiting to find out who killed Victor Oldham. You've been watching, haven't you?"

Beth wasn't about to admit that she only watched that program occasionally in order to keep up an intelligent conversation with her deceased father's brother, Uncle Ralph.

"Uncle Ralph, you know how long it takes for anything to happen on those soap operas. I'm just really glad that you keep me up to date. Now, the last time I saw it, the judge was going to make a final decision."

Uncle Ralph started coughing, recovered, and chuckled. "Well, it took the judge two weeks to figure out they needed to exhume that body. Old Victor's been in the ground two years. I wonder what they'll find out. I get so exasperated with these guys. It takes them so long to get to the point. Everyone else here in the home is just is as disgusted as I am. But all us old fogies are celebrating today."

Beth sipped her coffee. "They should celebrate. It's been a long wait."

"Sometimes the days are long in this place, and those soap operas seem to help. I know you must think I'm just an old man who doesn't have anything to do but watch soap operas. I want you to know that if I could get out of this bed by myself, I'd come over there and watch with you."

"Oh, I would love that! I need to get over there to see you."

"I'm not trying to put you on a guilt trip. I miss your dad. We spent a lot of time together."

Beth gulped. "I miss him, too. Funny you should mention him. It's been ten years today."

Uncle Ralph sniffed. "No, I didn't realize what day it is. Well, he's in a better place. How is your scoundrel of a husband doing these days? With the oil boom, he must be making the dough hand over fist. Even so, your dad sold ten times what Walt does. Of course, your father worked ten times harder than Walt does." He laughed.

Beth placed her cup in the saucer. "I refuse to listen to you talk that way about my husband."

"Hey, Beth, I call 'em like I see 'em. Always have; always will. I told your father the day I met Walt that he was a lazy gold digger." He sighed deeply. "I told your father what I thought, and he told me that you were in love and for me to keep my mouth shut."

Beth blinked away a tear and leaned back in her chair. "Father was a wise man. That was good advice. You should take it."

"You know I love you like a daughter. If I ever had one, I would have wanted her to be just like you. I don't know how you put up with all his garbage."

"I love you, too, Uncle Ralph. You've been wonderful to me and helped a lot since Dad passed."

"You know I always had a crush on your mother. I miss her, too."

Beth couldn't stifle her giggle. "Okay, let's not go there. I'm glad you called this morning. You have a good day."

"Now you need to keep watching *On the Horizon* and see what they find out. Promise me."

"I promise."

The same day
Zedlav, Alaska

Mary Lou stared at her cell phone. *Still no call from Bobby. Am I supposed to call him? What did he do for Christmas, and why didn't he call? Is he mad that I broke our date? What time is it?* She pressed her cell phone. Big numbers shouted 2:57 a.m. *That makes it five in Denver. Bobby is probably sleeping.*

Ugh! I've been here three days, and it's dark all the time. I can't spend another day in this room. I have to get out of here. She threw the covers off and sat up, then she snuggled back under the warm blankets. *It's too cold. I'm hungry. I'll just lay here until the restaurant opens at six. I'm so tired of being in this bed. I should have stayed up later, but there is nothing to do.*

She felt around the coffee table for the TV remote. *Success!* She pointed at the screen on the dresser across from her. Seconds later, the room lit up with an infomercial for NutriBullet, the new healthy way to eat. She watched as the pencil-thin, beautifully dressed young blonde stuffed bananas, cherries, and raw spinach into the mixing cup for a breakfast smoothie.

"I want eggs and bacon." The sound of her own voice startled her. Then she grinned at herself.

Alaskans do not eat smoothies. They can't. That would just not be human. They want warm food in the morning. Anyway, that's my take on this. Now, what did I do with that heating pad?

She switched the heating pad on high and curled around it.

The local news came on, and she realized that she had dozed off for a few hours. The young male news anchor announced that "With good luck, road crews may begin the huge job of removing the avalanche from Jackson Highway. This job is estimated to take at least a week. The avalanche is the largest ever to block the highway."

A week? Mary Lou covered her face with the pillow and screamed into it. "*Nooo!*"

She jumped out of the bed and ran into the bathroom to turn the water on in the shower. It took a few minutes before steam filled the room. After taking a hot shower and quickly getting dressed, she made her way down to a darkened restaurant.

The young hostess arrived in the hotel lobby. She shook snow off her down coat as she approached the entrance to the restaurant. "We'll be open in a few minutes. You can sit inside, if you like. I can get some coffee on right away."

"Coffee? Oh, that would be wonderful. Thank you." Mary Lou took a seat in the booth nearest the door. She held her head in her hands, supported by her elbows on the table. No one else was in sight. She rubbed her temples.

A young man walked in—the cook, she assumed. Several other people arrived and seemed to know where their assigned posts were for the job. The manager came with a large mug of coffee.

Mary Lou took the cup before the woman could set it on the table. "Oh, thank you. I need this."

"Have you had a chance to look at the menu?"

"I know what I want. Two eggs, over medium, hash browns, bacon, and… do you have cinnamon rolls? I am starving. It must be the weather."

The woman smiled. "I'll get that order in for you. Can I get you anything else right now?"

Mary Lou dumped sugar into her mug. She looked up and forced a smile. "I'm good. I need comfort food."

"Sure. I understand. I'm stranded, too. I'm just grateful that I work in a hotel restaurant. It could be much worse."

Mary Lou bristled at her cheerfulness. "Well, I want to go home, and I'm mad at God because He spoiled the holidays for me."

The woman grinned. "Mad at God, eh? That might be a bit extreme."

Mary Lou sipped her coffee. "He controls the weather, doesn't He? Given that fact, I think I have the right to be mad at Him right now." She leaned back in the booth and folded her arms.

The woman turned back toward the kitchen. "I'm not even going to go there."

Chapter Three

Friday, December 28
Denver, Colorado

Bobby Porter shouted to the dispatcher, "For crying out loud, Christmas is over!"

She replied, "You're too old to believe in Santa. It's not the real Santa who hijacked the car with a kid in it. There's an Amber Alert. The Red SUV is headed toward I-76, and you need to save that kid. Be aware that the Channel 9 News helicopter is already in the air."

"I see the copter." Bobby scanned the road below the copter to see the red SUV swerving through morning rush hour traffic. "I see the perp." He whispered a quick prayer: "Lord, help us save that kid."

The red SUV with Santa at the wheel roared past Bobby. Bobby took up the chase, hitting the sirens and lights as he accelerated to a speed in excess of ninety miles per hour. The SUV kept going.

Bobby reported, "He's weaving through traffic. Santa is not stopping for anyone. I'm at just over a hundred miles per hour, trying to keep up with him. Permission to pursue?"

"Back off and see if he slows down."

Disappointed, Bobby lifted his foot from the accelerator. He shook his head as he watched the SUV disappear into the traffic.

The dispatcher reported, "It's working. The copter reports that the perp is slowing down. We have pictures from the copter. He's out of the car. He's flagging down another car. Whoa—he just pulled the driver out and threw her on the ground. He's now in a—a 2008 silver BMW with Wyoming plates. Permission granted for full pursuit."

Bobby grinned and tromped on the accelerator. *Thank You, Lord. I pray that kid is okay. Help us stop this guy.*

He watched the BMW roar onto Interstate Highway 76. "I'm closing in on him."

"Back off a little. We've set up a roadblock at the next exit. Slow down to make the capture."

Bobby took his foot off the accelerator. "What's the word on the kid?"

"Just got a report that the four-year-old boy is fine. The father is here, and the mother is on her way. Officer Bailey is bringing him in."

Bobby saw flashing lights ahead of the BMW. "It's working. He's slowing—wait. Oh, no. He just crossed the median and is heading into oncoming traffic. Santa must be high."

The dispatch officer announced, "Here's Sergeant Wood."

Sergeant Wood's voice came over the speaker. "Will follow protocol and clear lanes. Continue pursuit."

Bobby Porter crossed the median, sirens and lights still blazing.

State Patrol cars had blocked entrances to the highway, and soon there was no other traffic, so Bobby floored the accelerator and caught up to the BMW. The BMW swerved through the ramp, hitting two patrol cars. Bobby followed him through the roadblock to a strip mall. The BMW hit the curb and crashed into McDonald's. Bobby pulled up behind him and jumped out of his car.

Patrons screamed and jumped and out of their seats, crowding toward the kitchen. Bobby pulled Santa out of the vehicle, pushed the man to the floor, straddled him, and pulled his arms back to cuff him.

A little girl pointed at the scene. "Mommy!" she screamed. "The policeman is hurting Santi Claus!"

Bobby pulled the perp to his feet and turned toward the little girl. "This isn't the real Santa." He shoved the man toward the patrol car.

The little girl's mother picked her up. "That's not the real Santa. He's a bad man pretending to be Santa. The real Santa is back at home at the North Pole."

The little girl's eyes widened as three more patrol cars approached the restaurant, sirens and lights blazing.

Bobby motioned to the officers. "I got this." He jerked his head toward the kitchen. "Those people need to be interviewed." He shoved the perp into the backseat.

Saturday, December 29
Arvada, Colorado

After picking up two newspapers from the porch, Eileen Stots used the key to open the front door of Mary Lou's home. She dropped the papers on the couch and turned on the kitchen lights. She peeked into the master bedroom. *Mary Lou obviously packed in a rush.* Clothes were strewn about the room, and the bed lay unmade.

Eileen made the bed and started hanging up blouses and pants that had been rejected for the trip. She hummed a Christmas carol as she worked. *Poor Mary Lou. I sure hope you get home soon.* After tidying up the house and watering the hanging spider plant, she sat on the couch and called Mary Lou's cell.

"Hullo." Mary Lou sounded drained.

"Hey, girl. I'm over here cleaning your house—after all, cleanliness is next to godliness. I thought I'd better check it out, since you didn't get to come home when you expected."

Mary Lou groaned.

Eileen put her feet up on Mary Lou's beat-up coffee table. "Hey, it's going to be all right. Do you have any news about when you can leave?"

"Nothing. I may be here until spring. But I am so glad you called. It's good to hear a familiar voice. Bobby hasn't even called."

"Bobby's been busy. He's the local hero, you know."

"What happened?" Mary Lou asked, voice perking up.

"He caught some guy dressed up as Santa in a high-speed chase. They guy had hijacked a car with a little boy in it, ditched that car, stole another one, and crashed into a McDonald's out by Denver International Airport."

"Santa? Christmas is over. Was he high?"

"Don't know—haven't got the details. Anyway, Bobby will call when he can. You could call him."

"I will not do that. I'm not playing the desperate woman. He can call me. I already had to break our date on Christmas Eve. I hope he's not mad. You know sometimes men can be so sulky."

Eileen focused on the Monet print on the wall across the room. "Yeah, well, I've never seen Bobby Porter sulk. What is your problem?"

"I want to hang up now."

Eileen shouted into the phone, "Mary Lou, don't you dare hang up! That's what you always do when the conversation isn't going your way. What is the matter with you?"

"Stop yelling! I can hear you. I'm going crazy, that's what! I am so depressed. This is torture, and nobody cares. Walt got his contract, so he's happy. He offered to let me use vacation time for the time I'm stranded here. I hate Walt."

Eileen held the receiver away from her ear, then brought it back to speak softly. "Mary Lou, that's Walt, and you've got to stop hating him. God loves him just as much as He loves you, and you're supposed to love Walt just like God loves you. Anyway, he can't take your vacation time today, because it's Saturday."

"Love Walt? That will never happen. Is it really Saturday? I thought it was Friday. All I do here is go down to the coffee shop and eat and come back here to my room."

"Isn't anyone else there?"

Mary Lou sighed. "Because of the holidays, no. There's an older couple and the people who work in the coffee shop. They got stranded, too. Thank Heaven they still have food here. I am so tired of bean soup. And it's cold."

Eileen sat up straight. "Surely there are some things you can be thankful for."

"Oh, please. No sermons, now. I can't handle it. God knows everything, so why am I still here when I want to be home so badly?"

"Aren't you thankful that you got the contract signed?"

"Of course I am," Mary Lou said, bristling.

Eileen added, "And you have a nice room."

Mary Lou countered, "I have a rustic room."

"Do you have hot water—"

"Okay, okay, I get it. I really do want to hang up now. Bye."

Sunday, December 30
Zedlav, Alaska

At two o'clock in the morning, Mary Lou woke with a start. Strange colored lights danced on the ceiling. Fear gripped her. Her eyes followed the path to edges around the drapes. She gingerly made her way across the room and peeked outside, not knowing what to expect.

The dark sky blazed with color. She caught her breath and threw the drapes open. *Amazing!*

After fifteen minutes, she walked backward to sit on the bed and stare out the window in awe at the Northern Lights. *This is incredible. I've never seen anything like this in Denver. Eileen would love this.* Wave after wave of color filled the sky. She laid her head on her pillow, all the time keeping her eyes on the window.

And then it was morning.

White light rays pierced the window, and Mary Lou knew she'd slept late. *It must be noon. I might as well keep sleeping. There's nothing to do but wait. But last night was incredible. I'll never forget what I saw.* She reached for her laptop to check her messages.

An email from Larry. "Hey, sis. We just wanted to thank you for the gifts."

Mary Lou sighed. *Bless Eileen. She delivered the gifts.*

Larry continued, "Sharon loves the slippers. Bunnies are one of her favorite animals. She says you're her favorite sister-in-law. Don't tell Eileen. Oh, and thanks for the croaking frog. I didn't know they could croak 'Santa Claus is Coming to Town.' The boys got a laugh from that one. They say thanks for their model planes. We missed you for Christmas. Hurry home.

"One time I thought I saw an eye doctor on an Alaskan island, but it turned out to be an optical Aleutian."

Mary Lou groaned. *Larry, you are so annoying with your puns.*

She replied, "Saw the Northern Lights this morning, and that's no joke."

Monday, December 31
Zedlav, Alaska

Another day in Alaska. Mary Lou took a hot shower and inspected the clothes she'd arrived in. She pulled on her black slacks and sweater. *These are getting pretty ripe.* She remembered seeing a washer and dryer in the hallway just past her room.

Sorting through her clothes was easy. Everything in her suitcase needed laundering. She found a plastic bag for dry cleaning on the rack just inside her door and filled it up. It was still dark. She felt like she was barely functioning, but she was determined to accomplish something that day.

She filled the washer with clothes, then she needed quarters. She left the clothes in the washer and went down to the lobby for quarters and soap. On her way back, she passed the older man—half of the couple that had also been stranded. He nodded, and she smiled back.

When she got to the laundry room, she found her clothes on the floor in front of the washer, which was ten minutes into the wash cycle. Her temper flared. *The old man did this! Men! How inconsiderate can you get?* The plastic bag was nowhere to be found. She gathered her clothes and went back to her room, making note of the fifty-two minute wait for the cycle to end. She dumped the clothes on her bed.

Time for breakfast. I hope I don't see them in the coffee shop. I don't know how I'll react. I might smack that turkey. She entered the coffee shop and found the nearest booth.

The waiter was familiar by now. "Good morning. What can I get you?"

"You can get me out of here!" Mary Lou grumbled.

He laughed. "Are you saying you want to go snowshoeing?"

Mary Lou grimaced. "Funny. I need coffee. And chocolate. Do you have any chocolate chip cookies?"

He rubbed his chin. "Uh. How about pancakes with chocolate syrup?"

She lit up. "Yes! That sounds perfect."

He brought her coffee within minutes. "Here you go. It's New Year's Eve, and we're having a little party tonight. Everyone who is stranded is invited. It starts at nine until after midnight. We're going to make snacks and serve cider and drinks of your choice. It's on the hotel, so you should come by."

Mary Lou sipped the coffee. "I just might do that. Thanks."

After her late breakfast, she went to the lobby to find something to read. She ended up with tourist magazines and brochures of all the sights to see in Alaska. She entered her room in time to take her laundry back, and she found the washing machine empty this time. She immediately started it and sat in the nearby chair.

The dryer churned. Mary Lou watched the clothes go round and round, trying to think of a way to let the offender know how displeased she was with what he had done, taking her machine. *The very idea. I should throw some chewed gum in there. That would fix him.*

She fished around in her purse and found a package of gum. She unwrapped a piece and stuck it in her mouth. While she chewed, she picked up a *People Magazine* and flipped through it. She added another stick of gum. When the gum was soft, she stood to open the dryer. A young man hurried past her to open the dryer. "Sorry, were those your clothes in the washer earlier? I am so sorry, but we're stuck here with twin babies, and I had to get those diapers in the wash. Again, I apologize. My wife is about to go nuts. We can't wait to get out of here. Let me pay for your laundry." He reached for his wallet.

Mary Lou swallowed the gum. "Oh, that's not necessary. It's fine."

He rushed out with the diapers. Mary Lou loaded the dryer with clean clothes. *Doing laundry for his family. Poor wife. I would be crazy, too, if I got stranded with twin babies. What a nice guy. Not many of those around.* She pushed the start button. *At least I'll have something clean for the party tonight.*

She spent the rest of the day watching boring television and walking the halls of the hotel. She went to the exercise room, and the older couple was using the treadmill and rowing machine. Finally she took a nap.

The buzz from her cell woke her. *A message! Bobby!* She rushed to open it and found a text from Joe. *"Thinking of you today as I'm home with family. Looking forward to your return. I owe you big time. We're surfing the net today to find a new piece of yard art for your backyard collection."*

You owe me—you got that right! It had better be a fantastic piece. I already have seven pinwheels. She dropped the phone onto the bed and dressed in her clean clothes to go down to the restaurant.

After a late dinner, she stayed for the party. It seemed everyone who worked for the hotel could play some kind of musical instrument. Two guitars, an accordion, a keyboard, and a washboard made up the ensemble. The man who had waited on her earlier sang a very good tenor. She stayed about an hour. *It's almost midnight in Denver.*

She went to her room and called Bobby. She waited expectantly until, after the fourth ring, she got the voice mail. "This is Bobby. Please leave a message."

She hung up. *All I wanted to do was wish him a happy new year. Where is he tonight? Is he celebrating? Maybe he's working. He would have his cell on.*

She went back to the lame party.

Tuesday, January 1, 2013
Zedlav, Alaska

Another day in Alaska. Mary Lou took a shower and dressed. She sauntered to the coffee shop.

The young man who'd waited on her the day before offered coffee. "Happy New Year."

His cheery smiled ticked her off. "Whatever."

"What can I get you this morning?" he asked, as if she hadn't snapped at him. "You seemed to like the pancakes yesterday."

She perked up. "Oh, yeah. I'll have what I had yesterday." *I can't believe I'm having pancakes with chocolate syrup for the second morning in a row. Has my life come to this?*

It was still dark outside when she got back to her room. Her room had been made up, and everything looked neat and in order. The nightstand looked as if something was missing.

Her cell. It was gone.

Where could it be? She searched the floor around the nightstand, then she got down on her hands and knees and looked under the bed. *There it is! Oh, thank God! My only connection to civilization.* She strained to reach it. Her fingers touched the edge, and she pushed herself under the bed to grasp it.

When she had retrieved it, she sat on the bed and automatically checked her messages. *A text from Bobby! How did I miss this? I was up until after midnight.* She clicked on the message.

"Happy New Year. I waited until it was midnight in Zedlav. I miss you. Can't wait to see you when you get home. Hope you're having fun tonight."

She laid flat on her back on the bed. *Bobby! I missed your text.* She touched the call button and listened to his phone ring four times. She hung up. *No, I'm not leaving a message. He can call me back. I'm the one who is stranded.*

Thursday, January 3
Zedlav, Alaska

Mary Lou dug out the notebook she had begun to journal in, for lack of anything else to do. She wrote in her best penmanship, *I feel so trapped. I am trapped. I hate this place! It is so dark and cold all the time and everywhere.*

I hate Walt. He is such a jerk. Seriously, Mr. Feldman offered to fax the contract to Denver. Instead I had to fly here, and I faxed in the contract. Really, if I didn't have so many bills, I would look for another job. A different job. I have no idea where I could work that would pay me as well or give me the sense of accomplishment I get when I close a multimillion-dollar deal. If only Walt would retire. Some people retire early. Right?

I do like Joe, and I think he really does try his best. I'm glad I could come here instead of him. He's a good guy. There's not many like him around. His family would have missed him terribly if he had been trapped here for as long as I have. Nobody misses me like that. Sure, Eileen misses me, but she's got her own life, and I'm just her sister.

Larry's busy all the time with Sharon and the kids. They say they miss me, but I probably wouldn't even have seen them after Christmas for a month or more. Mom and Dad know that I'm fine and that I'll be home someday. That's just life.

Then there's you, Bobby. I thought we were a couple. I guess I was wrong about that. I mean, Eileen says you've been very busy, but if you really cared for me, you'd have at least called me back. Your call record shows that I called. I should be mad. I AM mad. I am not calling you again. You've hurt me by ignoring me. One text on this whole trip. I think I may not see you again.

Sadness clutched her. Tears soaked her face. *Bobby, you're a jerk! You're just as bad as Walt. You both treat me like dirt.*

Chapter Four

Saturday, January 5
Zedlav, Alaska

The phone rang in Mary Lou's room. "This is the front office downstairs. Miss Stots, you will be pleased to know that the highway will be cleared late this morning. A shuttle will leave for the airport at noon. Please let us know if there is anything else we can do anything to assist you."

Mary Lou choked. "Thank you so much. I will be down to check out."

The same day
Denver, Colorado

Bobby Porter had put in a long day on the streets of Denver. One domestic situation, a drunk driver, a speeder through a school zone, and then a robbery at Kum & Go made the day go fast. Snow made driving difficult, at best. He was glad to get home after putting in another unexpected twelve-hour day. Picking up the slack for the vacationing personnel made the holidays fly by.

He changed into his comfy sweats. In the kitchen he found leftovers from the New Year's dinner his mother had sent home with him. "Oh, now, I know you're not going to let this food go to waste. Here, take this, and some of this, and this." He replayed her going around the table, dipping into each dish to fill a large plastic bowl. Now he appreciated her efforts. He took the lid off the bowl and stuck it in the microwave oven while he retrieved a soda from the refrigerator.

The microwave tinged, signaling that his food was ready. Bobby carefully picked it up with a paper towel to protect his hands and sat on the couch in front of the TV. *I should call Mary Lou, but I'm beat. I'll probably mess up if I talk to her. Besides, I need to get some sleep. I'm on the late shift tonight.* He took the last bite of supper and fell asleep.

Later the same day
Denver International Airport

The empty baggage claim area echoed. Mary Lou stared at the conveyor belt moving past her. Her late flight had come in even later than expected. She spotted her bag and lifted it off the carousel. *Ugh! How could this thing get heavier? I certainly didn't buy any souvenirs. That four-hour layover in Seattle didn't help. Now if I can just get to my car. Hope the shuttle is still running. It is nearly midnight. This nightmare is almost over.*

She rolled her bag out door number five thirteen and shuffled to the third aisle to wait for the USAirport Parking shuttle. *Oh, it is so cold. I think it's colder here than in Alaska. How can that be?* She threw her arms around herself to hug her body. She remembered her parking ticket and called the number on it.

"USAirport Parking."

Mary Lou could see her breath as she talked into her cell. "I'm waiting for the shuttle. Can you tell me how much longer? Are you still coming? It's cold out here."

"Oh, yes. Ten minutes."

Mary Lou wanted to scream that ten minutes was a long time when she was standing outside but restrained herself. "Thank you."

Twelve minutes and thirteen seconds later, she saw the shuttle round the corner at the end of the terminal. It lumbered toward her at glacial speed. As far as she could see, she was the only person outside the terminal. *Really? You couldn't move any faster? It must be ten below out here.*

Finally, it stopped in front of her. The door swung open, and the warm air embraced her as she entered. She handed her parking slip to the driver so he could find her car in the sea of snow-covered automobiles at USAirport Parking. He closed the doors, and she collapsed in a seat, closing her eyes and cursing Walt Pederson.

Sunday, January 6
Denver, Colorado

Bobby Porter activated the light and sirens on his patrol car to initiate the traffic stop. It was twelve forty-five, and he had been sitting on the shoulder of I-25 when the car raced past him at ninety-five miles an hour. Bobby read the license plate to the dispatcher as he pulled the late-model Hummer over. He requested a 10-28. The dispatcher entered the information into the NCIC database and instantly received the pertinent information—the type and color of car, the dates of license, and to whom the car was licensed. The car was not listed as stolen or wanted. Everything seemed in order. The dispatcher relayed the information to Bobby. The Hummer pulled far off the shoulder, away from the light traffic.

Bobby felt the knot in his stomach tighten as he walked up to black-tinted windows. He hated tinted windows, especially at night. The habitual questions raced through his mind as he approached the driver's side. *Does he have a gun? Does he have a hostage? Is the driver dangerous? Has he been drinking? Is this a setup? Is the vehicle carrying illegal drugs or weapons? How will the driver react to getting a citation? Will he become combative?*

The black window slid down, and a muscular black man stuck his head out the window and smiled too brightly. "Hey, there. You got me. I know it."

Bobby hesitated a second until he could see into the car and that the man had both hands on the steering wheel. "May I see your driver's license and proof of insurance?"

"Sure, man, no problem." The man pulled down the sun visor and retrieved his registration and insurance information. "Hey, man, my license is in my wallet."

Bobby could tell from the few words spoken that the man was sober. "Go ahead."

The man got his wallet from his back pocket. Bobby took the documents back to the cruiser and called dispatch for a 10-27, driver's license check on Mark Phelps. Nothing came up out of the ordinary, so Bobby routinely requested a printout of the NCIC report. He would need it when he got back to the station for his report. He dreaded the paperwork for even a normal traffic stop.

Mr. Phelps accepted the citation without comment.

Bobby got back in the cruiser and waited for Mr. Phelps to leave.

As soon as the black Hummer got up to speed, a car roared past doing over ninety miles an hour, and he activated his lights and sirens. That vehicle looked all too familiar. *Mary Lou!*

Mary Lou pulled over immediately.

He threw the cruiser into park and strode up to the open driver's window.

Mary Lou blinked back tears. "Oh, Bobby, I was hoping it was you. Thank God." She broke out in a full-blown meltdown.

He opened the car door and put his arms around her. "Hey, it's all right."

She sniffed and looked up. "Get in the car. It's freezing out there."

He walked around to the passenger seat. *That's Mary Lou, the pragmatist. Get out of the cold, dummy.* He grinned and felt light as he got into the car beside her.

She turned and embraced him, burying her head in his shoulder. "That's better. I feel better now. Oh, I've missed you so much. Why didn't you call? Do you have any idea how isolated I felt? Alaska is a horrible place."

He patted her hair and pushed her away to look her in the eye. "I'm glad you're back. I missed you. But I'm on duty right now. Mary Lou, you know you were speeding."

Her face went innocent. "I was?"

"Over ninety miles an hour."

She dried her eyes and blew her nose. "Oh, I just wanted to be home. Home in my own house, in my own bed. It's been nothing less than hell the last two weeks."

Bobby sighed. Everything in Mary Lou's life was larger than life and more awful than life or, in good times, better than life. He leaned back in his seat. "I need to get back in the cruiser. You slow down the rest of the way home." He patted her hand.

She grabbed his hand. "Is that it? Bobby, when are we going to see each other again?"

He rubbed his forehead. "It's been busy. I'm not sure when I'm off."

"What?" she shouted. "I've been in hell over Christmas and New Year's and you can't even figure out when we can go out? We didn't see each other over Christmas or New Year's Eve or New Year's Day. I hate this!" She grabbed the steering wheel and banged her head against it.

He reached out to stop her. "Let me think. Let's see. It's Saturday, and—"

Mary Lou screeched, "It's Sunday!" She pointed at the clock on the dashboard and sniffed, then whined, "It's 1:30 a.m. on Sunday."

He relaxed. This was Mary Lou in her tensed-out mode. "Monday—Monday, I'm off. That's tomorrow. I can pick you up at seven. Can I take you to dinner Monday evening, Princess?"

Her shoulders went down, she wiped her eyes, "Yes, I'd love to see you tomorrow evening."

Monday, January 7
Arvada, Colorado

Mary Lou powdered her nose. Bobby would be on time. She flipped through the blouses in her closet for the tenth time and decided to change her top. She glanced at the clock. Six fifty-eight. She slipped on the blouse and glanced in the mirror. *That's better.* She smiled at herself and walked into the living room as the doorbell rang.

She opened the door. Bobby stepped in, and they hugged, long and tight. Mary Lou kissed him, and he held her close.

She inhaled his cologne. "Mm, you smell good."

"It's one of my new essential oils. Sandalwood. Glad you like it." He reached to help her with her coat.

"I sure do." *I could take this relationship to the next level right now. You are the sexiest man in the universe. The only time you look better is when in uniform, and that cologne may drive me to do something shocking tonight.*

Stop it, girl, you'll scare him to death. You were in Alaska too long.

He opened the door for her. "I made reservations at the Greenbriar. Hope that's all right."

She glowed. "I love it. I haven't been there for ages. It's pretty special. Are we celebrating?"

Bobby laughed. "Just that you're back in the lower forty-eight."

Mary Lou and Bobby got into his aging Range Rover. She snuggled into the seat as Bobby turned the key and the engine roared to life. He turned toward Boulder and Left Hand Canyon.

The Greenbriar was packed, as usual. The hostess led Mary Lou and Bobby to a table in the back of the dining hall, next to the doors to the kitchen.

After they had been served, Bobby smiled. "Mind if I say a prayer?"

Mary Lou blushed, put down her fork, and quickly bowed her head. "Go ahead."

"Lord, Creator and Sustainer of the universe, we just want to thank You for this day and for Mary Lou's safe return. Thank You for who You are and what You did for us on Calvary. Thank You for Your provision in all things. We praise Your Name and ask Your blessing on this evening. In Jesus's Name, Amen."

Mary Lou lifted her head and looked around to see if anyone was watching. Everyone seemed involved in their own conversations.

Bobby lifted his glass of iced tea. "To life!"

She lifted her tea, and they clinked glasses. "I'm so glad to be home. I guess I've told you that a dozen times already tonight. Being with you is what I dreamed about when I was stuck in Alaska. I mean, it was awful, and not hearing from you made it worse."

Bobby sipped his tea. "I'm sorry. A lot has happened since we last saw each other. I guess I need to get you caught up."

Mary Lou loved the way his eyes lit up.

He blurted, "I converted."

The remark frightened her. "What do you mean? Converted to what?"

"Remember that we had a date you had to cancel the night before you left for Alaska? One of the guys at work—you may have heard me mention his name before. Alex."

She shook her head.

"Anyway, Alex and I went over to Hacienda Colorado to get a bite to eat. We had a good visit, and it ended up with him inviting me to his Bible study. I told him I wasn't interested, and he proceeded to tell me about Jesus." Bobby rushed on. "And right there, we prayed, and I took Jesus as my Lord and Savior. My feet have not touched the ground since. Between work and Bible study, it's been quite a ride. But I have to tell you—Bible study has been incredible. I have learned so much. I mean, my parents raised me Christian, but I never knew Jesus the way I know him now."

Speechless, Mary Lou could only blink.

"The thing of it is," he continued, picking up speed. "Well, I want the same thing for you. Jesus is real. He wants to save you from sin and call you His own. You can pray and ask Him to forgive you of all of your sins, and He can do that because He took them on at the cross. He will forgive you and guarantee you a place in Heaven for eternity."

Mary Lou's eyebrows shot up. "You're witnessing to *me*? I can't believe you don't know that I'm Christian. How *dare* you decide what my belief system is! Excuse me. I need to go to the rest room." She wiped at her eyes and stood.

He grabbed her hand as she passed him. "I'm sorry. I didn't know."

She jerked her hand away and strode to the ladies' room.

Ten minutes later, Mary Lou returned to the table. "Don't worry. I'm better now."

He put down his glass. "I'm glad. I didn't mean to offend you."

She reached for her glass and flatly said, "I forgive you."

Bobby grimaced. "I've been doing a lot of thinking about us and about my career and…well, a lot of things."

She leaned forward. "What? There's more? What are you taking so long to tell me? Just tell me. You know I can't take all this mystery."

He sucked in a deep breath. "All right. Here it is: I've been offered the job in San Diego that I interviewed for last October. Remember when I had to go for the oral examinations?"

Mary Lou blinked. "I remember, but they didn't call you, and I thought it was done. I thought—"

"It was never over. It just takes time for them to get all the background checks and so forth done. I accepted the job last week, and I will be moving to San Diego within the next few days."

Mary Lou lost her appetite. She couldn't speak. She sat there, stunned.

"I didn't want to tell you this while you were in Alaska, but there's another reason I'm going at this time. You see, I care very much about you. To be honest, I'm falling in love with you."

Hope surged into Mary Lou's heart. The conversation wasn't turning out the way she'd feared.

Mary Lou felt her shoulders relax. *Oh, Bobby, I agree. Don't stop talking. Yes, I will marry you and move to San Diego. Just ask, you dope!*

Bobby took her other hand. "The only problem with that is that—well, now, please don't take this the wrong way."

Mary Lou squeezed his hands. "Go on. I want to hear what you have to say."

Bobby smiled a sad smile. "When Alex and I talked, I told him all about you and how wonderful you are. He told me that it sounded like I might be having impure thoughts about you. The more that we talked, the more I knew that what he said was true. Then this job came up. And the more that I think about it, I'm pretty sure it is a God thing. I need some distance to grow spiritually, and your beauty distracts me."

Mary Lou summoned her brightest smile. "If that job is what you want, then you should go for it."

Bobby glanced down at the plate in front of him then back at her. "The job is important, of course. But more important is for you to understand where I'm coming from." He squeezed her hands back and took a deep breath. "I'm afraid that we're unequally yoked, and I couldn't live like that. You may be the woman God wants me to spend my life with—it's just that, if you are that woman, it's the wrong time. I hope to move back to Denver sometime in the future."

Mary Lou let go of his hands. She found her voice and heard herself ask, "Unequally yoked? I told you I was a Christian."

He reached across the table to take her hand back. "That is great news, but our spiritual priorities are different. Jesus means everything to me, and I don't believe you have that same commitment."

She clasped her hands together in her lap. Her shoulders lifted, along with her voice. "'Spiritual priorities'? What does that even mean? I'm a Christian. Tell me what you want." She felt her back arch. "So I'm not good enough for you?"

"I didn't say that at all. It's not about being good enough; it's about being able to have a right relationship with the Lord and being ready to do whatever He asks for the rest of our lives."

She threw her napkin on her unfinished meal. "I'm ready for something, Bobby. I'm ready to end this conversation. Take me home." She went to get her coat.

Bobby caught the waiter, paid the bill, and hurried outside to see Mary Lou standing in the parking lot beside the car.

Snow had begun to fall. The light from the streetlight glowed around her. She was hugging herself and shivering in the cold. The sight made him want to take her in his arms to comfort her, but he knew better. He was the reason for her hurt.

He pressed the button on the key fob and unlocked the car from a distance. She was in the car by the time he reached it.

Chapter Five

After getting home from work, Mary Lou walked three houses down to Eileen's house for dinner. It had been a furiously busy week. She had volunteered for extra jobs and helped people out with their own projects so she wouldn't have time to think about Bobby. She was exhausted and looking forward to tonight. Her sister had always been the cook of the family. *I hope it's her eggplant Parmesan. She knows that's my favorite.* Mary Lou rang the doorbell.

The thick aroma of eggplant Parmesan escaped when Eileen opened the door. "About time you got here. I hate it when I cook a meal and have to serve it cold."

Mary Lou walked into the kitchen nook. "Oh my, you have everything ready."

Eileen heaved a sigh. "Yes, sit down so we can pray and eat this wonderful—if I do say so myself—meal."

Mary Lou grinned and took a seat. "You pray. I'm not sure I'm speaking to God right now."

Eileen shook her head. "I'll pray over dinner, but you're going to have to explain that remark after."

Eileen bowed her head, and Mary Lou followed suit. "Thank You, Lord, for this food and all Your provisions that make our lives better. Thank You for my sister. Amen."

Then Eileen passed the huge platter of eggplant Parmesan to Mary Lou. "Now I want to know what all this 'I'm not talking to God' stuff is about."

Mary Lou piled the sumptuous food onto her plate. "Bobby dumped me." She took a bite of her favorite dish and shifted gears. "Mmm. You sure know how to cook."

Eileen handed her a napkin. "Don't you try to change the subject by mooning over my cooking. What happened with you and Bobby? I know he didn't just dump you. There had to be a reason. Now tell me the whole story."

Mary Lou wiped her mouth. "There's nothing to tell. Oh, yeah, get this—he took me out to dinner to witness to me. Can you believe it? He didn't even know I was Christian. How does that grab you?"

Eileen put her fork down. "Wow. But you are a Christian. He didn't dump you because you're a Christian. Tell me the rest. Come on, now."

"He gave me this song and dance about how he had a long talk with his friend Alex who basically told him I wasn't good enough for him."

Eileen frowned at her.

Mary Lou took a deep breath. "I guess there is more to it. Bobby says people who plan to spend their lives together need to start out on the same spiritual level. Bobby just became a Christian on Christmas Eve, and yet he considers himself living at a deeper spiritual level. Men are so arrogant. Then he says that he thinks I might be the woman he wants to spend the rest of his life with, but… I am so ticked off at him. I don't care if I ever see him again."

Eileen took a sip of water. "Is that why I haven't been able to get ahold of you this week, other than texting?"

Mary Lou shrugged. "Oh, that. I've been incredibly busy. I took on some extra projects at work. I'm completely reorganizing my filing system and renaming all my files so that they will coincide with Joe's. Then I started a manual for the other agents to follow as far as office procedure in our department—"

"Stop!" Eileen banged her hand on the table. "You always do this. Whenever you can't handle something, you dive into work. You'll reorganize Joe's files and everyone else's in the office rather than face the problem."

"The problem? There's no problem. Bobby turned out to be a jerk, that's all. I'll get over it. I am over it."

Eileen leaned forward. "You're not over it—but that's not even the issue here. You're missing the elephant in the room. It's not about Bobby. It's about God. Think back. Remember when we used to go to church together every Sunday? Remember when you had lost your job, and you didn't know what you were going to do? And we prayed, and we went to church, and you went home, and you prayed. Do you remember how you leaned on God? Remember how you got this job? They had never had a woman in their sales department until they hired you.

"You cried out to God after that interview because you wanted that job so badly. And because if you didn't get it, you didn't know how you were going to make your next house payment."

Mary Lou got serious. "I do remember that time. It's been five years."

"It *has* been five years," Eileen said. "Right after you got that job, you got too busy to attend church regularly. I understand that you have to miss now and then, but months would go by. You poured yourself into your work to prove yourself to them. And then you met Bobby."

Mary Lou went into defensive mode. "I've only been dating him a few months."

Eileen grimaced. "Only *dating* a few months. True. Listen, baby sister, you had your eye on him for at least six months before that. It took all of your energy to get him to ask you out. And now it's taken all of your energy to get him to ask you to marry him."

Mary Lou shrugged. "Well, he never asked me to marry him."

Eileen picked up where she left off. "No, he didn't ask you to marry him, but he said he loved you or that he thought you were the woman he would like to spend the rest of his life with. The problem is, you lost sight of God. All you can think about is what Mary Lou wants. You've been lusting after this poor man for almost a year. You've backslid. You need to get back to God. 'Trust in the Lord with all your heart and lean not on your understanding; in all your ways acknowledge Him, and He will make your paths straight'— Proverbs 3:5-6. You need to learn to trust God for whatever may happen in the future."

Mary Lou began to clear the table. "I should have known that you'd start throwing Scripture at me. If trusting God for everything is so great, why are you still single? Why aren't you happily married to some rich, handsome guy?"

Eileen smiled. "God is my partner. If and when He decides I should marry, He will bring the right man into my life. Until then, I cherish the gift of being single. Being single allows me to focus more on Him. I have a wonderful relationship with Him, and I am happy with where He's put me—'for such a time as this,' Esther 4:14."

Monday, January 14
Arvada, Colorado

"I could kill him," Mary Lou shouted into her Bluetooth. Hot breath clouded the frosty windshield in front of her.

"Mary Lou Stots, you do not talk like that," her sister reprimanded her. "'Do not let any unwholesome talk come out of your mouths, but only what is helpful for building others up according to their needs, that it may benefit those who listen'—Ephesians 4:29."

Mary Lou squinted and brushed the clouded windshield with the back of her glove. "I know it's wrong. I'm sorry. I wish I didn't feel this way, but you should have my job for just one day and see how he treats me. Oh, dear God, You don't have to make him suffer. Just make him disappear."

Eileen scolded, "Mary Lou, stop talking like that. God's not the only one who could be listening to this conversation. You're upset. Now say you didn't mean what you said. Besides, if Walt disappeared, you wouldn't have a job."

Mary Lou felt her eyes drip. "I know it's wrong, but I hate the man."

Eileen sucked in a breath. "You need to get a grip, girl. What brought all this on?"

Mary Lou sniffed and turned the defroster on. "I just sat through the most demeaning, demotivating sales meeting ever. Walt viciously attacked me, made fun of me, and embarrassed me in front of the rest of the team. Sure, he owns the company, but he's not even my direct boss. Joe's my boss. It's hard being the only woman in sales. I'm selling more than anyone, yet Walt constantly beats up on me. I don't understand it."

Eileen cleared her throat. "Are you at home?"

"I'm driving." Mary Lou pushed the button on the console to open her garage door. "I just got to the house."

"I'm coming over."

Mary Lou drove her Nissan Rogue into her double-car garage. "Thanks, but right now I need someone to take my side."

"See you in a minute; you know I'm always on your side." Eileen hung up.

Mary Lou got out of her car and walked up the two steps to the door to her living quarters. She pressed the garage door button and entered the white-tiled laundry room of her modern two-bedroom home. She crossed further white tile through the kitchen to her small gray-carpeted home office. She laid her purse and briefcase on the desk, tore her coat off, and threw it into the desk chair. After that she made her way to the living room, unlocked the front door in anticipation of Eileen's arrival, kicked off her shoes, and flopped on the blue-flower-print couch.

She took a deep breath and forced the tension to leave her body. "Oh, that's better." She closed her eyes.

Two minutes later, a quiet knock announced Eileen's arrival.

"Come in, Eileen! It's unlocked."

Eileen entered and sat on the arm of the couch. "Are you all right?"

Mary Lou sat up. "I'm at the end of my rope. Can't you tell? I'm so ready to quit this job. If I didn't make so much money, I would leave. Walt is unbearable. Usually Joe stands up for me, but I think even he's getting tired of all the drama."

Eileen slid from the couch arm onto the cushion. "Does Walt have a woman problem?"

Mary Lou scooted over to give Eileen more room. "What does that mean?"

Eileen shrugged one shoulder. "Some men can't work with women. It's a pride thing. Women scare them. And with you being so successful, Walt could feel threatened."

"Threatened? He hired me. How could he be threatened? He owns the company. Besides, Walt Pederson is twice my size. He takes every opportunity to make fun of how short I am. No, you're wrong there."

Eileen grinned. "Yeah, well, elephants are afraid of mice. Go figure."

Mary Lou welcomed the humorous thought. "Oh, I should remember that one. Next time Walt teases me about being short, I'll just call him Dumbo." She giggled. Then her face turned somber. "He would fire me. But you might be right about the woman thing. His wife is the quietest woman."

Eileen nodded. "I'll bet he's intimidated her into submission. She's as tiny as you are—no, she might be an inch taller than you. I remember her from high school. Not exactly a wallflower. She always had the popular girls around her. You know, the beautiful people. She was not the quiet woman she is today. I saw her and Walt at the country club a few weeks ago. Talk about Mutt and Jeff. But tell me—what happened today? What brought out all this anger?"

Mary Lou sucked in a deep breath. "Walt's looking at the sales numbers for last year. From my monthly observations, I should be leading the team by quite a bit. Especially after the Zedlav, Alaska, fiasco." She smiled to herself. "I've had a very good year. Anyway, he called a sales meeting just before quitting time to give his projections for year-end totals. About a month ago, Walt announced that the prize for top sales this year is a cruise to the Bahamas. Anyway, everyone's excited to hear their numbers. I would love to win a cruise."

Eileen leaned back into the couch. "Okay. Why are you so mad?"

"Because, after we got in there, he spent an hour telling us that he wasn't going to give us the numbers until Friday. Then he said for us to get out of the office and make some lucrative deals for this year. He stuck out his foot and tripped me as I left the room. I fell flat on my face. I can still hear everyone laughing. And he says, 'She's all right. Didn't fall far.' He treats me worse than a dog."

"The Bible says, 'In your anger do not sin'—Ephesians 4:26. Be careful what you say and do when you're angry."

"I'm not going to do anything stupid. I like my income and everything else about the job. Besides, my credit card bills are staggering. Suing him would only make my life more miserable. Thank Heaven I have a sister to talk to. Otherwise I'd go nuts."

Tuesday, January 15
Denver, Colorado

Before going into her office the next morning, Mary Lou stopped by Joe Gillespie's office. She stuck her head in the door. "How we get any work done around here is a mystery to me."

Her boss looked up from his computer. "Are you referring to all the practical jokes and partying? Well, yes. They certainly impact productivity."

The latest joke had been on Joe. His expense account had been returned by Accounting, and Walt had brought it up at the meeting in front of all the agents. Mary Lou would never forget how the room literally shook as the six-foot-four three hundred-pound Walter Pederson used his booming voice to accuse Joe of abusing his expense account by including a new suit as a business expense. The look on Joe's face had been priceless. Obviously, he didn't have a clue as to what Walt was ranting about.

Walt loved center stage. Mary Lou remembered bracing herself, thinking that Walt would fire Joe. Instead Walt ended the tirade by telling Joe that if he needed a suit that bad, he would donate one of his personal suits to Joe. Walt's roaring laugh then filled the room, and the rest of the men nervously joined in. Joe could fit in Walt's suit with ample room left over for any of the other men in the room to join him.

Later, Mary Lou found out one of the salesmen had doctored Joe's expense report as a practical joke.

Joe and Mary Lou shared the disability of being "vertically challenged," as Walt referred to their heights. Joe's stocky frame and dark, curly hair only added to his good looks. Between their similarities and the camaraderie from suffering from Walt's frequent remarks, Joe counted on her for input every now and then.

Mary Lou shook off the remembrance. "Especially the practical jokes."

Joe answered her with a serious expression. "Our job is to sell. What Walt does is his business. We need to sell enough to keep up with expenses, and that's a challenge at times. That's not why I called you in here. I wanted to give you a heads up."

Yes, about what?"

"Walt hired another salesperson."

She tilted her head. "He hired another salesperson? Why? We've got too many now."

Joe grimaced. "He didn't consult me. You know Walt. This fellow is originally from Texas, and I guess he knew Walt in college. In any case, Denny Adams starts Friday. I'll be sending a memo out this afternoon. You're assigned to show him how we do things here."

Chapter Six

Friday, January 18
Denver, Colorado

Friday morning, Mary Lou made a special effort to get to the sales meeting early, anticipating her cruise to the Bahamas. One by one, the other members of her department ambled into the sterile conference room and found seats at the oversized table. Joe sat next to her. After all nineteen of them had arrived, Walt Pederson appeared in front of them.

Another man, unfamiliar to Mary Lou, walked into the room and took a chair against the wall. He nodded at Walt. Walt nodded back and smiled.

Mary Lou pressed her five-foot frame deeper into her chair. *Is Walt Pederson the cross I must bear? God, I want You to deal with this man. After working for him for five years, I still have no idea what he will do or say. Just look at him, standing up there like he's You.*

Walt Pederson stood at the whiteboard in front of the conference table with his "I'm CEO of International Enterprises and you'd better sit up and take notice" attitude. He sucked in his gut and loudly asked, "Seven salesmen and one woman make up the sales and marketing team for International Enterprises. Four of you are sales support. Joe, this is your team. What is wrong with this picture?"

An uncomfortable silence begged him to answer his own question.

Ten excruciating seconds later, he bellowed, "Not a one of you guys can sell. That's what's the matter!" His face crimson, he slammed his fist down on the conference table.

Joe Gillespie, the sales director, stood up. "Walt, I have to disagree with you. Mary Lou sold far beyond what either one of us predicted this year. You admitted that yourself when we calculated the year-end sales."

Walt looked down his nose. "Who asked you, Gillespie? Are you saying we need more women on the sales force?" He let out a loud snicker. "This isn't a bake sale, Gillespie. Think about it—we sell heavy equipment for oil drilling. It's a man's business." He glared at Mary Lou.

Mary Lou felt her face get hot. *What is wrong with him? He thought I'd be a "nice addition to the sales department" five years ago when he interviewed me. What? Was I not supposed to sell product? Every time I sell something, he makes money. Why can't he be nice to me?*

Joe sat back down. "We've met our quotas, and more."

Walt set his fists on his hips. "You guys didn't make your quotas." Then he pointed at Mary Lou. "She did. I saw the individual sales reports, and she made up for what your guys missed. Your guys are not pulling their weight." Walt glanced at the man sitting against the wall. "This will change."

Walt glared at Mary Lou and shook his finger in her face. "And you—no more sleeping with clients."

He did not just say that. Her shoulders tightened. *Sleep with a client? Is that what he thinks it takes to close a deal?* Shocked, she could only blink in reply.

Then Walt looked around the room at the men and laughed. "You guys need to do whatever it takes to close. Now, down to the reason for this little get-together. Top salesperson for 2012…" He put on his reading glasses and looked around the table. "Drum roll, please."

Everyone tapped the desk until Walt held up his hand for them to stop. "The winner and still champion, Mary Lou Stots."

Mary Lou stood up to receive the dark plaque Walt held out to her. Then he snatched it back before she could take it. "Mary Lou, stand up. Oh, you're already standing." He roared a laugh, and the others joined in, except for Joe.

Walt handed the plaque to Mary Lou in a grandiose gesture. She grasped it and held it out in front of her. She inspected the gold lettering on the polished walnut board. It read, *International Enterprises, Salesman of the Year 2012.* Under that, she read her name: *Mary Lou Sluts.*

Sluts? She blinked to clear her eyes and inspected the third line a second time. *They misspelled my name. For crying out loud, did Walt do this on purpose?* Heat crept into her cheeks.

Salesman of the year? Do I look like a man? She put on her best business smile and muttered, "Thank you." She sat and placed the plaque face down in her lap.

Walt continued, "As you know, the prize for first in sales is a four-day cruise, so Mary Lou will be taking a luxurious cruise to the Bahamas. Everyone give her a hand." His smile bordered somewhere between evil and conniving.

Later the same day
Denver, Colorado

A bit unnerved after the meeting and still smarting from the "no more sleeping with clients" and the "Sluts" error, Mary Lou sat in her office. She brought up her computer to look at her client messages. *Happy cruising to me! I can't wait to get out of here.*

Mary Lou was about to shut down her computer when a message flashed up. It was from Joe, asking her to come to his office.

When she got there, the strange man from the sales meeting sat across from Joe.

Joe stood as she entered the room. "Mary Lou, I'd like to introduce our new salesman. This is Denny Adams."

Denny stood. His handshake felt firm and sure.

She smiled. "Welcome to International Enterprises."

"Thank you, sweetheart." Denny's slight Southern drawl sounded endearing and a little condescending. "You're the number one in sales. Congratulations."

"Oh, yes. I saw you at the meeting."

Denny chuckled. "Walt just couldn't wait for me to get on board. He asked me to stop by and observe the meeting. It was very interesting."

Joe sat, and Mary Lou and Denny sat across from his desk. "Mary Lou, I wanted you to meet Denny right away because he's eager to know more about what goes on here. You're probably the best one to show him the ropes, since you've been here over five years." He looked at Denny. "I started three years ago, and I'm still getting information from Mary Lou."

Denny leaned back and looked Mary Lou up and down. "Next week's going to be a 'short' week, pardon the pun."

Mary Lou grimaced.

Denny continued, "Walt says the office will be shut down Monday for Martin Luther King Day. Maybe you could come in for a few hours Monday morning and help me get oriented."

Joe's forehead wrinkled. "Denny, the office is closed. No one will be here. I don't think—"

"Walt said she'd be happy to help out," Denny interrupted. "Now come on. She could come in Monday, at least for part of the day."

Joe, still frowning, said, "That's not—"

"Let her decide. What about it, Mary Lou. You're a team player, aren't you?"

I'm better than a team player. Mary Lou shrugged. "Sure, I can come in a few hours on Monday. I'll have to leave by noon. I'm having dinner with family."

Denny smiled at Joe and then looked back at her. "Sure. I didn't know you were married."

She felt the hair stand up on the back of her neck. "I am not married. I still have a life." She tried to keep her tone even on the second sentence.

Denny slapped his knee. "All right, then. See you Monday at eight!"

Evening, the same day

Friday night, Mary Lou asked Eileen to meet her for an early dinner at Chili's, and afterward they went shopping.

On Saturday, Mary Lou cleaned house, did more shopping, and cleaned house again. At eight thirty, she fell into bed, exhausted by the activities of the day. Before she fell asleep, she thought of Bobby and about what could have been. She missed him.

Sunday, January 20
Arvada, Colorado

Sunday morning she slept in until nine a.m. and barely had time to dress and get to church on time. A light overnight snow thinly covered the ice from last week's frozen rain, making driving treacherous. The church parking lot looked half empty; her tires crunched ice as she pulled into a space near the entrance. Eileen waved from the front door and then ducked inside, keeping warm until Mary Lou joined her.

Mary Lou quickly closed the door behind her. "Man, it is cold out there."

Eileen turned toward the sanctuary. "The wind makes it worse."

Mary Lou wrinkled her nose and closed her eyes, "I see fluffy white flakes floating to the ground outside my window, while basking in the warmth of a fire in the fireplace."

Eileen nudged her and put her finger to her lips. "Shush. The service is about to start. I'm so glad you came. Did you forget your Bible?"

Mary Lou accepted a bulletin from the man in the foyer. "Oh, no, I left it in the car," she lied. "There's no way I'm going back outside."

She followed Eileen to the fifth row of pews from the front, where they always used to sit. They took their seats as the praise team started playing "What a Mighty God We Serve." The words on the screen in front of them made it impossible not to join in singing.

Half an hour of praise songs passed, and then Pastor Don Elliott came forward with his message for the week. The tall, thin man stood in front of the group, adjusted his thick-rimmed glasses, and opened his Bible.

He surveyed his congregation and spoke. "The message today is titled 'The Power of Prayer.' Prayer is the greater part of worship. When we pray, we acknowledge our thoughts and desires to the King of the universe. This is good, and this is what our Lord wants us to do. Let me reference the Scriptures; turn in your Bibles to Philippians chapter 4, verse 6." He paused a few seconds, then read, "Do not be anxious about anything, but in every situation, by prayer and petition with thanksgiving, present your requests to God." Let me explain this verse to you. It is not a plea. It is a statement, a command. You don't see any question marks there, do you?"

Eileen shared her Bible with Mary Lou.

Pastor Elliott continued, "Prayer is the most powerful weapon we have against the enemy. And, as you know, the enemy comes in all forms. He is so tricky, he can be in the midst of us in an instant, plant deception, and disappear before we're aware of him. He can camp out on our front mind and cause immediate and lasting depression. With prayer, we can throw it off. Because it is the power of God that heals and protects us.

"It's also the evil one who is responsible for sickness. Again, prayer is the most powerful weapon you can use to fight illness. Jesus Christ is the Great Physician. Yes, it's all right to pray for God to help your doctor. And the doctor can diagnose and operate. You can have a successful operation, but the doctor can't heal. Healing comes from God."

Mary Lou nudged Eileen and whispered, "Is that true?"

Eileen wrote on her bulletin and pushed the note over so Mary Lou could read, *God made our bodies so that they heal. When someone has stitches, they heal because of what God does, not what the doctor does. Only God heals.*

Mary Lou took Eileen's pen out of her hand and wrote, *That must be why people heal at different rates; everybody is different.*

Pastor Elliott moved on. "We should always pray for the men and women in our military. They've agreed to defend our country at whatever cost it takes. Once again, we can thank the enemy that we have such a thing as war. It is our duty as children of God to appeal to our Heavenly Father to protect our servicemen and women. And always pray for those in authority over us." He looked down at the children in the front row. "For you, it means to pray for your parents."

He turned a page of his notes. "And when we think of persons in unfamiliar and distant places, we must not forget our missionaries. Always be praying for those holding up the Word throughout the world. These men and woman have sacrificed their lives for the hope of the world. They get little help and nearly no recognition, and yet their battle is to further the Kingdom. Pray for the persecuted Church—these are the missionaries that are under constant threat of their livelihood and, in fact, even their lives."

Then he looked back at the rest of the congregation. "We don't always agree with those in authority over us, but we are called to pray for them and to submit to them. Look here at Romans chapter 13:1-3, where it says, 'Let everyone be subject to the governing authorities, for there is no authority except that which God has established. The authorities that exist have been established by God. Consequently, whoever rebels against the authority is rebelling against what God has instituted, and those who do so will bring judgment on themselves. For rulers hold no terror for those who do right, but for those who do wrong. Do you want to be free from fear of the one in authority? Then do what is right and you will be commended.'"

Other than Joe, Walt's the only person I can think of right now that is in authority over me. I must admit that I am afraid of Walt. Joe would never fire me, but I'm afraid Walt will fire me, and I'll lose the best-paying job I've ever had. Trouble is, he changes the rules all the time. I can hardly keep up. And he's just an angry man. He's mean and ugly to everyone. He's the most ungodly man I know. It seems wrong to say Your name and his in the same sentence.

She focused back to Pastor Elliott, who was saying to turn to the book of Second Timothy, chapter 2:1-6. "I urge, then, first of all, that petitions, prayers, intercession and thanksgiving be made for all people—for kings and all those in authority, that we may live peaceful and quiet lives in all godliness and holiness. This is good and pleases God our Savior, who wants all people to be saved and to come to a knowledge of the truth. For there is one God and one mediator between God and mankind, the man Christ Jesus, who gave himself as a ransom for all people."

Pastor Elliott looked up from reading. "Sometimes our candidate doesn't get elected, or we end up working for someone we don't agree with, but we should always pray for the person in authority who is making decisions for us and for our nation.

"Prayer is never limited to our immediate problems. Our God is much bigger than that. Oh, He can and will answer each and every need we pray about, but He wants us to be involved in more than just those around us. Pray for your enemies, those who offend you and degrade you."

Mary Lou frowned.

"We are commanded to love our enemies, and how better can we show our love for them than to pray for their salvation and deliverance?"

She felt her back stiffen. *Like I could pray for Walt Pederson. He deserves something, but it's not my prayers. I refuse to pray for him. He's beyond lost.*

Chapter Seven

Monday, January 21
Denver, Colorado

Mary Lou got to the office at a quarter to eight. She nodded and flashed her badge to security as she walked past the stocky young man into a deserted hallway. Her heels clicked on the tiled floor, and the sound echoed through the empty building, occupied only by security personnel. She arrived at her office and turned on the light. *Denny should be here any minute.*

She unbuttoned her coat and hung it on the hook just inside her office. Then she sat behind her desk and brought up her computer. She listened for Denny's footsteps. *In the meantime, I can check on client status for the year.*

Before long, she became deeply engrossed in strategic planning for the new year.

She jumped at the sound of Denny knocking on the wood frame of her open door. She glanced at the clock on her computer—nine fifteen—then looked up at him. "Oh, you startled me. You're late."

"Hey, sorry. I got held up at the apartment. I got a call from the moving company. My stuff isn't here yet."

"What stuff? You mean you just moved here?"

He plopped down in the chair across from her desk. "Didn't Joe tell you? I'm from San Diego, originally from Texas. I just moved here kind of last minute. Everything is up in the air. The moving company is stuck in Glenwood Springs. How far is that? I mean, how long could it take? They've driven in snow before."

He's from San Diego. That's where Bobby is. Wow. I wonder if they know each other.

Now, that's just dumb. I am not going to ask. Bobby's been there, what, two weeks? What do I care, anyway? They could be best friends, as far as I know. What difference does it make? "I heard on the news this morning that there's a storm in the mountains. Just be glad they don't have to go over Monument Pass."

He cocked his head, "Where's that?"

Mary Lou turned toward her computer screen. "Never mind. Let's get down to work. I have to leave by noon. Do you want to work here or in your office?"

Denny grinned. "I have an office?"

She shrugged. "We'll work here. I'm sure Joe will have your office ready by next Monday."

"Well, I would hope so. Walt starts me out with a measly eighty-five thousand base salary, after he begs me to come on board, and I don't even have an office."

She controlled her surprise. *Eight-five thousand? He's getting ten thousand more than I make, and I've been here five years!* "Where did you get your MBA?"

"MBA, me? No, I barely got through undergraduate school at CU. When I got that degree, I was finished. School is not my thing. I never could get motivated. I guess if they had paid me to go to school, I would have done much better. It wasn't hard work, just boring."

Mary Lou struggled to keep from frowning. *He is not an MBA? Joe has got some explaining to do—or perhaps he doesn't know. Yes, it's Walt, up to his tricks again. This time, he's going to make it right. A woman doing the same job as a man demands equal pay—it's the law. Since I've been here five years, I should be making a lot more than a newcomer.* "Okay, then, Denny. Let me give you an overview of how a sale works here at International Enterprises."

After two hours, Denny leaned back in his chair. "Let's take a break. Thanks to you I'll be ready to jump in."

Mary Lou put her pen down. "Did Joe mention who your clients would be?"

Denny raised his eyebrows. "Not yet. I'm hoping for a client in the Middle East. Wouldn't that be cool? I'd love to go to Kuwait."

Inwardly, Mary Lou rolled her eyes. *He's never met a client, and he wants to go to Kuwait? Please.*

Denny kept talking. "Where ever he assigns me, I'm pretty sure that not much is going to get done before we go on that deep-sea fishing trip."

She tilted her head. "Deep-sea fishing trip? Never mind. It's late, and I have to go."

Denny stood. "You've already forgotten about the trip you won? Walt says we're going to head out in a few weeks."

She frowned, unable to hold back. "Nobody said anything about a fishing trip. I won a cruise."

Denny walked toward the door. "All I'm saying is what Walt told me. I guess it's going to be a combo. He told me that we're taking his mega yacht, *The Adventurer.* I'm going to love this job. See ya." He turned to go to his car, which was parked in Walt's space.

That evening, Mary Lou had dinner with her parents, her sister Eileen, her brother Larry, and his wife and kids. After dinner, they played board games and then hand and foot canasta until midnight.

Saturday, January 26
Arvada, Colorado

Mary Lou wanted to sleep late that weekend, but she woke early. It was finally the weekend! She wrapped her plush new robe around her. *Oh, Mom, this robe feels absolutely divine. You could not have gotten me anything better for Christmas. I love it.* She fixed her morning cup of coffee.

From her kitchen table, she watched the news on the TV in the living room as she sipped her coffee.

At seven, the phone rang. *Who would be calling me at this hour?* She checked the caller ID, then picked up the phone. "Eileen, what's up?"

"Want to go up to Winter Park with me? I've got a friend who's working at the Viking Lodge. She said she could get us a deal on a room."

Mary Lou's interest piqued. "Did you say 'a deal'? Sounds good to me. So what's the plan?"

"We could stay cheap for two nights and ski for two days. We don't have to ski the whole time, but my friend said she could get us discount passes for two days."

Mary Lou glanced at the snow outside her window. "So you want to leave… when?" She'd tried to keep busier than usual since Bobby left. The ski trip with her sister would solve a lonely weekend.

"Now. We can get there in time to ski all day today. Then we would check in to the Viking Lodge. Come on. You need a change of scene."

"You're right about that. Okay, I'll dig out my skis. I assume you're driving."

"Hallelujah! Praise the Lord! I'm excited. We're going to have some fun."

Later that morning

Eileen tooted her horn as she pulled into Mary Lou's driveway behind the opened garage door. Mary Lou smiled, waved, and carried her ancient K2s out to secure them on top of Eileen's car. She breathed out fog as she struggled with the last clip of the ski rack. "Man, this is a tough one."

Eileen stepped out of the car. "You need help?"

"Ouch!" Mary Lou snatched her hand back. "No, I don't need help." She forced a laugh. "I just pinched my finger in the clip. Didn't break it—just pinched it. It's secure. It's all good."

Eileen wrinkled her brow. "You're sure you're all right?"

Mary Lou brightened. "I. Am. Fine." She stuck her forefinger in her mouth. "Just a pinch." She pulled her finger out of her mouth and inspected it. "I am so ready for this trip. Let me grab my bag." She ran back into the garage.

Eileen turned the radio to her favorite radio station and listened to the strains of "Wild Thing" while she waited. *Wow! I haven't heard that song for a long time.*

Minutes later, Mary Lou hopped in the car. "Oh, wait a minute. I have to use the keypad on the house to close the door. Too many things to remember." She laughed. "I really needed to get away. This is great."

She jumped out of the car and hurried to punch in the garage door code. The door rumbled as it made its descent.

Mary Lou flopped into the seat and exhaled. "Finally. Sorry about all the confusion. Let's get out of here."

Eileen looked at Mary Lou's lap. "Seat belt."

Mary Lou pulled the strap across her and snapped it into place. "Got it. Okay, now I'm ready. Sorry."

Eileen laughed. "Oh, stop saying you're sorry. We are on our way." She backed onto the street and headed toward I-25.

Mary Lou tilted her head. "What's that you're listening to?" She wrinkled her nose. "Is that 'Wild Thing'? Are you kidding me? That *is* 'Wild Thing.'"

Eileen put on a serious face. "You've never complained about my music preferences before. What's wrong with 'Wild Thing'?"

"Uh, you're not serious."

Eileen held her expression. "I'll have you know that it is rated as one of the greatest hits of all time—by *Rolling Stone* magazine, no less."

"Who *are* you? And what have you done with my sister?"

Both of them burst out laughing.

Eileen stuck out her bottom lip. "Can't I go back to my youth, once in a while?"

The radio announcer broke in with "And that was 'Wild Thing' by the Troggs, rated number two hundred fifty-seven on the *Rolling Stone* magazine's list of the top five hundred greatest songs of all time. It's Oldies Day here at 119.4 Radio. Now for a change of pace, sit back and enjoy the strains of 'A Summer Place.'"

Eileen listened as Mary Lou hummed along with the radio. She leaned back in her seat. "Today is far from summer. Right now the wet road isn't a problem, but from the looks of those clouds on the mountains, it could get slick."

Snow stuck to the median and ground around the highway. Freezing temperatures and falling snow could easily overtake the chemicals that kept the roadways free from ice. Eileen kept her eyes on the road. Less than five minutes later, they took the ramp onto the highway.

Eileen passed the snowplow and crept into the flow of traffic. Merging onto I-76 via exit 216, she turned toward Grand Junction.

Six miles later, she was on I-70, heading into the mountains. Tiny snowflakes lightly sprinkled the windshield.

"Looks like we're going to get more snow," Eileen said, interrupting the music they'd been listening to. "If it doesn't get any worse than this, we'll be in great shape." She readjusted her seat belt across her chest.

Mary Lou looked up from her cell phone. "I was just looking at the forecast. You're not going to like this. Didn't you check before we left?"

"Hey, it's winter. Snow might happen."

Mary Lou turned the radio off. "Uh, I'm sorry, but the forecast is calling for a foot or more of snow in the high country."

Eileen turned on the windshield wipers as the flakes thickened. "Oh, they say that all the time so skiers will flock up here to ski. It's just a commerce thing. You're in marketing. You know how that works. I swear, all those weather forecasters are on the take."

Mary Lou grimaced. "Humph. On the take, eh? Take a look at the oncoming traffic."

Eileen glanced across the median. Snow-covered vehicles braked as they traveled down the seven-percent grade into Denver. A large clump of ice broke off an eighteen-wheeler and rolled into the white space between them. "Yikes! Glad I'm not following that truck. But really, Mary Lou, don't worry. We know how to drive in snow. I mean, we do it every winter. That's why I drive an Outback."

"That reminds me. I'm sorry, but I am so looking forward to my cruise."

"Oh, yeah. When are you leaving?"

Mary Lou rolled her eyes. "I don't know. Mr. Control Freak, Walt, will let me know when he's good and ready, and not one minute sooner. That's why I haven't even asked. But I am so ready."

For the next hour, they listened to a popular radio talk show and commented on opinions of the people calling in.

Eileen turned onto the ramp to U.S. 40. Snow was blowing full blast into the windshield. She squinted to see the two wheel tracks in front of her.

The car swerved.

Mary Lou grabbed the handle above her door. "Watch out!"

A second before they would have gone into the ditch, the wheels found traction and stopped sliding.

Eileen screamed, "Thank You, Lord! Thank You for Your protection!"

Mary Lou released the grab bar. "I'm sorry, but I think we should stop in Empire."

A snowplow pulled out around them.

Eileen squealed. "Yee! You talk about God's provision. We're going to follow this baby all the way to Winter Park." She fell in behind the snowplow.

"I'm glad you're driving. Still, the next thirty miles—"

"Mary Lou, just think how great the powder's going to be. You don't get this all the time. It is going to be great!"

"Only twenty-nine miles to go. I hope we make it."

Eileen gripped the wheel. "It will take a while. The snowplow is going thirty-five miles an hour, and I am not going to pass him."

"No, no. I don't want you to. There's no hurry. We can get half-day passes today."

An hour later, the Subaru Outback pulled up in front of the Viking Lodge.

Eileen pulled off her sunglasses. "Let's check in and unload. I want to lie down for a few minutes. Then we can take the shuttle to the lift."

Mary Lou pulled up her soft leather boots. "Good idea. I can't believe the sun is out. It is gorgeous. Half an hour ago, I was ready to go back home."

Chapter Eight

Later the same day
Winter Park, Colorado

They checked in and carried their bags to their second-floor room. Rustic light fixtures accented log walls and furniture made out of thick branches. The two queen-sized beds left plenty of room for the sofa and overstuffed chair with side tables.

Mary Lou dropped her backpack on the bed nearest the door and flopped on the sofa. "Yay! We made it."

Eileen stretched out on the bed. "Just need a few minutes to switch gears." She flexed her hands. "I've got to stop gripping the wheel when I get nervous. My hands feel numb."

"It's cold in here." Mary Lou jumped up to flip the switch next to the fireplace, and flames immediately leaped to attention. She felt the warmth. "Now, that's more like it."

Eileen sighed. "Oh, that's nice."

Mary Lou watched Eileen close her eyes and fall asleep. *Well, I guess that drive would wear me out, too.* Mary Lou quietly began unpacking her things. She put her fuzzy pajamas under her pillow, her slippers on the floor beside the bed, and her backpack inside the spacious closet. She took her toiletries bag into the large bathroom.

The countertop and double sinks left ample room for Eileen's things, even after Mary Lou took out her toothbrush, cleansing cream, and moisturizer.

She heard Eileen moving about in the main room and sauntered out of the bathroom. "That was a short nap."

"Oh, I didn't mean to go to sleep. How long was I down?"

"Only a few minutes. You want to rest more? We can ski tomorrow."

Eileen rubbed her eyes and looked at the sun reflecting off the snow outside the window. "Oh, I'm ready. 'This is the day the Lord has made. Let us rejoice and be glad in it'—Psalm 118:24. Let's get out there!"

Mary Lou grinned wide. "I'm ready."

They grabbed their gear and caught the shuttle to the lifts. After donning ski boots and skis, they hurried to the main lift. They were third in line, and after it swooshed down and picked them up, Mary Lou gazed out at the scene before them. Sparkling snow diamonds greeted her. She took in a deep breath and exhaled a puff of fog.

At the top of Mary Jane Mountain, they eased onto the ski run. Just a little wind at the top of the mountain swirled snow around them. Soon they would be protected from the wind by the mountain.

Eileen chose the run marked with a blue square, meaning an intermediate slope. If Eileen had picked the black diamond, Mary Lou would have been game to try it, but she knew very well that she was not ready for an advanced run.

It turned out to be a perfect day for schussing down the mountain. The powder came up to Mary Lou's knees in places. She enjoyed watching Eileen cut through the powder in front of her.

In no time, she found herself back at the base of the mountain, waiting in line for the lift. *That went so fast. What a beautiful, beautiful day. Lord, You have truly blessed us.*

Eileen showed a toothy smile. "This is amazing."

Mary Lou tapped her poles into the snow beside her. "Just great powder—I didn't even get down to crust. It's the best ever." Then Mary Lou shoved Eileen away from the line. "Watch out!" she shouted, as a kid shot past. "Sorry, Eileen. That Never-ever about plowed into you."

Eileen steadied herself. "Thanks, but how do you know he's a newbie?"

"I saw him on the learning slope with a group of students. He was trying to snowplow, but he forgot that he should be traversing."

Eileen laughed. "I forgive him. We've all been there." She looked over at the young man, whose face had turned red from the cold.

An older man—Mary Lou thought it could be the boy's father—raised his ski pole at Eileen. "Sorry. He's just learning."

She waved back. "No worries." She turned toward Mary Lou. "Daddy's cute. Don't you think so?"

Mary Lou took a second look. "Uh, yeah, I guess so." *Men. Who cares? Bobby took the life out of me. I could care less about men.*

The lift they were about to get on was a quad, and Eileen and Mary Lou ended up with the boy and his father.

The man sat next to Eileen. "Hello, I'm Kurt, and this is Logan. Logan, say hello to the woman you nearly knocked over a few minutes ago." Kurt chuckled.

Logan, still red from the cold, looked up. "Sorry, ma'am. I'm just a beginner. It's my first time here. Today is my twelfth birthday."

Eileen smiled bigger than Mary Lou thought necessary. "Happy birthday, and don't worry about it. All of us have been there. One time I tried to snowplow on ice and knocked down the whole line of people waiting in line to get on the lift. Boy, was I embarrassed!"

The boy looked across the quad at Mary Lou. "When I came down the hill, I thought you were one of my classmates and lost my focus. When I got close enough to see that I'd made a mistake, it was too late, and I almost crashed."

He thought I was a classmate? It's a good thing he's on the other end of this thing. He might find himself on the ground. She looked down. *It's probably a good twenty feet down. Okay, I've got to stop thinking like that. The kid made a mistake.*

She glanced at Eileen's radiant face looking at Kurt. He was smiling back at Eileen as if he were smitten.

What is this? Mary Lou felt left out. *Is it old home week or what? What is going on here? I think Eileen is flirting.*

Mary Lou felt suspicion rise up in her. A married man, having some fun with her sister? And Eileen was enjoying every bit of the attention. Mary Lou spoke to the boy over the wind. "How nice of your father to bring you skiing on your birthday. Where is your mother?"

The boy smiled. "She hates snow."

Kurt laughed. "He's my nephew. Every once in a while, he gives his single—and lonely—Uncle Kurt some company. He's full of life and enthusiasm. A great kid. He's game for almost any new experience."

Eileen jumped right on that, asking, "Why are you so lonely, Uncle Kurt?"

He dramatically pouted at Eileen. "I own my own company with a very capable staff. I simply have too much free time. I'd give about anything to have someone to share it with."

Mary Lou blinked. *Are you kidding me? Is this guy trying to pick her up? We came up here to ski, for Pete's sake.*

Kurt chuckled. "Can I take you and your friend to dinner later?"

Eileen giggled. "Well, of course we can go to dinner." She looked at Mary Lou's scowling face. "We'd love to—right, Mary Lou?"

Mary Lou attempted to recover. "Let's talk about it."

Kurt straightened up to dismount the lift. "Okay, I'll meet you at the warming house at seven o'clock."

They reached the summit, and each of them got off the lift.

Mary Lou skied up next to Eileen. "What are you doing?"

"I'm having fun. Remember what that's like? Come on, Mary Lou. Lighten up." Eileen pointed her skis down the hill. "Try to catch me!"

And away she flew down the mountain.

Mary Lou stood at the summit. *I can't believe I came up here with a thirty-five-year-old sister, and she turned into a teenybopper in less than the bat of Rambo's eyelash. Really. I am going to have to sit through an evening of flirting in front of his twelve-year-old nephew. Or will they set me up with him? After all, he did think I was his classmate. What is he, a sixth grader? Eileen, you are going to pay for this one.*

Mary Lou traversed the trail slowly, so as to miss meeting their new friends at the lift again. Just before getting to the bottom of the hill she looked up to see Eileen, Kurt, and Logan going up on the quad again.

They waved at her, and Eileen shouted, "Meet you at the room later!"

Mary Lou spread a big fake smile across her face and waved back. "Okay. Have fun!"

Later the same day
Winter Park, Colorado

After five more runs down the intermediate slopes, Mary Lou took off her skis and made her way to the shuttle. A five-minute ride took her back to the Viking Lodge, where she immediately went to her room and took off her ski gear. She sat in the overstuffed chair and rubbed her knees. *I am getting too old for this. My knees ache, and my nose is running. A smart person knows when to quit.*

She went to lie down on the bed. *Ah, I could go to sleep right now.*

The door flew open, and Eileen pranced in. "I have to find something to wear. I didn't even bring makeup. We're going to meet Kurt for dinner. I can't wait to find out more about him. Don't you think he's just the cutest guy?"

Mary Lou wrinkled her nose. "I'd say that you think he's cute enough for both of us. Obviously, it doesn't matter what I think."

Eileen smiled sweetly. "He invited both of us to dinner. Hey, when was the last time you got a free dinner? I think you're jealous. I know one thing—if Bobby was here, you'd go in a minute. Now get ready. Let's go have a free dinner."

Mary Lou scowled and chose to ignore Eileen's mention of Bobby. "You know as well as I do that there is no such thing as a free dinner or lunch. I just hope this doesn't cost you too much. The last time you fell in love was less than six months ago. That lasted two weeks."

Eileen took off her coat and boots. "You're right. I can't argue with that. And that was the greatest two weeks. I really thought I was in love again."

Mary Lou wrinkled her nose. "Well, that's just fine for you, but every time you break up, I have to go through it with you. I don't know if I'm up for it. The highs are so high, but the lows are devastating."

Eileen took off the rest of her ski gear and walked toward the bathroom. "Hey, we're not getting married. We're having dinner with you and Logan. I think you can stop him from sweeping me off my feet, thank you very much." She slammed the bathroom door.

A few minutes later, Mary Lou heard the shower running. *There is no getting out of this. I might as well change and get ready. I'm sure going to find out as much as I can about this guy. If he hurts my sister, he will pay.*

Evening, the same day
Winter Park, Colorado

It was seven o'clock. Mary Lou and Eileen walked into the restaurant, looking left and right for Kurt and Logan.

Mary Lou nudged Eileen. "Didn't I tell you there were no such thing as a free lunch? Don't feel bad. It looks like a great place to eat. We can have dinner without them."

Eileen shrugged. "It's beyond me why they didn't show up. I just knew he was being sincere. He seemed like such a nice guy."

A voice behind them said, "And he is such a nice guy."

They turned around to see Kurt's smiling face.

Mary Lou looked around Kurt. "Where's Logan?"

Kurt looked behind himself, as if looking for his nephew, then turned back to face Mary Lou and Eileen. "Logan is tired and didn't want to be bored with the conversation of adults. After a light snack, he chose to go to the arcade. I'll pick him up after dinner. That way both of us get to do what we want to."

Mary Lou frowned. "Shouldn't he have an adult with him? I mean, anything could happen. And you say he's your nephew? Aren't you worried?"

Kurt laughed and pointed toward a large glass window wall. "The arcade's right there in the room next to us. I can see him from here. Let's find the table near the window, and he'll be in my sight the whole time. I happen to know that he's in love with that game he's playing right now."

The hostess arrived and seated them at a table in the perfect spot. Kurt could see Logan playing in the arcade, and Mary Lou could make sure he was watching Logan. And Eileen sat next to Kurt with that silly smile on her face.

Dinner lasted well over an hour. Mary Lou counted every second. It was painful to watch Eileen and Kurt in the dance of getting to know each other when her love life had crashed and burned so recently. *Unequally yoked, blah, blah, blah! What an excuse. But I have my work and I'm actually glad for that. Bobby and Walt—men are such jerks. No wonder God tried again.*

Mary Lou expected Kurt to ditch her and Logan for a few minutes alone with Eileen after dinner. But after they ate, they went to the arcade and met Logan. Kurt was very attentive, asking Logan if he had a good time, what games he played, and such. The conversation seemed to go on forever as the youngster related every detail of every arcade game he played that night. Mary Lou was exhausted when Kurt told them good night at the front of the restaurant.

Back at the room, Eileen went on and on about how much she had enjoyed the evening. She didn't mention the fact that Kurt had not brought up the subject of when they would see each other again, but Mary Lou let it go. She was tired, and it was time to go to bed. She wanted to get up early and be the first one on the slopes.

Sunday, January 27
Winter Park, Colorado

The next morning, Mary Lou made it first to the summit. The sun was excruciatingly bright. A light crust had formed on yesterday's powder. *It's good to have my ski mask.* She looked down at the newly combed hill. *Not a ski trail on it! Love being able to make the first marks in fresh powder.*

When she'd left the room that morning, Eileen still slept. *No doubt dreaming about her future.* Mary Lou had chuckled, shook her head, she whispered, "You're going to have to catch up with me today. I'm out of here. Sweet dreams."

Mary Lou enjoyed the solitude and the quiet of the morning. *There's nothing quite like feeling the presence of the Lord within His magnificent creation. This is so beautiful.* She traversed down the intermediate slope at a lazy speed, enjoying the sound of her skis slicing through the fresh powder.

She heard someone shouting her name and turned to see Logan.

"Miss Mary Lou, is that you?" He squinted. "It is you. Want to race down the hill?"

No, she didn't want to race down the hill, but she had to admit that Logan was as charming as his uncle Kurt. "Okay, I'll race you. Ready, set, go!"

They took off in a cloud of snow. Mary Lou skied as fast as she could. No way could he be keeping up with her. She caught a glance of him only a few feet behind her.

She turned back and couldn't hold back her scream. She was about to take a flying leap off an expert ski jump. She hadn't seen it in her path before, but now she was on the jump, with no recourse but to complete it.

Having never been on a ski jump, Mary Lou didn't have time to be afraid or reconsider. She flew off the end of the jump and landed in a heap of snow, in a tangled mess.

She could not move. Her skis were wrapped around each other.

"Mary Lou! Mary Lou, are you all right?" He sped up beside her.

The wind was knocked out of her. She struggled for air. Finally she gasped out, "I don't know."

Logan was on his knees beside her. "Let me help you." He tried to pull her up.

Mary Lou felt pain shoot up from her ankle. "Logan, we're going to need more help. Go get someone. Go to the bottom of the hill and ask them to send the EMTs."

Logan's face went white. "Yes ma'am. Yes, ma'am. I'll go right now."

He was still on his knees.

Mary Lou calmed her voice and repeated, more slowly, "Logan, I need you to stand up on your skis and go down to the bottom of the hill and ask them to send EMTs or the ski patrol or somebody that can help. My ankle is hurt. I can't ski."

His eyes widened. "I'll go fast."

He took off down the hill. A minute later, Kurt was by her side. "I was on the lift. Logan had gone on ahead of me. I was kind of waiting around to see if I would see you and Eileen, and I got on a later lift. When I looked down, I saw Logan on his knees, then I saw you. Are you all right?"

Mary Lou could not keep the tears out of her eyes. "I hurt my ankle. It really hurts. I could feel pain shoot all the way up my leg. Oh, it hurts so bad."

"Let me help you. This may hurt. If it's too much, tell me, and I'll stop." He leaned over and popped her skis off, allowing her legs to lie on the snow, untangled.

"That's better, thank you." she took a deep breath.

The EMTs arrived. They checked her injuries, applied a splint to her leg, and lifted her onto a sled gurney. The two men took each side of the gurney and carefully slid it down the hill. When they got to the bottom of the hill, they pushed it onto a cart, and then pushed the cart into the back of an ambulance.

Kurt stuck his head in behind them. "Can I come along? Logan and I would love to keep you company."

Mary Lou wrinkled her nose. "You and Logan can go back to the lift. I am going to be fine. But thanks for offering."

The EMT slammed the door shut. Kurt and Logan waved as the ambulance lumbered toward the hospital.

Eileen showed up at the emergency room minutes after Kurt's call. "What did you do? I can't believe you left me in bed this morning. And now this. Can't trust you by yourself, can I?"

Mary Lou breathed in. "It's all better now. They just took X-rays to see if I broke my ankle. I scratched up my leg somehow, but the real injury is my ankle."

The nurse came in with the X-rays and nodded as she walked toward Mary Lou's bed. "You are lucky today. You didn't break it. But it's a sprain. So we'll fit you with a boot, and you really shouldn't put any weight on it for a while. You're getting a brand-new pair of crutches." She smiled.

"I really don't feel that lucky today." Mary Lou grimaced as the nurse started wrapping the tan Ace bandage around her ankle.

The nurse shrugged. "It could've been a lot worse. We see a lot worse all the time. Now, you want me to send something with you for the pain?"

Mary Lou stiffened. "I don't like to take medicine. I don't like to take pills. I'm really not in that much pain now, so I think I'll be all right."

The nurse laughed. "You're not in that much pain right now because the EMTs gave you something when you were in the ambulance. Remember?"

Mary Lou rubbed her forehead. "Yes, I forgot for a minute. But I did take a pill."

The nurse handed her a bag. "You should probably take something with you. When you wake up in the middle of the night, you'll have it."

Reluctantly, Mary Lou accepted the little bag of four pills, along with a prescription for more in case she needed it.

Eileen took the bag and prescription and helped Mary Lou get up on the crutches for the first time. "Praise God. You know He protected you today. This could have been a lot worse. 'Cast your cares on Him, for He cares for you'—1 Peter 5:7. Look, they had to give you the child size to fit your height. Isn't that cute?"

Mary Lou frowned at her. "Really, Eileen? I don't think that's funny. Let's go back to the room so I can put my foot up."

Once they got back in the room, Eileen started packing to go home.

Mary Lou watched for a minute. "Put those clothes back. There is no reason for us to go back home. We can leave in the morning. I'm not going to work tomorrow. I'm taking a few days off to baby this ankle. Right now I'm going to put my foot up and enjoy the fireplace and the view out the window."

Eileen pulled out her cell phone. "I'm texting work to tell them I'll be in late tomorrow. That way we can drive back in the morning. You come up with the best ideas!"

Mary Lou hugged the sofa pillow to her chest. "You go skiing. Find that Kurt guy. He was looking for you, this morning."

Eileen brightened. "You saw Kurt? He was looking for me?"

Mary Lou rolled her eyes. "Yes, that's what I said. He was out this morning, looking for you. Oh, and he still has Logan with him."

Eileen was already putting on her coat.

After Eileen left, Mary Lou focused on the lovely fire, burning brightly. In the flames, she pictured the cruise boat. *I won a cruise. As soon as we get back to work, I'm going to ask Walt when I can leave. He and Denny can go on their fishing trip, but I won a cruise. I could use this recovery time on the deck of a fancy cruise ship in the Bahamas.* She closed her eyes and pictured herself in a lounge chair wearing large diamond-studded sunglasses, a book in her hand, with the emerald ocean spread out before her. She smiled at the vision. *I can't wait. It's mine, and I'm going to take it. I won it, fair and square. I'm going to enjoy every minute of it, and I'm not going to give one minute of thought to Bobby Porter.*

Chapter Nine

Wednesday, January 30
Denver, Colorado

Mary Lou's first day back at work came way too soon and turned into a real challenge. The fact that she had yet to have a good night's sleep since the accident did not help matters. Also, leaning on the crutches hurt her armpits. She could take the big boot off, but then she had to be extra careful not to bump the ankle or forget and use it. She dreaded running into Walt, who would make her the butt of his harassing jokes.

She got to her office without anyone seeing her except the security guard at the front door. She sat at her desk and laid the crutches on the floor beside her desk.

Shortly thereafter, Joe came in. "I got the message that you would be out extra days. Did you have a good vacation?" He saw the crutches. "Oh no, what happened?"

Mary Lou shrugged. "Ski accident. No big deal. Just sprained my ankle."

Joe picked up one of the crutches and examined it. "Must've been a pretty bad sprain. How long are you going to be on crutches?"

Mary Lou resituated herself in her chair. "Probably just this week. It's a lot better than it was even yesterday."

Joe handed her the crutch. "Walt wants us in the conference room. I'm not sure what it's about."

Mary Lou wetted her lips. "We need to talk."

"Sure, but Walt doesn't like to wait. We should go in there now."

Mary Lou didn't move. "I don't like to complain, but I've worked here five years. My base pay is seventy-five thousand a year, and I'm not complaining about that. But I came in Monday morning, when the office was closed for a holiday, to work with a new employee—I would call that above and beyond what is required, yet I willingly did that. And what did I find out?"

Joe tilted his head. "What?"

"My new colleague, Denny Adams, told me his starting salary is eighty-five thousand a year—and by the way, he *was* complaining. Now, I could understand it if he was hired at a higher level than I am. But he's not. We are basically doing the same job. And because I've been here five years, I'm training him."

Joe raised his eyebrows and folded his arms. *Perhaps Joe didn't know until now.* "I'll look into it."

Mary Lou fingered her desk pad. "I don't want to even start a conversation about discrimination, but you know as well as I do that a woman who is doing the same job as a man should get the same pay. Or maybe you don't agree with that?"

"You know better than that. Give me some time. I'll talk to Walt about this when the time is right. And speaking of time, we need to meet him now." He picked up her other crutch and offered them to her.

She scooted her chair out, revealing the oversized boot on her right leg.

Joe moved closer. "Here. Let me help you."

Mary Lou took the crutches and placed them under her arms. "I've got this. I'm just slow. You go ahead. I'll meet you in the conference room."

Joe shook his head. "I'll walk with you."

They made their way down the hall toward the conference room. Joe walked to the side and slightly behind Mary Lou. Her crutches took up more than half the hallway space.

When they got to the conference room, Joe leaped out in front of her to open the door. She entered a room already occupied by a frowning Walt, a smiling Denny, several agents, and one of the secretaries preparing coffee at the bar in the back of the room.

Walt boomed, "What happened to you?"

Joe pulled out a chair, and Mary Lou clumsily sat down, laying her crutches on the floor beside her chair. "Just a little ski accident," she said. "Sprained my ankle. It should be better soon."

Walt responded by reaching into the box of glazed donuts, taking a huge bite, and remarking with his mouth full, "It better be, because we're leaving on this cruise a week from Friday."

"What do you mean, 'we' are leaving on this cruise?" Mary Lou asked, stunned. "I thought *I* won a cruise."

He took another huge bite of the doughnut, leaving about a quarter of it secured between his thumb and forefinger, and spoke again through a mouthful of doughnut. "You did win a cruise."

Mary Lou shot back, "So what is this 'we' are leaving?'"

Walt swallowed his mouthful and laughed. "We're taking out my mega yacht, *The Adventurer*, for little cruise and deep-sea fishing in the Bahamas. Mary Lou, you'll be happy to know that I've arranged for Denny and Joe to come along. There's plenty of room on the yacht, don't worry. You'll have your own stateroom—after all, you did win."

Mary Lou needed coffee. But in order for her to get a cup of coffee, she would have to back out of her chair, pick up her crutches, and navigate around the huge conference table to the bar at the back of the room.

Her mouth was dry. Her head was beginning to throb. And she was resisting the urge to yell at Walt.

Calmly and slowly, she said, "So I won a cruise, and you guys are going deep-sea fishing on your yacht."

Walt shook his head. "I'm certainly going to be sure you have the proper gear for deep-sea fishing. No doubt I'll have to order something custom-made because you're so short." He started laughing.

Mary Lou held her hands under the table on her lap. She started pushing back the cuticles on each finger as she decided how she should respond. This was her trip. She won it, fair and square. *Seems like Walt and Denny, the old college buddies, want to make it into a holiday. The only reason Joe is invited is to make it look like business. I'm sure Walt's getting some kind of tax refund by using his yacht.*

I'll figure out a way to enjoy this trip, one way or another. This is my trip. I won it. I am going to have it. But I'm sure as heck not going to deep-sea fish. Mary Lou finally looked up from her calendar. "So it looks like we're leaving on February eighth."

Walt sat down and crossed his legs at the knee. He rocked back in the office chair. "Now, that's the spirit. Rule number one. No talking about business while on *The Adventurer*." He slapped his knee. "We're going to have us some fun."

Mary Lou cringed. *Yeah.*

Mary Lou leaned over to pick up her crutches. She straightened up and started to make her way around the table to the coffee urn. "Oh, and Walt—don't invest in custom deep-sea fishing gear for me. I'll find something to do."

She made it to the coffee urn, drew a cup of Nantucket blend, and added some cream and little sugar. She was stirring it when Walt announced that the meeting was over. She took a deep sip of her coffee, because there was no way she could walk with her crutches and carry the cup coffee.

She looked longingly at the cup, saying her good-byes. Then she turned on her crutches to navigate around the huge conference table to go out the door and to her office.

A voice behind her said, "Here, let me bring your coffee to your office."

She felt a rush of deep-seated gratitude. She turned around to say thank you and met Denny's eyes head on. "Oh! Denny." She found it impossible to hide her surprise. Denny didn't seem the type to help out. "Thanks, that would be very nice. I appreciate it."

He followed her to her office, cup in hand. After they got there, he set the coffee on her desk while she struggled with the big boot, her office chair, and the crutches.

She smiled. "Thanks again, Denny. That was very considerate."

Denny shrugged. "No big deal. I've had crutches before. It's not fun. I do hope you don't have to take them on the cruise."

"Oh, I have no intention of taking crutches on that cruise. The doctor told me a week with the boot, and after that, we'll see."

Denny turned, gave a thumbs-up, and headed toward his new office down the hall.

What a surprise. Denny Adams has manners? Could have fooled me. What am I saying? Maybe he's not such a bad guy after all.

Friday, February 1
Denver, Colorado

Joe stopped by Mary Lou's office. "Walt just sent a memo. Have you checked your email? In any case, he's calling a big meeting in the main conference room. He wants all salespeople there. Sorry you have to get up, I know it's not easy getting around right now."

"It's much better. Look." She turned her chair toward him and showed her the bootless right leg. "No more boot."

"Hey, that's great. Let's go see what Walt's up to."

They went to the main conference room, where a large conference table filled the room. All the salespeople were there, along with several sales support people.

Mary Lou found a seat near the door. *What is this all about? I can't imagine what grandiose scheme Walt's come up with.*

The sales agent sitting next to her nudged her. "You're in the know. What's up?"

Mary Lou shook her head. "I don't have a clue, but it looks like we're going to find out real soon."

Walt strode into the room. He took his usual stance at the head of the table in front of a whiteboard. He smiled condescendingly, looking down on his minions. "Thank everyone for coming today."

Thank everyone for coming today? Since when has Walt thanked anybody for anything?

"I wanted you all here to share my exciting news!"

Stop playing these games to try to make yourself look good. I need to get some work done. All I needed was one more useless meeting to make my day.

Suddenly, Walt was standing over Mary Lou. "Mary Lou, this meeting is all about you."

What is he up to now? About me? What did I do now? Is he going to fire me?

Walt bellowed with a laugh. "You've been here, what over five years? How the time flies. It seems like just yesterday that I saw you come in to interview. Right away I knew that you were a winner! I knew you would be an excellent salesman for International Enterprises."

He took a step back and addressed the group. "And was I right? Do I know what I'm doing? I would say I know how to pick them. Here she is salesman of the year, third time in a row."

Someone began to clap, and soon applause filled the room.

Walt's face reddened slightly. "I guess we all agree. She deserves something besides a cruise to the Bahamas and a walnut plaque. I won't wait any longer. I don't want to keep everyone in suspense." He held out what looked like a check.

Mary Lou took the check and held it out to see. She gasped.

Walt puffed up and announced, "The company is giving Mary Lou a check for ten grand. Mary Lou, this is for your outstanding performance as a salesman for International Enterprises. Please take this with our gratitude and best wishes. Also, I would like you to know this will be reflected from this year on as an increase in your salary."

Mary Lou couldn't believe her eyes or ears. *So this is what happened when Joe told Walt about their conversation.* "I—I don't know what to say." She wanted to rip him seven ways from Sunday, but she knew better. *What an ass.*

"You needn't say anything. This is money you earned last year." Walt leaned back and shouted, "Now do it again this year!" He looked around the room. "You are dismissed."

Salespeople filed out of the room until the only ones left were Mary Lou and Joe.

"Listen, Mary Lou—I promise I did not know this was going to happen. The day you told me about it, I went to Walt and confronted him with this injustice. He told me he would fix it. Well, you know Walt. He fixed it. In his mind, he's done the right thing."

In. His. Mind? Mary Lou groped for words. *In his mind, he did the right thing?* "My big reward for all my contributions is the same salary as the new guy. Whoopee. Walt sure knows how to motivate people. That man is stupid, crude, and has about as much tact as an earwig."

Joe shook his head. "I hate to say this, but as long as we work for Walt, we both know what kind of man he is, and I'm going to leave it like that."

Mary Lou answered, "Enough said."

Sunday, February 3
Arvada, Colorado

Bright sunlight poured into Mary Lou's bedroom. She woke with a start and rolled over to look at the clock. *Nine o'clock. I must have been exhausted. I've been burning the candle at both ends lately. I need to get going. I'm burning daylight, and there's lots for me to accomplish today.* She threw the covers off and headed for the bathroom to shower. *At least I can walk without those crutches.*

As she stood under the warm shower, her plan for the day took form. *First I'm going to clean out the junk drawer in the kitchen. I can't find anything in that mess. Then I'll start on my closet. That thing could sure use an overhaul. After that, I'll clean up the home office and do some much-needed filing. Yes, and then I could read* War and Peace *before bedtime.*

Eileen's right. I always get super busy doing nothing when I can't face what I need to. Lord, help me get it right. I need to drive up to Lookout Mountain this morning and just meditate on You, my Creator. It's February, so there won't be many tourists. I'll take my Bible and just spend time with You, Lord.

In less than twenty minutes, she was in the car headed up I-70 to Lookout Mountain. The skies were brilliant blue, with a few white clouds. *Thank You, Lord, for this beautiful day. I really am grateful for this day and for the many blessings that I take for granted every day. Thank You for Eileen, who keeps me on track and reminds me that I need to be in tune with what You want for my life.*

She turned on the radio, and the sound of rock music pounded the dash. *Not today. I want something a bit more spiritual.* She switched stations and ended up at 910 AM on the dial. She heard the music and a voice singing, "Put Jesus first in your life and turn your life around." The music stopped, and the announcer said, "Dr. Robert Dallenbach from Alma Temple in Denver, Colorado."

Dr. Dallenbach gave a short inspirational message. Mary Lou had nearly reached Lookout Mountain, but she abruptly turned her car around at the next exit. She searched Google to find Alma Temple at the Denver address listed on the broadcast. Soon she found herself parking in front of the large building with the domed roof. The call letters of the radio station, KPOF, hung over the front of the church.

She entered and saw a man at the pulpit giving the invocation. Mary Lou walked to the front row and took a seat in front of the altar. She glanced up at the stained glass window behind the pulpit. There stood Jesus. He grasped a staff in one hand and held a lamb in the other. Sheep surrounded his feet.

Mary Lou felt a tear trail down her cheek. *You are my shepherd. Dear Jesus, I am your lamb, one of Your sheep.* The congregation stood to sing "The Old Rugged Cross." Mary Lou knelt before the altar and wept.

She and Eileen had prayed the sinner's prayer, along with nine of their friends at the campfire on the last night of a church camp. After her conversion, she went back home and attended church regularly for years. Then somewhere, along the way, she resumed her old life. But her sister had changed. She wanted to go to church all the time.

Mary Lou asked for forgiveness for forgetting God and retaining a selfish life filled with meaningless things. The more she prayed, the more she cried. The service continued as though the congregation was used to people crying at the altar.

She felt as if this was her time—her time to change and to get right with God, and she wasn't going to leave this altar until she was finished.

After nearly an hour, she felt a tap on her shoulder.

The figure in the stained glass window stood beside her. "Welcome home, My child."

Jesus pointed to a white-haired lady in the fifth row of the congregation. "She will be your mentor. Do not fear. Everything will be fine."

A wave of peace and love washed over Mary Lou. She stood up, drying her eyes, and returned to her seat in the front row. She sat through the ending prayer, staring at Jesus in the stained glass window.

As soon as the service ended, she proceeded to the pew where the white-haired lady sat.

Mary Lou took a deep breath. "This may sound strange, but Jesus just told me that you would be my mentor."

The woman put her arm around Mary Lou. "Oh, my child, there is nothing strange about it. I saw Him tap your shoulder and point to me; I'm Mrs. Cunkell. I knew that this would be a special day. Now give me your car keys, and one of the boys will bring your car up to the hill. You're coming with me. We have a lot to talk about. We're going to start in the Book of Mark."

Tuesday, February 5
Westminster, Colorado

Mary Lou walked into the Family Christian Bookstore on a mission. She strolled over to the Bible section. Bibles filled the cases from floor to ceiling. She was overwhelmed by all the different translations and choices.

Lord, in the past I've read Your word. I admit that I haven't read it very seriously. I read my Bible cover to cover the first year after I was saved. I don't remember much about it. Now I want to know You, not just read the Bible and know about You. Mrs. Cunkell says a study Bible would help.

One of the store clerks approached her. "Can I help you find something?"

Mary Lou breathed a sigh of relief. "I need a new Bible. The one I have is what I got when I first became a Christian. That was back at church camp a long time ago. I have a teen version, and I think it's about time I got a good study Bible."

The woman smiled kindly. "Is there any reason you want a study Bible in particular?"

Mary Lou admired the leather bindings in front of her. "Yes, there is. The woman I'm studying with suggested that it would be helpful."

The store clerk pulled four Bibles off the shelf and took them to a nearby table. She opened each one of them and showed Mary Lou the different ways they were laid out, the different type, and other features.

Mary Lou picked one of them up. "This is nice." She flipped through a few pages. "I want something that connects the Living Word with me living today, now."

The woman nodded picked another Bible off the shelf. "I think this is what you want. It's a Life Application Study Bible. See, the notes suggest ways to apply the Scriptures to your life in today's world. It's a popular version."

Mary Lou took the Bible from the woman and opened it to look at one of the Scriptures Mrs. Cunkell had talked about. Mary Lou liked the way the notes explained the passage.

The clerk said, "This gives information on Bible life and times, plus it goes a step further to show you how to take it personally. It's the one I use in my quiet time."

Chapter Ten

Friday, February 8
Ft. Lauderdale, Florida

At four o'clock in the afternoon, Mary Lou walked across the dock to the one hundred ten-foot mega yacht, *The Adventurer*, in slip *A*. The slight breeze caused her to shiver as she approached the boat. Denny and Joe led the way.

Walt popped out the aft hatch onto the rear deck. He faced his little group of minions. "Before I take you on the tour of the boat, I want you to notice the name on this ship. It's *The Adventurer*. That's what life is all about—adventure. Every time I take her out, it's an adventure."

Denny Adams admired the craft. "You know how to name them, boss. She's a beauty."

Joe Gillespie nodded in agreement as he scrutinized his surroundings.

Walt motioned to the man on the upper deck. "Come down here. I want you to meet my employees."

A Middle Eastern man of medium height with a stocky build climbed down the metal stairway. His crisp white uniform, complete with a gold-decorated ship captain's hat, blazed against his dark skin. He spoke with a slight Arabic accent. "We are ready to leave port when you give the order, boss."

Walt puffed up, obviously loving being called boss. He walked over and put his arm around the captain's shoulders. "This is our captain, Kiral. His name means 'supreme leader,' but you can call him Captain."

Kiral nodded at the group.

Denny stepped in and offered his hand. "I'm Denny."

Joe stuck out his hand. "Joe."

Kiral nodded and shook hands with Joe and Denny.

Mary Lou squeezed between Denny and Joe, extending her hand. "I'm Mary Lou. I'm so glad to meet you."

Kiral smiled brightly and shook her hand. "Happy to meet you, Mary Lou."

Walt walked toward the steps to the top. "We'll leave in a few minutes. First, I want you to give them a tour. I'm going to check in with the missus."

Mary Lou wondered why Beth Pederson had come on the cruise, but she was glad there would be another woman. Then it occurred to her—*I'm sure the master suite should go to whoever won the prize. Unless, of course, the owner of the ship and his wife are on board. Well, okay.*

Kiral bowed slightly. "As you wish. Then he faced the group. Please follow me."

Mary Lou jumped directly behind Kiral with Joe and Denny, who were jockeying for second and third place following the captain.

They ascended the white metal staircase along the outside of the upper cabins. Soon they found themselves in the captain's roost, which had a large steering wheel in the center.

Kiral took the wheel. "There are a few things you should know when you are on a ship. Have any of you sailed before?"

We are all from landlocked Denver, Colorado. Sure, I sailed for an hour on Lake Estes, but this is very different.

Kiral continued, "As I look out onto the sea from the helm, starboard is on my right, and port is on my left. It would be good if you remember this. Starboard and port, right and left. You should note that you entered this ship on the main deck."

Mary Lou's stomach growled. *How embarrassing. I wonder how long before dinner.*

She figured that Kiral must have heard her stomach, because he immediately let go of the steering wheel and made for the door. He motioned for them to follow. "I will show you the galley."

Sumptuous smells had Mary Lou's mouth watering as she followed Kiral down a carpeted stairwell in the middle of the bridge. One flight of steps later, they found the galley. The smells told them that it was the kitchen without him saying anything.

Kiral squeezed to the back wall, allowing all of them to see two men—one at the grill, the other pulling ingredients from the cupboard. "This is the ship's galley. This kitchen is laid out to make the best use of limited space. As you can see, overhead cabinets and storage help with this. Also, you will notice bars to keep the cook from falling onto the hot stove. Most equipment here is what we call 'gimbaled.' Gimbals keep the stoves upright with respect to the horizon despite the ship's pitching and rolling, should we hit rough waters. This keeps liquids from spilling while the cook makes our meals."

The rich, dark-cherrywood cabinets and black granite bar looked like a modern kitchen, except for the very tight quarters.

Off the kitchen, the dining room table, set like something from Buckingham Palace, seated eight. Kiral rushed past it. "We will return here after your tour."

He took steps down to the lower level and opened the first door on the port side. "Miss Mary Lou will be in the guest suite on the forward deck. This one is for the men."

Mary Lou choked back a hallelujah.

The men inspected the two single beds in the room.

Joe smiled. "Thanks, Kiral. It looks perfect."

Denny peeked into the head. "Hey, we got a shower."

Kiral told them they could freshen up and meet in the dining room. Then he escorted Mary Lou to the guest suite, next door.

Mary Lou was pleasantly surprised. It offered a queen-sized bed, a full bath with tub, and a settee beneath a large porthole. "Wow, this is nice. Are you sure it's not the master suite?"

Kiral laughed. "Oh no. The master suite has the king-sized bed for Mr. Walt."

Mary Lou smiled and closed the door after the captain. She lay down on the bed, testing the mattress. *Perfect. Not too firm, not too soft. I'm going to sleep well tonight. I can't wait for bedtime, and as hungry as I am, I dread spending a meal with the rest of the gang.* A minute later, she got up, washed her face, and headed to the dining room.

Perhaps she had been on the bed for more than a minute. Everyone already sat at the table when she arrived. She took the only empty chair, which happened to be next to Walt. Seconds later, an older man dressed in a service uniform came around and filled their water glasses.

Walt sat at the head of the table, with Beth across the corner next to him.

As soon as his glass was filled, Walt picked it up and poured it on the floor between him and Beth. "Edmund, I don't drink water while on *The Adventurer*, and you know it. Scotch on the rocks." He dropped the empty glass, and it bounced off the carpeted floor.

Edmund quickly picked up the glass. "Yes, sir. Immediately, sir."

Walt looked at Denny. "One for you, too?"

"Sure," he said quickly.

Edmund disappeared around the corner and returned in less than a minute with the two drinks. "Drinks for anyone else?"

Mary Lou glanced at Beth. Beth bit her lip and looked into her plate.

Joe raised his hand in a stopping gesture. "I'm fine, thank you."

Walt raised his glass to Denny, sitting at the opposite end of the table. "Here's to deep-sea fishing and yachting."

Denny seemed unaware of the tension in the room.

Mary Lou wondered how they could be so insensitive. Walt raised his glass to Denny, but fixed his eyes on Beth. "To a week of adventure."

Beth forced a smile.

Another man dressed in a waiter's uniform served each of them a bowl of hot conch soup. Mary Lou waited for Walt to start before she picked up her spoon. She was starving, and it seemed to take forever, but finally the boss took a sip of his soup.

Immediately Mary Lou lifted a spoon of the hot soup to her mouth. The creamy base soothed her hunger pangs. The second spoonful of soup exploded with flavor. This time, she tasted the creamy tomato base with small chunks of sea conch.

She couldn't help but express her pleasure. "This is delicious!"

Joe put down his spoon. "We don't get soup like this in Denver. This is real seafood."

Walt grabbed a hot roll from the basket in the center of the table. "Wait until you get the entrée. I've instructed the chef to spare no expense on meals this week. I like gourmet cooking, and our chef is from one of the best restaurants in Ft. Lauderdale. He's on board for this cruise—bribes helped, too." Walt broke out in his overpowering laugh.

Denny mimicked Walt's laugh, and Mary Lou got a slight wave of nausea observing the sucking up. *Really, could you be more obvious?*

Joe smiled. "After tasting this soup, I have great expectations."

Walt bragged about outfitting *The Adventurer* with special equipment for deep-sea fishing. "We don't even have to leave the yacht. I've attached special holds for our catch and custom rigging for holding our poles off the aft deck."

The men listened in rapt attention. Mary Lou could care less about how the boat was rigged. And as far as the mechanics—*Please. Boring.* She thought of Mrs. Cunkell. *How would she handle this trip?*

Edmund appeared and took everyone's empty bowls, followed by the other man with a tiny whisk brush, who cleared each setting of any breadcrumbs.

Edmund returned, carrying plates with green leaves of some kind. On the side, a small flower—Mary Lou thought it was an orchid—was stuck in some kind of sauce.

Walt took a huge bite of food and talked with his mouth full. "Mary Lou, how was your flight?"

A bit unnerved that Walt would give a fig about whether or not she'd had a good flight, she hesitantly answered, "Fine, I guess."

He wiped his face with the white cloth napkin. "I brought the guys in on the company jet. My secretary tried to contact you, but I guess you had already left."

I'll bet he tried to contact me, like an aphid contacts a preying mantis. So they took the company jet. I should be mad, but I believe I prefer flying commercial to spending another minute in the presence of these guys.

Mary Lou dug into her food. "I took an early flight to hang out and see some of the local sights."

Joe, always the peacemaker, took a sip of his water. "We missed your friendly face. Anyway, what did you see around Ft. Lauderdale?"

She didn't want to share any information about what she did away from this little group, but Joe was being polite, so Mary Lou decided it was the least she could do. "I hung out at the Riverwalk. I shopped a little and went to the Museum of Discovery and Science. It was just a relaxing afternoon."

Joe smiled. "I thought you'd be on the beach."

Mary Lou relaxed her guard a little. "I didn't get to the beach. But I do love the sound of the waves."

"I used to go to the beach on Coronado Island," Denny broke in. "Man, just get me a good beach chair and a six pack. It's like being in Heaven."

Everyone finished their entrées, and Edmund and his helper were clearing the table. Once again, the white whisk broom came out. After that, Edmund appeared with flaming dessert and coffee.

Mary Lou noticed through the large porthole behind the table that it was dark outside.

Edmund served the cherries jubilee. One bite into that scrumptious dessert, and Mary Lou really was in Heaven. As soon as she was finished, she felt satisfied and sleepy.

She also felt Walt's hand on her knee.

She jumped up and slapped him across his surprised face. "How dare you! Don't ever do that again!"

He feigned innocence. "What? Are you nuts? What are you talking about?"

Mary Lou wheeled around and stomped to her room.

As soon as she closed the door behind her, she lay on the bed. *Walt is such a creep.*

Was I imagining it? Did Walt really have the guts to put his hand on my knee with his wife sitting on the other side?

One deep sigh later, Mary Lou must have fallen asleep, because when she opened her eyes, she saw the moon reflecting off the waters outside the porthole. She found her cell phone and checked the time. *Three sixteen a.m.* She fumbled to find the light and then dug through her bags to find her pajamas.

Up one step behind the bed, and she was in the tiny bathroom—the "head," as the captain had called it earlier. She soon discovered it was not called a dressing room for a reason. She bumped the wall with her elbow twice as she tried to quietly slip into her pajamas. She sucked in a deep breath, remembering that Joe and Denny were on the other side of the thin wall.

Once she succeeded in getting dressed, she braced herself against the sway of the boat, made her way down the one step, and fell into bed. The last thing she remembered was wondering what the morning would hold.

The same time,
In the master suite of The Adventurer

Beth lay alone in the king-sized bed. For the one hundredth time, she counted the tiles in the ceiling. *Lord, please protect him. Walt's such a fool when he's out drinking with the guys. Who knows what they're doing? They're probably peeing off the back of the boat and laughing themselves silly over it. Lord, when will he ever grow up? Will he ever find the true meaning of life? Will he ever find You?*

Lord, You know I've spent the better part of twenty-four years hanging in there, asking You to come to him, begging for him to accept You. I have remained faithful in the hope that through my faith he would be saved. Father! He doesn't even know I exist, let alone You. Right now he's out there, partying with his employees like they are his best friends.

I don't think he has a real friend in the world.

Chapter Eleven

Saturday, February 9th
Off the coast of Florida

Sun reflected off the water outside the portholes on either side of Mary Lou's bed. The boat rocked, and she closed her eyes again, feeling a little like a baby in a crib.

Do mega yachts ever capsize? Not that this is too bad, but the little sway reminds me that we are on water. She groaned. *Last night was such a catastrophe. Walt is such a jerk. How could he have the guts to grab my knee with his wife sitting on the other side of him? And really, after working for him for the last five years, he knows me well enough to know that I would never tolerate such activity.*

What is wrong with me? She glanced at her cell phone. *Time to get up and join the rest of the group for breakfast. Another day with the people I'm forced to be with every day of the week. Really? This is my prize? Walt, you sure have a messed-up idea of what a girl would like for a prize. Just like the plaque. Salesman of the year. Really, Walt? Do I look like a man to you? I guess not, since you made a pass at me last night in front of your wife.*

Mary Lou tried to shake off her anger, but it rose up again from someplace deep inside her. *I have to get rid of this before I go up to breakfast. Maybe if I think about something else…*

Okay. Got it—the wonderful time I had at the last church retreat in Dallas. That was some night of me and Eileen just singing and praising the Lord. Hallelujah! I feel better already. Yes, Eileen would find ways to enjoy this trip.

Mary Lou jumped out of bed. The boat shifted, and she knocked her head against the hull. *Ouch! That hurt.* She rubbed her head and made her way up the one step into the head. After taking a warm shower and drying her hair, she dressed and found her way to the upper deck to the salon. The smell of fried bacon and pastries led her all the way.

Keenly aware that she was probably the last to arrive, Mary Lou approached the large silver coffee urn. She looked around the room. *I guess I'm not the last one here. I'm sure Walt's waiting to make a grand entrance. But Beth is here, so he probably won't be long. I'm starving.*

"There she is…" Denny broke out singing the Miss America refrain. "I thought you'd fallen in. You went to bed early last night. I didn't think you could sleep much longer. We've been speeding across the ocean all night while you were sleeping."

Mary Lou gave him her brightest smile. "I slept well, thank you. I assume you did, too." *After consuming who knows how much liquor last night, you probably snored like a hog.*

No, now I need to clean up my thinking. I don't really know what Denny did last night. As far as I know, he went to his room shortly after I left.

He slapped her on the back. "I got up about an hour ago. I just love the salt air, especially when the boat is moving. Love it."

She stepped away from him and addressed Joe, who was sitting across the room. "Did you guys stay up late last night?"

Mary Lou couldn't help noticing Beth's piercing glance toward Joe as he answered, "Not really. Anyway, I probably went to my room an hour after you did. Denny and I couldn't keep up with Walt."

Beth looked back to the magazine she'd been reading.

Denny ogled the food stacked on the self-service bar. "Where's Walt? Are you all waiting for him? Not me. I'm hungry."

He picked up a plate off the bar and chose two sweet rolls, then he filled his cup with the most robust-smelling coffee.

Denny took a deep whiff of his steaming cup. "Now that's good coffee. I can tell before I even taste it." He took a sip. "Yeah, I was right."

A Moment Later
In the Main Salon

Beth stood up from her cushioned seat. She went to the coffee bar and filled a cup without speaking. She glanced at the entrance, poured cream from the tiny stainless steel pitcher, and added sugar.

Joe found a plate and went to the hot bar, where he piled on scrambled eggs and bacon with a big spoonful of hash browns. "Sea air has a way of bringing on the appetite. It must be all that oxygen in the air. Not like Denver, where the air is thin."

Beth went back to her seat and her magazine. She obviously had nothing in common with these employees of her husband's. *Where is he?* It was rude enough that he had never returned to their stateroom last night, but missing breakfast was beyond embarrassing. *It is so like him. What has caught his attention that he's forgotten about breakfast? Where could he be?*

She pretended to be engrossed in her magazine and double-checked that she was holding it right side up.

Edmund entered with a covered silver platter. He placed it on the bar, then lifted the metal dome. "Hotcakes, anyone?"

Soon hotcakes covered Mary Lou's plate. She put her coffee down on the side table next to the sofa. "My weakness."

Edmund offered a steaming silver pitcher. "Hot maple syrup, miss?"

"Wonderful." She watched him pour an ample amount of the thick syrup.

"Thank you, Edmund. That's perfect." She set the plate next to her coffee.

Denny gulped his coffee and finished chewing another sweet roll. "Beth, please go see what's keeping Walt. He should have been up here by now. Maybe he fell asleep in that big tub you guys got in the master stateroom."

Beth slapped her magazine down on the small table next to her chair. Without speaking, she marched out the door onto the deck. She walked around the deck and up the stairway to the captain's cockpit. "Captain Kiral, would you be so kind as to inform Mr. Pederson that his guests await his arrival in the main salon where breakfast is being served?"

Kiral blinked. "Of course. I will tell him." He motioned to his first mate to take the helm and immediately went to find Walt.

Beth took another path to her stateroom so as not to see the rest of the passengers again. She held the faintest hope that Walt would be there, but as soon as she opened the door, she knew that he wasn't.

Back in the main salon, Denny and Joe stared at the waves outside the large windows. The few moments of silence held tension, and finally Denny said, "If Walt wants to fish today, he'd better get with it. We're burning daylight."

Joe finished his coffee and proceeded to the bar for a refill. "He hasn't shared the schedule with us, so fishing must start tomorrow. He said we'd start before daybreak on fishing day. Didn't he tell us that on the way?" He looked over at Mary Lou.

"Don't look at me. I wasn't with you on the way down here, remember?" She attempted to hold back the bitterness at being left out once again.

Joe rubbed his forehead. "Oh, that's right. Well, that's what he said. Perhaps he started without us."

Joe and Denny shared a chuckle at the thought of Walt getting up early and fishing without them.

Kiral entered the salon and looked around the room. "Has anybody seen Mr. Pederson?"

The three of them answered simultaneously, "No."

Kiral frowned. "I can't find him anywhere. Would you mind looking in your staterooms, please? He has to be somewhere."

Mary Lou stood. "He'd better not be in my stateroom."

Denny and Joe walked down the narrow stairway to the lower deck. Mary Lou followed and stopped a few steps up from them at her room. She gingerly opened the door, half believing Walt might be inside. She saw the wall-to-wall bed, small dressing table, and step to the head. She walked to the door of the head and stopped.

Should I knock? Oh, come on now. He is not in there.

Mary Lou slowly turned the handle and pushed the door open. The room remained as empty as she had left it only an hour before. She breathed a sigh of relief and closed the door.

Mary Lou made her way back to the upper deck and the main salon.

Beth sat on the long sofa with Kiral standing over her, saying softly, "If he is on this boat, I will find him." He left to search *The Adventurer* once again.

Denny and Joe came up from the lower deck, shaking their heads.

Joe said the obvious: "He's not anywhere down there. I don't know where else to look."

After a few moments, Kiral returned.

Denny turned to Kiral. "We've looked everywhere. We even checked the engine room. No sign of him."

Kiral faced the group. "Ah, yes, the engine room. Well, he is not on the boat. We must notify the authorities. Obviously there is a man overboard."

Beth's eyes widened. "Man overboard? What do you mean?"

"I am bound by profession to contact the authorities when someone disappears from the boat. Excuse me."

Mary Lou followed Kiral up to the bridge. He called the authorities while she took a seat on the long bench behind the captain's perch.

"You want to talk with me?" he asked. "There is nothing I can tell you. The man may have fallen overboard. As far as I know, that's exactly what happened."

Mary Lou sat next to him. "Oh, no. I guess I just wanted to talk to someone other than the group. You see, I feel so bad for Walt. He probably had too much to drink. Oh, I hope he was saved."

Kiral's brow furrowed. "Saved? If he was saved, he would be here. Someone would have brought him to the boat."

"No, no—I mean 'saved' as in 'going to Heaven.' I'm a Christian."

"Yes, and I am Muslim."

"Well, Christians are taught that if anyone accepts Christ and repents of their sins, they go to Heaven when they die. There everything is made right. There is no pain, no sorrow, and all the people we loved that accepted Christ are there."

Kiral nodded. "I have heard something about that. You think Mr. Pederson was saved?"

Mary Lou grimaced. "You can tell if someone's a Christian, most of the time. They do lots of good things for other people, and they talk about God." *I wonder how well Kiral knew Walt. Maybe he knows some good thing Walt did. Surely he had some redeeming qualities.*

Kiral raised an eyebrow. "That does not sound like Mr. Pederson."

Mary Lou scrutinized the helm. "I have to agree with you, and that makes me sad, because you really don't want to go to the other place."

"That would be hell, right?"

Mary Lou turned toward Kiral. "Yes, that's right. But nobody has to go there, because Jesus died to forgive us our sins. And if we pray to him, He will forgive us, no matter what we've done."

Kiral looked into her eyes. "No matter what?"

"No matter what. I mean, even murderers get forgiven and have life in Heaven after they die."

Kiral frowned again. "Really?"

She stood up. "Yes, really. But when someone confesses their sins, they have to really mean it. They have to change. They can't go on sinning. They do good things from then on, like help the poor and give to the church. Oh, and go to church and read their Bibles."

The short-wave radio crackled, and Kiral got up to answer. "This is *The Adventurer.*"

Later the same day,
Off the Florida coast

Mary Lou returned to the main salon and observed that Beth had changed from the arrogant boss's wife to a frightened, even frail woman. *Is she really concerned about him? Should we be? What could have happened to him?*

Mary Lou excused herself and decided to take a look around by herself. She took the stairway down to the lower deck and passed her own stateroom. She tried the door of Denny and Joe's stateroom and found it locked.

Then she walked through another hallway and found herself in front of a small hatch that resembled the door to the head in her room. She pushed on the handle, and it opened to the engine room. She found the room immaculate, with everything in its proper place. It nearly sparkled and looked like a picture in some kind of mechanical magazine.

She carefully stepped inside and walked past the engines to a small alcove with a desk and maintenance schedule pinned to a bulletin board above it.

She pushed through another door and found herself on the rear deck, near the swim deck. Everything looked pristine. She shrugged and made her way back to the main salon.

Kiral returned to tell them that the authorities would soon be on board.

Within minutes, Denny pointed out the window. "Look—there's the Coast Guard."

The ship pulled close, and two men jumped onto *The Adventurer.* One of the men approached Captain Kiral. "Officer Gooding, U.S. Coast Guard. We are responding to your call. Please follow the Coast Guard vessel to the Key West port. We will interview your passengers separately."

Kiral showed Officer Gooding to a private office off the captain's cockpit. First he asked that Denny sit in the chair across from him. "Denny Adams, right?"

Denny nodded. "That's right. I've known Walt for twenty-five years, and he just hired me to work for him recently."

The officer had a note in his hand. "I understand you attended college with Walt—and, in fact, were roommates."

Denny smiled. "That's correct. How did you get that information?"

"We try to be as thorough as possible, as quickly as possible. Is there anything you want to tell me about what happened last night?"

"I don't know what you want me to say. We had a few drinks, then Joe and I left Walt on the upper deck. We shared a room, and we were anticipating an early morning of fishing."

"So you were with Joe Gillespie all night?"

"Yes, I certainly was," Denny said defensively. "You can ask Joe."

Officer Gooding pressed on. "And the young woman, Mary Lou. I understand she and Walt had a confrontation at dinner last night."

"She and Walt often have confrontations, as far as I can tell. But I can assure you that she did not push him off this boat."

"How can you be certain?"

Denny chuckled. "You can ask Joe. He will tell you the same thing. The walls between the sleeping quarters are as thin as paper. When Joe and I came into our room, we could hear Mary Lou snoring like she was sawing logs. We laughed so hard we thought we might wake her. But then she kept us up all night."

Officer Gooding did not smile, but he took notes. "And Mrs. Pederson—do you know where she was all night?"

Denny leaned into Gooding's face. "Listen, here—you leave her alone. She would never harm her husband. She's the best thing that ever happened to him. She's been nothing but a loyal and steadfast wife to him for the last twenty-four years."

Gooding's eyebrows shot up. "And what kind of relationship do you have with this woman?"

"This woman is a friend. I knew her in college. Remember, Walt and I were roommates."

"And what is your relationship with Mary Lou Stots?"

Denny shook his head. "She is a coworker. I met her when I came on board with International Enterprises."

Gooding wrote something. "We are finished for now. Please tell Mr. Gillespie to come in."

Denny left the office, escorted by another officer, and told Joe that Officer Gooding was waiting for him.

After Joe had substantiated everything Denny reported, he was asked to tell Mary Lou to come to the office.

She entered, and Gooding closed the door behind her. She took the seat he indicated to her.

"Miss Stots, we are questioning each of the passengers in regard to their relationship with Mr. Pederson. How would you describe your relationship with him?"

Mary Lou closed her eyes for a good ten seconds. "I am very sorry this happened to Walt. But I have to say that he and I were not friends. I worked for him, and he made sure that I was aware of that every day I had any contact with him. The only reason I was here is that I won a contest for top sales last year."

Gooding nodded. "We know. Now please tell me what happened last night."

She took a deep breath. "I don't know. I was tired from traveling here—I mean to Ft. Lauderdale, and I was hungry, and... When we finally had dinner, Walt made a pass at me. I got mad and went to my quarters and went to bed."

Gooding took more notes. "He made a pass at you?"

She squirmed. "Yes, he put his hand on my knee at dinner. And his wife was sitting right next to him on the other side. I was so stinking mad at him. What do you expect? I am not that kind of woman. I slapped him in the face. I'm still mad at him about that. Right there in front of his wife."

Gooding adjusted his glasses. "What difference did it make if she were there?"

Mary Lou grimaced. "I respect her as his wife."

Gooding looked at his notes. "I see. Has anyone ever told you that you snore?"

After a few more questions, Gooding told Mary Lou to ask Beth to come in to talk with him.

Mary Lou sat with Denny and Joe while Beth was with Gooding.

Denny smiled at Mary Lou. "Don't worry; it's going to be all right."

Mary Lou glared at him. "Oh, yeah. I heard that you and Joe had to listen to me snore all night."

"Denny was just trying to help," Joe said. "At least we know where you were all night."

Denny burst out laughing.

Joe frowned at him. "Denny, there is nothing to laugh about. Walt is missing."

Denny muffled his laugh. "Sorry, it isn't funny. It really isn't. Mary Lou, you should thank me. At least you have an alibi. After what happened at dinner, you needed one."

She went to the head before she said something she might regret.

Chapter Twelve

Later the same day

As soon as *The Adventurer* reached the dock, more officers boarded. Soon afterward, Kiral called over the PA system. "The authorities have asked everyone to please meet in the main salon."

Everyone hurried to the salon to hear what would happen next. Two officers stood by as Officer Gooding made the announcement. "We are convinced that none of you know what happened to Mr. Pederson. We believe that Mr. Pederson exited *The Adventurer* late last night or early this morning. He may have been under the influence of alcohol or drugs. We have alerted headquarters. They have sent search crews to find him. It is not hopeful, since it's been hours since he disappeared."

Beth tilted her head. "Exited? What exactly does that mean?"

Officer Gooding paused for a second, then faced her. "It means that we believe that Mr. Pederson either fell or jumped overboard."

Mary Lou cringed at Denny's obnoxious voice behind her. "Well, Walt is a fighter. If anyone could survive, it will be Walt."

Officer Gooding noted that there was blood on the swim deck where Walt may have 'exited' the yacht. "He may have slipped and hurt himself. We will test the blood. I must tell you that the likelihood of his survival is slim."

Beth couldn't help but speculate. "Especially if he had been drinking."

Kiral murmured to Gooding, "The life raft and tender boat are on board. There is no place he could have gone."

Joe motioned to speak in Gooding's ear. "Are there sharks in these waters?"

Gooding only nodded and ordered everyone off *The Adventurer.* Mary Lou hurried down to her stateroom and threw everything into her bags. She didn't want to be on this misadventure for one more minute than necessary. She just wanted to go home to Denver.

Kiral strode ahead of her as Mary Lou lugged her bags off *The Adventurer.*

"Kiral, wait up!" She caught up to him and took a deep breath to recover. "What are you going to do now?"

Kiral shifted the large duffel bag from his shoulder to the pavement. "Oh, do not worry about me. It is no problem. I may look for another yacht to captain, or I may take a break. It is not a problem."

Mary Lou sensed tension in Kiral's body language. He seemed to be forcing himself to talk with her. Something just seemed wrong. She shrugged. *Curious. Maybe he wants to talk about Walt?* "I really didn't know Walt very well, even though I worked for him for five years."

Kiral nodded. "He was an eccentric, for sure."

Meanwhile, inside the salon of *The Adventurer,* Beth sat next to Gooding. "I can't leave without Walt. I know you're going to find him soon."

Gooding took off his hat. "I'm so sorry to have to tell you not to get your hopes up. It does not look good for a rescue. Look out there. You see how big the ocean is? You were out to sea. To be sure, we will do our very best. But in the interim, you should go home. If we find him, we will bring him home. So go home and do what you need to do to get ready for him."

Beth rubbed her forehead. "I don't know what to do."

Gooding stood to leave. "Helicopters have already searched the area you were in, with no signs of him or any clothing or anything that might lead to him. You should go home with the men you brought with you. We will keep in contact."

The same day,
Key West, Florida

Mary Lou couldn't wait to get home. She caught the Keys Shuttle to the Ft. Lauderdale airport. The flight to Denver International Airport seemed longer than when she'd flown out to Ft. Lauderdale. After the aircraft landed, they waited fifteen minutes to get to the gate, and then it took forever for the cabin door to open.

Her seat, 20B, won the prize for the most uncomfortable location on the plane, and Mary Lou stood as soon as she could. She sprinted toward baggage claim as soon as she made it through the gangway, barely clearing the little old lady in front of her.

Hurry up and wait. It looks like luggage from four different flights is coming in here. Come on, now. I want to get home. She checked her cell phone to see the time. *10:40 PM. I won't get home until midnight at this rate.*

Half an hour later, the first bag from her flight popped up, then glided down the ramp for luggage pickup. Mary Lou had checked in early for the flight, so she relaxed her shoulders and accepted the fact that her bag would probably be the last one off.

Joe had kindly offered her a ride back on the company jet, but she wanted to get away from her coworkers. She needed time alone to process the events of the last twenty-four hours. For once, she was glad that she was the outsider and that she had her return ticket.

Her purple alligator bag slid down the ramp and landed on the conveyor belt at the other end from where she stood. She took a deep breath and decided to wait for it to make its way back to her. The bag approached slowly; she leaned over and neatly retrieved it.

An icy blast of wind descended upon her as door five hundred thirteen quickly retracted, opening to a dark and wet series of islands. She pulled her coat around her, bent her head down, and made a dash for island three to wait for the USAirport parking shuttle.

Once there, Mary Lou stood alone, looking up and down the street. No bus. She checked her cell phone for the time again—a quarter after eleven.

Ten minutes later, ears frozen, she summoned her numb fingers to check her cell for the time and temperature once again. *Nineteen degrees. Shades of my return from Alaska. I give up.*

The USAirport bus rounded the corner at the end of the terminal just as she decided to go back inside, and she changed her mind. The shuttle seemed to travel at snail's pace until it finally heaved to stop in front of her. Doors opened, and she gratefully climbed into the warm bus.

The same day
Key West International Airport, Florida

Denny jumped into the International Enterprises Learjet and turned to extend a helping hand to Beth. He had called the pilot in advance to make sure he would be there when they were ready to return. Her face was ashen, and his heart went out to her. Once inside, she collapsed into the comfortable forward seat, obviously not wanting to face anyone.

Joe stepped inside the hull, and the copilot secured the door behind him. The pilot already had the engine running. They were next in line for takeoff, and the pilot immediately taxied to Runway Two. In five minutes, they were in the air.

Denny stared at the emerald waters below. He was still in shock that Walt wasn't flying back with them. *Beth must be caving.*

Denny touched Beth's shoulder in front of him. "Beth, can I get some coffee for you?" He knew full well that the flight attendant would take care of her, but he wanted her to know he cared and that he was there if she wanted to talk.

Beth patted his fingers on her shoulder. "I'm doing all right, Denny. Thanks. I think I'm just going to close my eyes, maybe take a little nap. It's been an exhausting few days."

"Sure." Denny leaned back in his seat.

He looked at Joe across the aisle, who was reading something on his computer. *That Joe never stops working. No doubt he's reading company reports. Well, good for him. This was supposed to be our getaway. Yeah, this was going to be the male bonding, deep-sea fishing trip of a lifetime on Walt's twenty-two-million-dollar yacht.*

Denny had met Walt when they were seniors at the University of Colorado, the most partying school in the United States at the time, and Walt was helping them keep that position. Graduation was coming up, and Walt was worried about his chemistry paper. Denny ended up accepting an exorbitant payment to do it for Walt.

He was rich, and I was poor, Denny rationalized. *I had the ability and was willing to give up a few nights of partying to do it for him, and I needed the money.* But the worst part of getting to know Walt—the very worst part of it—was that Walt was dating the cute redhead Denny had fallen for the first time he saw her the year before. He had never even asked her out because she was Episcopal, which was too close to Catholic for his Southern Baptist heart. *Besides, Walt asked her out first.* He tried to brush the memory off, but it came back.

Denny closed his eyes and saw Beth when she was just twenty years old, coming out of the gym, hair wet, eyes glistening, and laughing with her girlfriends. *She was full of life, so different from today.* He had seen the change when they boarded the jet to come to Ft. Lauderdale. She'd seemed fragile even then, but now, even more so.

Over the years, God removed his prejudice against Catholics. He actually endorsed some of the policies that the Church publicized—no premarital sex, no abortion, marriage being between a man and woman, and no divorce.

Beth was the reason he had never married. He'd waited. He knew living with Walt couldn't be easy, and even though he would have denied it, he was waiting for the inevitable breakup. Year after year, he made himself content with changing jobs, traveling, and whatever else he could do to keep her off his mind. Yet year after year, he kept tabs on the divorce announcements. Hers never surfaced.

Walt, I won't ever say that I'm glad you're gone, but I believe everything happens for a reason. I am going to be here for her.

Monday, February 11
Denver, Colorado

Monday morning seemed nothing less than surreal. Mary Lou arrived at her office at the regular time. *It feels weird walking by Walt's office, knowing that he's dead. Or do we know he's dead? I guess he's dead. It doesn't feel like he's dead. But he must be dead. No one has heard from the Coast Guard.*

She observed two office secretaries, chatting across their facing desks in the reception area. They stopped talking as Mary Lou passed them.

Mary Lou noticed that Joe's office door was open. She peeked in to see him working at his computer. "Good morning, Joe."

He tore his eyes from the computer screen. "Good morning. How are you doing today?"

She sighed, "Everything seems surreal this morning. How about you? Any news from the Coast Guard?"

Joe stood and walked toward her with his empty coffee cup in his hand. "Nothing yet. I'm playing it moment by moment as the day unfolds. Who knows what will happen in a day? We sure had no idea a fishing trip would turn into a tragedy."

I had no idea my cruise would turn into a tragedy.

Joe continued, "Hopefully today will be a better day. In the meantime…" He lifted his cup. "I'm ready for a refill, but we need to talk."

She stepped away to unblock his way through the door as he made his way to the coffee bar down the hall. "I'm going to need a good strong cup of coffee, too. But first I need to drop these off at my office." She lifted her laptop case and purse.

He gave her a thumbs-up. "Meet me back here when you're settled in."

Mary Lou unloaded in her office, set up the laptop and started it, then placed her purse in the bottom left drawer of her desk, which also held her box of chocolate chip cookies.

She found her coffee cup from last week where she'd left it. It had a brown circle around the inside bottom where the last few drops of coffee had dried. She grabbed it and headed past the coffee bar to the tiny kitchen to wash out her cup. Once she had it clean and fresh, she went around the corner to fill up with the office blend.

Denny stood at the large coffee pot, filling the largest mug she'd ever seen.

"That must be twenty ounces," she said.

He looked up. "It's a beer stein I got when I was in Germany a few years ago. Actually, I got two of them. One is not for coffee."

Inside she snickered, feeling superior to the man who had to drink coffee from a beer stein. "Don't get them mixed up. It wouldn't be pretty," she said dryly.

Denny finished at the coffee spigot and then dumped half a cup of cream into the stein. "Oh, yeah. That would be bad."

She filled her sparkling-clean mug. The smell of the coffee in the cup comforted her. *How does one get to the point where they look forward to the office coffee? I must be working too hard—that or I'm still in a state of shock about Walt.*

Wonder what's going on in Denny's head. They were such good buddies.

She headed to Joe's office. Denny followed, and that irritated her. *Couldn't I just once have a private conversation with my boss without you horning in?* She stopped at Joe's door and turned to see if he was still behind her. He was on her heels. *Crumbs!*

Joe stood up from his desk chair. "Come in, both of you. We should probably have a short meeting before Beth gets here."

Denny's eyebrows shot up. "Beth's coming? She seemed very upset when we left Ft. Lauderdale. You think that's a good idea?"

Joe sat down as Mary Lou and Denny sat across from him. "Of course I don't think it's a good idea, but that's not my call. She is his only heir, and they owned this company together. You know what that means. In any case, after the memorial service, she plans to take an active part in running the company."

Denny frowned. "What does that mean? She's going to be CEO?"

Joe leaned back in his chair. "For us, it means she is now the owner of the majority of the stock in the corporation. Walt's been at the helm since her father died ten years ago. Now she needs to make some decisions soon. Everyone in the corporation will be wondering what's next. We just have to wait and see."

Denny leaned back and rested his ankle on his other knee. "No doubt she'll need me to help run the company. Who was closer to the man than me?"

Joe frowned. "It's not a popularity contest, Denny."

Mary Lou chimed in, "You've barely been on board. What do you know about running International Enterprises?"

Denny puffed up. "I'm up for the task."

Joe's weary expression spoke volumes as he said, "I'm sure you could do it, Denny. But until we hear from the Coast Guard, I wouldn't be making any plans."

Mary Lou couldn't let that one go by. "I'm sure Joe is a more likely candidate for CEO."

Joe's intercom buzzed, and the receptionist said, "Joe, Mrs. Pederson just called to reschedule your meeting to next Monday."

Tuesday, February 12
Lakewood, Colorado

Beth answered the phone to hear the voice of Officer Gooding from the Coast Guard. "I called to let you know that the search for Mr. Pederson has been called off. Mr. Pederson is presumed lost at sea."

Beth's hand went to her heart. "Lost at sea. Could he still be alive?"

Officer Gooding responded slowly, "I am so sorry to say this, but it is doubtful anyone would survive the storms at sea the past two days. We will continue to investigate, but so far nothing indicates foul play." He cleared his throat. "Or that he intended to hurt himself. There was no suicide note."

Beth took a deep breath. "No, Walt would never commit suicide. He enjoyed life to the fullest."

Officer Gooding's voice quieted. "The conclusion is that it was a tragic accident at sea."

Chapter Thirteen

Wednesday, February 13
Denver, Colorado

Beth found herself in the office of her father's old friend, the Honorable Judge C. Elmore Wiesel. She sat across from him at his spacious desk. He had heard the news before she got there.

"Dear Beth, I am so sorry for your loss and what you're going through. Your father and I were such close friends. He's been gone ten years now, but I promised him I would look after you the last time I saw him. He was so ill."

Beth sniffed and pulled a tissue from the box on his desk. "I miss my father. And now…"

Beth felt tears well up for the first time since Walt went missing. "I feel so alone. I don't know what to do. The Coast Guard stopped searching for him. They say he could not have survived, being so far out to sea. I have accepted the fact that he was drunk and probably drowned. I hope he didn't suffer. I just don't know what to do now. Can you help me with this? I mean, the authorities in Florida said that a federal judge would have to declare him dead because they never found the body."

The judge cleared his throat. "Actually, Beth, I thought you might need me. I took the liberty of getting copies of the reports the Coast Guard made during their investigation. With the kind of accident it was, and with me personally knowing that Walt was prone to drinking too much—"

"But does that have to be in the report? I mean, I don't want to tarnish his reputation. He did drink too much, but I think he was fighting depression. He would never admit it, but I remember his doctor even telling him he should go on antidepressants."

"Yes, that is also a factor. What do you think happened?"

Beth twisted the tissue in her hand. "I can see Walt just getting roaring drunk and falling off the boat. I can see that."

Judge Wiesel cleared his throat again. "We shouldn't speculate, but I think he got drunk and started playing out some fantasy. I believe he probably didn't mean to fall off the boat. You know when Walt partied, it always included lots of booze. I sure don't think he just jumped into the ocean."

Beth blinked away a tear. "I don't think so, either. You're right—he probably lost his balance or something and simply fell into the ocean. I know he wouldn't just jump."

The judge called in his secretary. "I'll need the forms to declare Walter Pederson legally dead. Please bring them right away and I will fill them out." He turned to Beth. "Everything is going to be all right. Once we get this filed, you can go ahead with the memorial service and start the healing. The fact is, they may never find his body."

Beth sniffed. "I know, I know." She shook her head and blew her nose. "I want you to know that I'm not here because I'm worried about insurance or having to have him declared dead so I can remarry or anything absurd like that. We've had the insurance policies just over ten years, so they don't care. I just want some kind of closure."

Judge Wiesel's finger tapped the papers in front of him. "It is within my power to declare Walt Pederson dead, and I'm going to take advantage of that today. I'm ruling this an accidental death. We will file the necessary forms today."

Saturday, February 16
Denver, Colorado

Mary Lou found a parking spot two blocks from St. John's Cathedral. Thankful that she was a little early, she got out, locked the doors, and headed toward the church. She rounded the corner at fourteenth and Washington and saw strings of people making their way up the steps of the church. She noticed Joe and his family crossing the street ahead of her and caught up with them. She had asked Eileen to come with her, but Eileen was busy. *No doubt hanging out with Kurt.*

Mary Lou smiled at Joe's wife. "Is it all right if I sit with you?"

Joe answered, "Of course. Look at all these people. Probably everyone who ever worked for Walt is here."

His wife snickered. "I'm sure all the news coverage has something to do with it."

Joe put his arm around her shoulders. "Okay, Linda. Mary Lou knew him, too. It's not necessary to condemn him for her sake."

Mary Lou stepped up the curb. "He's gone, and perhaps the priest has found some good in Walt that we missed."

They joined the crowded sanctuary and found seats near the back.

What is that by the altar? Mary Lou stood up for a better look. "Joe, Linda—is that a casket? Did they find his body?"

Joe stretched his neck to see over the people in front. "It is a casket. They must have found his body…or something."

Linda wrinkled her nose. "You mean some part of him."

The organ began playing a mournful dirge. Mary Lou couldn't take her eyes off the vertical lines of pipes in the front of the sanctuary. She hadn't been in a church with a real pipe organ in a long time.

After a full ten minutes of the same song, the music stopped. Between the couple in front of her, she could see the priest, dressed in long white robes and with a long white shawl draped around his neck, approach the pulpit.

"We are gathered here today to honor Walter D. Pederson. Walt is survived by his wife and soul mate, Beth Pederson. Walt was one of those rare people called a Colorado native. He was born in 1965 in Arvada, Colorado, back when Arvada was mostly acreage. Walt grew up on a small acreage with his parents and a sister who died about five years ago. Walt loved sailing and racecars. Beth says he never liked to work on them, but he loved to drive them."

A chuckle rippled through the congregation.

"Beth and Walt met at Colorado University and fell in love. Shortly after Beth graduated, they were married in this very church. Walt loved business and spent many hours working with Beth's father, who taught him the ropes. In 2002, after the death of Beth's father, Walt Pederson took the reins of International Enterprises as owner and CEO.

"Walt loved to travel. He loved adventure—in fact, that's what he named the second love of his life, his mega yacht, *The Adventurer*." The priest paused and took a step back from the pulpit. He took a deep breath and stepped forward again. "Walt found it most satisfying to watch the business grow and personally interview and hire most of the personnel. He will be missed."

Then the priest left the pulpit and made his way to the front of the closed casket. Mary Lou sucked in a deep breath as he grasped the handle and pulled it open, exposing a plush white satin lining.

Mary Lou breathed a sigh of relief. *Who wants to see a dead body, even at a funeral? Especially a victim that's been in the sea for days.*

The priest turned toward his audience. "Beloved friends and relatives of Walter Pederson, it is with great sorrow that we acknowledge his passing. The sorrow extends beyond the death of a dear friend but to the core of our hearts as we reflect on this horrible accident and how life can end at any second.

"When death happens suddenly and unexpectedly, we search for answers. Many times we try to blame others. Sometimes we even go so far as to blame the person who passed.

"So an accident happened. We must ask ourselves what part we played in Walt Pederson's life. Was there something we did or didn't do, something maybe we felt led to do and didn't? Now suddenly Walt is gone, and our opportunity to have done that deed is gone."

Mary Lou squirmed in her seat. *Really, Mr. Priest? You're blaming us for what happened to Walt? I mean, we weren't friends, but there's no way I would've wanted him to die. Even after that stunt he pulled at dinner that night, I never would've wanted him dead. Grabbing my knee—well, that was Walt at his usual one-too-many-drinks self. I never wished him dead. Did I? Maybe I thought something like that, but Lord, You know I didn't mean it.*

The priest had raised one hand with a notepad in it. "Ladies and gentlemen, you will find a notepad in the seat pocket in front of you with pens and pencils. As a gesture of closure, I would ask each of you to write a note to Walt. You might want to write something you never got to tell him, or perhaps ask him something you never got to ask. You may have words of well wishes for him, or you may have words of wisdom for him. Your message may be about anything— any unfinished business you had with Walt Pederson."

"We will take about ten minutes for you to think about what you want to say, then as we exit down in front and pass the empty casket, I would ask each of you to place your note in the casket. These expressions of closure will be buried at Memorial Gardens in a graveside service following this service."

Mary Lou retrieved a notepad and pen, as did everyone in her row. She stared at the casket and attempted to collect her thoughts. *Walt, what on earth could I write that would give me closure? You were a hard man to work for, you exploited me, and you took advantage of everyone around you. You made fun of me and belittled me every time I was in your presence. I can't write anything like that. If I could afford it, I would have walked out of that office and told you to go to hell a long time ago.*

She put the pen to paper. *Walt, you wanted more than this world could give. I hope the other side holds everything you ever wanted . . . and is as good to you as you were to me.* She ran a line through it. *No, that's not what I mean.* She tried again. *Walt, sorry you were such a small, greedy person here on earth. Since you couldn't learn on earth, maybe God will get through to you in Heaven.* She read her note. *More likely you're in hell, Walt.*

Oh, shame on me. I have to change my attitude. Walt is dead. Don't speak ill of the dead.

Sunday, February 17
Alma Temple, Denver, Colorado

Mary Lou arrived at church just as the service began—promptly at eleven o'clock, because the service was broadcast live on radio. She found Mrs. Cunkell third row from the front, in the center of the pew. Mrs. Cunkell smiled and handed her a bulletin as Mary Lou sat beside her.

Mary Lou whispered to her, "I have a lot of questions after the service, if you have time."

Mrs. Cunkell nodded and kept her eyes on the pulpit.

The worship leader said, "Let's all stand and sing 'Because He Lives' on page two hundred fifty-six in your hymnal."

They finished the song, and a young woman came to the pulpit and led the congregation in prayer. "Lord, we ask Your blessing and seek Your face as we worship here this morning. We praise You, because only You are holy and only You are worthy to be praised. We ask You to heal the sick among us, to comfort the needy, and to touch us with Your Holy Spirit. We pray for those suffering around the world in Your name. We pray for our military, our national leaders, and our loved ones. In the Precious Name of Jesus, Amen."

They sang a few more hymns, and Dr. Dallenbach approached the pulpit to deliver his message, "Forgiveness."

Mary Lou could hardly believe the sermon. Every word seemed to be directed at her. She needed to forgive Walt for the way he had treated her. She needed to forgive Bobby for leaving her. She needed to forgive Eileen... She kept thinking of grudges she needed to release.

As soon as the service was over, she thanked Dr. Dallenbach for the wonderful message. Then she and Mrs. Cunkell spent the afternoon engrossed in Bible study on the hill.

Monday, February 18
Denver, Colorado

Beth Pederson stuck her head into Joe's office. "Good. You're here. Meeting in the CEO's office in ten minutes."

Her diminutive figure continued down the row of offices and entered Walt's office. She stopped just inside the door and took in her surroundings. *I haven't been here ten times in the ten years since Dad died. This was Dad's corporation. This used to be my father's office.* She walked around to sit behind the desk.

Once she was sitting, with her large purse on the floor next to the chair, a picture on his desk caught her attention. She picked it up for a closer look.

In the picture, she wore a yellow pantsuit and a large straw hat. She remembered the picture—they had been on vacation on the island of Eleuthera in the West Indies. Walt had wanted her to wear her bikini for a photo shoot, but she refused and showed up in her favorite outfit instead.

She felt a tear on her cheek and wiped it away with her fingers. Then she set the picture down and dug in her purse for a tissue. After drying her eyes and blowing her nose, she went to the adjoining bathroom and freshened up.

She silently spoke to the woman in the mirror: *Today is important. This is not the time to be emotional. You must look strong. In a minute, three people are going to walk in here. You need to let them know that you are in charge. You are not a weepy widow. You are Walt's first mate, and he needs you to pick up where he left off. Straighten up, Beth. You can cry later.*

She heard a knock on the office door and went to answer. Mary Lou, Denny, and Joe all smiled expectantly.

She opened the door wide. "Come in, and we can begin."

Beth returned to Walt's familiar chair.

Mary Lou sat across the desk from her, closest to the door. Joe sat next to Mary Lou, and Denny pulled up a chair from near the sofa.

Denny spoke first. "Beth, let me extend my heartfelt condolences. I know I speak for all of us when we say we're going to miss Walt."

The sound of Walt's name coming from someone else brought dampness to her eyes, but she fought it off. "Thank you, Denny. The memorial service is over. Today is about International Enterprises."

Mentally, Beth relaxed. *He and Walt were such good buddies in college. Even after Denny moved away, Walt would find time to go see him if he had business in San Diego. Yes, I know you and my husband partied when he was there on so-called business.*

Denny leaned back. "Of course it is."

Joe stepped in. "Beth, what can we do to help?"

Beth smiled. "Tell me how I can get a cup of coffee around here?"

Mary Lou and Denny jumped up simultaneously. Denny took a giant step around Mary Lou and beat her to the door. "I'll get it— two creams, right?"

Beth was visibly pleased. "Right." *You get points for remembering how I take my coffee, Denny. That is a surprise.*

Denny returned in less than thirty seconds. "Lucky you. They just brewed a fresh pot."

Beth took a sip of coffee, then set the cup on Walt's Denver Broncos coaster. "Today I am announcing the new CEO of International Enterprises."

Mary Lou, Denny, and Joe all leaned forward with rapt attention.

Beth savored the moment, then she continued, "I've decided that the Pederson name should continue to lead the corporation. As of today, I will be in this office as CEO. In order to continue the positive practices of the corporation with as little disruption as possible, I will need your help. That being the case, I will announce a small reorganization at this level."

"Joe, you will be my right-hand man and general manager."

Joe sat straight in his chair. "Thank You, Mrs. Pederson. I won't let you down."

Beth smiled at him. "You can call me Beth."

Then she turned to Mary Lou. "Mary Lou, you will take Joe's place, since you've led in sales ever since you came here and the other agents respect you."

Mary Lou blinked. "I'm director of sales and marketing?"

Beth blinked back dramatically. "Yes, Mary Lou, you are director of sales and marketing."

Beth turned to Denny. "Joe is general manager, Mary Lou is director of sales, and I know Walt trusted you, so I am pulling you out of sales. I need a consultant for a while. Later, we will decide where to place you.

"This meeting is adjourned. A memo will go out this morning concerning your new responsibilities. Now, go do your jobs."

All three of them stood and backed out of the office.

Beth pushed the number for the accounting office.

The same day

Mary Lou turned out of the office to go down the hallway. *I always thought she was a snob, but today she seemed human. I thought she didn't like me, but she promoted me. What's that about? How wrong can a person be? Maybe she's shy, and it comes off looking like arrogance. I could have sworn she was arrogant. She was such an upper-class snob in high school. Maybe I was jealous. Oh, Lord, forgive me. I don't want to be jealous of anybody. And thank You so much for Your favor. I got promoted!*

Mary Lou got to her office and took a moment to let it sink in. *Walt would never have made me director of sales and marketing. Never, never, never.*

Chapter Fourteen

The same day,
with the accountant

Joan Gregg, the corporate accountant for International Enterprises, spent more than two hours explaining the finances of the corporation to Beth. International Enterprises, one of the top manufacturers of oil and gas drilling equipment in the world, had kept pace with the economic conditions only because of her sharp instincts. Walt often deferred to her advice, especially in tough economic times.

Joan indicated a list of figures on the computer screen in front of Beth. "Our largest accounts continue to support baseline expenses. Other accounts add to our capacity for research and development."

Beth picked up on new information quickly. "I see that our largest client has been in the news lately for not meeting federal requirements on their last offshore drilling project."

Joan nodded. "Unfortunately, they cut some corners to meet a time constraint. However, the fines involved are a drop in the bucket for them compared to what they will realize. I believe they factored in that expense before they committed the crime. Often that happens."

Beth didn't want to seem innocent and hoped her surprise at the company's habit of breaking the law didn't register on her face. "Count the cost, right?"

"Exactly."

Beth pointed at a column of figures on the screen. "What is this Eastern Surface CAP Expense account?"

Joan squinted at the numbers. "It looks like this account was initiated two years ago. It shows five million dollars went into this account, and now the balance is zero."

That doesn't answer my question. "What's the Eastern Surface CAP Expense mean?"

Joan paused. "It could be some R&D—research and development—fund. Although it's not really that much money for R&D. Walt worked with many scientists and inventors. Who knows what he was up to? We'll find out."

Indeed, who knows? I have a bad feeling about this, and I don't want her to catch on. "Thanks for all your help today. I believe I have a good idea regarding the finances of the corporation." She stood up, giving Joan the signal to leave.

Joan gathered up the profit-and-loss statements she had carried in and exited, saying, "Happy to help out. Please accept my profound condolences, Mrs. Pederson."

"Thank you, Joan. Everything is going to be all right. It's just going to take some time."

After Joan left, Beth continued searching the computer screens and going over accounts. She kept going back to the Eastern Surface CAP Expense. Exactly five million dollars had been taken from the account days before they left for Ft. Lauderdale.

Eastern Surface CAP Expense. E. S. C. A. P. E.!

Her nerves came to the surface. *Escape? Is that what it means, Walt? Is this your escape account? What were you escaping from? Was it me? And why did you have to embezzle five million dollars to do it?* She gulped.

Oh, Walt, did you escape from me? Are you still out there somewhere, alive?

Her stomach churned. She looked up at the clock and noted that it was five thirty. She had put in her first full day. Her first full day at the office, and she was exhausted. She just wanted to go home and go to bed.

She picked up the mail on the way home and reclined on the sofa as she sorted through a stack of envelopes. One envelope's return address indicated it was from Walt's insurance company. She wasn't concerned about insurance, but she was curious how much he'd left her.

She popped open the envelope. The letter stated that an agent would be by in the near future to deliver a check for ten million dollars. Evidently, Walt had upped the original one million-dollar policy to ten million five years before, due to how valuable he was as a CEO.

She closed her eyes. *It has been such a long day. I really can't deal with this right now.*

Her gaze went from the letter to the reflection in the picture window, and she sucked in a breath. *Walt!*

She blinked. *Unmistakable. That's Walt!* She dropped the letter. She sat up straight and spoke to the reflection. "You are dead. You are not real. You are a figment of my imagination."

He gave his "I can charm anybody" smile and walked clearly into view. She turned away from the reflection to see him standing in front of her.

He shrugged nonchalantly. "What you see is what you get."

She covered her eyes and shook her head. "No, you can't be alive."

He took a step toward her and held out his arms. "Would it be so bad if I were alive?"

She threw one of the sofa pillows at him. "You monster. You never loved me. All you ever did was use me to take my father's money. You might as well have been dead."

He laughed out loud. "Your father's money made you beautiful, doll."

He leaned over and picked up the letter off the floor. "And this is what I came back for. You're going to help me."

"Why would I? After the hell you've made my life. It's a wonder I have a shred of self-esteem left."

He glared down at her. "The luckiest day of your life was the day you married me."

He reached for her. She jumped up, knocking over the coffee table in front of her. He roared with menacing laughter.

She sprinted across the room to the stairway and glanced back to see him step behind her. Beth pushed her strength and took the stairs as fast as she could, her short legs straining. She reached the top floor and turned toward the door of their bedroom, pausing long enough to see him topping the stairs.

She ran into the bedroom and slammed the door, throwing the dead bolt almost simultaneously. "Go away!"

He pounded on the door. "I'm not going anywhere."

Beth desperately looked around the room for a weapon. *Anything, is there anything I could use to protect myself? A baseball bat in the bedroom? Never. I don't think we've ever had one in the house.*

She ran to what had been Walt's side of the bed and yanked open the small drawer in the nightstand. Her eyes widened at the sight of a pistol. She grabbed it and was surprised at the weight. She turned back to see the door buck each time Walt kicked it. The door snapped back into place with each blow, but it was weakening.

She glanced at the door to the attached bathroom. It would be suicide to get trapped in the small, windowless room.

Bam! A fist ripped the door wide open, and Walt stepped through the doorway.

She grabbed the pistol with both hands, shifting to the shooting stance her father had taught her many years ago. "Get out of here, I will shoot you." She narrowed her eyes and lowered her voice. "Walt, I will shoot to kill."

He stepped toward her. "You don't have the guts. You don't have what it takes to kill someone in cold blood."

She racked the slide to be sure there was a bullet in the chamber and shouted, "How could I kill you anyway, Walt?"

"You couldn't. You still love me."

She ignored the statement and gulped. "How can someone kill a dead man? Remember? You're already dead. You made sure of that. All I have to do is shoot you and get rid of your body."

She thumbed the laser sight to life. "I could find any number of people that would love to help me get rid of your dead body."

He raised his hand toward the gun barrel and advanced toward her. "Don't do it. You can't do it."

She pulled the trigger. One shot rang out, then another, then another, then another.

Beth's eyes flew open. She realized she had not moved from the sitting room. The letter from the insurance company was on the floor beside the couch.

It had been a dream. Just a dream. She wiped sweat from her brow and sat up, dazed. She looked toward the front door, which someone kept banging. She attempted to get herself together and ran her fingers through her short hair as she walked toward the door. She peeked through the curtain at the side and saw her neighbor Sandy standing there with a bowl of something in her hands.

Beth opened the door and held out her hands to take the bowl. "Oh Sandy. What is this?"

Sandy handed the bowl to Beth. "Are you all right? I must have knocked ten times after I rang the doorbell. I heard it ring from out here. I wouldn't have kept pounding on the door, except I could see you lying on the couch. I was beginning to get worried."

Still recovering from the dream, Beth turned to carry the bowl into the kitchen. "Come in, Sandy. I must have been in a deep sleep."

Sandy followed her through the foyer. "Oh, I am so sorry."

Beth set the bowl on the kitchen table. "I didn't mean to fall asleep. Busy day at the office."

Sandy picked up the bowl and headed for the refrigerator. "It's a fruit salad. I hope you like it. It needs to stay chilled."

Beth opened the refrigerator door. "I'm sure I'll love it. In fact, it looks perfect for tonight. Would you like to stay and share it?"

Sandy slipped into the chair at the table. "Sure. You could probably use some company."

Beth got out plates and forks. "What would you like to drink?"

"Water's fine. Can I help?"

Beth set two glasses for water at their places. "Sparkling?" She retrieved a large bottle of Perrier from the refrigerator.

Sandy held her glass out while Beth poured. "Lovely. Thanks."

Beth filled her own glass and sat. She took a helping of the fruit salad that partially filled her plate and scooted the bowl toward Sandy. "This is very nice. You didn't have to do it."

"I know. I just want you to know that I've been thinking about you."

The house phone broke into their conversation. Beth squinted up at the phone on the wall and read the caller ID. *Ralph Burns.* "Oh, Sandy, I apologize, but I have to take this. Ralph is my uncle, and he's in a nursing home. We haven't talked today, and with everything that has been going on—"

Sandy waved her hand. "Please, go ahead. I understand. Take your time."

Beth jumped up and grabbed the phone before the next ring. "Uncle Ralph, how are you doing today?"

She listened for a minute and motioned to Sandy. "My neighbor Sandy is here. Do you mind if I put you on speaker, and she can say hi." She pressed the speaker button.

Uncle Ralph's deep voice didn't sound like someone in a nursing home. "Hey, Sandy. Nice to meet you."

Sandy put down her fork. "Hello, Mr. Burns. It's my pleasure."

"Call me Ralph. Mr. Burns died about thirty years ago. That was my father." His laugh filled the room.

Sandy raised her eyebrows at Beth, and they joined his laugh. "Okay, Ralph."

"Hey, Beth, did you get to watch *On the Horizon* today?"

Beth grimaced. Her soap opera watching days were most likely over, but Ralph had nothing to do. The episodes entertained him. The least she could do was add comment and discussion to his day. "Missed it today. What happened?"

"Hey, Sandy, did you see it?"

Sandy shook her head. "No, Ralph. I don't get to watch in the afternoons."

"Well, Inspector Foss made them dig up the casket."

Beth shrugged at Sandy and spoke into the speaker. "I knew he would, but I thought he was going to do that a few weeks ago. Law enforcement can be very thorough, even on soap operas. Did they do an autopsy?"

Ralph coughed then shouted, "The casket was empty! Everyone here is so ticked off."

Beth looked at Sandy, who held her hand over her mouth to keep from laughing at the old man's frustration.

Uncle Ralph continued, "That was a cheap trick. It took six months for them to come up with that? And now none of us know what really happened. What a disgusting bunch of writers."

They could hear Ralph speak to someone else in his room. "Oh, all right. Then his voice got stronger as he spoke back into the receiver. "I have to go. It's time for meds. Talk to you tomorrow. Bye, Sandy. Nice talking with you."

Beth took the phone off speaker. "Good night, Uncle Ralph."

She hung the phone back up on the wall. "Sorry, but like I said, he's in a nursing home."

Sandy smiled. "And you talk to him every day. I am so impressed."

Beth held up her hand. "No, no. I don't talk to him every day. He loses track of time. He believes that, but I do try to make sure we talk at least once a week. If he doesn't call in a few days, I'll check in with him." She smoothed out her napkin. "I'll have to catch up with *On the Horizon* before I call him again. Perhaps I can find a website with a synopsis of the episodes."

Friday, March 1
San Diego, California

At five o'clock in the afternoon, Kiral Nadeem slid behind the wheel of his newest toy, a blood-red, fully loaded Lamborghini. Since the night Walt Pederson had disappeared, Kiral had been on a roller coaster. He'd tried Vegas, but his luck ran short, so he found a bungalow on the coast near La Jolla Cove in Southern California. He slowly backed the showpiece onto the street then turned to press the pedal for an accelerated start.

Lazy days and trolling nights left had Kiral in a bit of a trance. It was the first time that he had not either been in school or working full time. It didn't take long for him to discover that the later he stayed out at night, the later he slept in, leaving the day shorter and less lonely.

Kiral didn't have a friend in the world.

He pulled up next to a gold Cadillac convertible that had the top down, and he peeked across to see the driver. A cute young blonde smiled back at him and waved, then took off just as the light turned green. He caught up as she turned left to follow the coastal highway. He let up on the gas and coasted to the next light. Kiral's stomach growled as he made his way to his favorite starting point for the night, George's at the Cove. Delicious entrées with exceptional wine offerings had become routine the last few days.

He parked at the back of the parking lot, away from other vehicles, lest one scratch a speck of the gorgeous paint off his Lamborghini.

No way was valet parking laying a hand on that car. The short walk would do him some good; and in fact, it felt good to stretch his legs.

Once inside and seated at a table on the rooftop deck overlooking La Jolla Cove, he immediately asked for a bottle of Blackbird Arise, the 2009 merlot he'd grown quite fond of.

He drummed his fingers on the table as the breeze ruffled his dark hair for the two minutes it took the waiter to return with his order. He felt nervous that night, and he couldn't figure out why. After his order arrived, he leaned back, closed his eyes, and took a long sip of the smooth wine. Still savoring his drink, Kiral opened his eyes to see the waiter standing at his table, waiting for him to order. He quickly ordered the braised Colorado lamb shank with butternut squash risotto, sweet onion raisin relish, and mint-marinated feta.

Kiral took another sip of wine as the waiter walked away and tried to focus back on those calming sea waves. The sight reminded him of his last few moments with Walt Pederson. For the first time since he had left *The Adventurer* three weeks earlier, his mind flashed back to that night.

Kiral had walked in on Walt in the engine room. So far as he knew, Walt had never been in the engine room before. It caught him by surprise. "What are you doing here?"

Walt stood over the inflatable Zodiac dressed in a full-body wetsuit, complete with fins on his feet. He glared at Kiral. "What do you mean, what am I doing here? I own this ship. Go away."

Kiral moved closer and stole a glance at the raft and the large duffel bag beside it.

Walt slowly reached for the bag. "Kiral, this is none of your business. But since you unfortunately stumbled in here at the most inopportune time, I will make it well worth your while to never speak of this night again."

Kiral had been still trying to make sense of what he had walked in on when he answered, "As you wish, sir."

Walt retrieved the large duffel bag and unzipped it. "No, I mean this is serious business. I will pay you fifty thousand dollars to forget you ever saw me tonight. And if I ever hear that you told, I promise you—I will find you, and I will kill you."

Kiral could tell from Walt's tone that he would do exactly what he said. He watched in amazement as Walt dug through the bag, which was stuffed with money.

Walt stuck a stack of bills in Kiral's face. "Now, take it and get out of here."

Kiral felt his knees weaken. "Yes, sir." He took the money and turned to leave.

"Kiral."

Kiral turned back around.

Walt gave him his most menacing look. "Remember what I said. If you ever tell what happened here tonight, I will kill you."

Kiral's blood ran cold. "Yes, sir."

Walt swore and waved him off. "Get out of here."

He took the money and immediately went to the bridge. He stood in front of the helm and processed what had just happened. *If Walt is leaving in the middle of the night, what is all the money for? He is a very rich man. Suppose Walt wants to take all that money and disappear?* Kiral held up the money Walt had given him. *If this is fifty thousand, he must have millions in that duffel bag.*

If he's going to disappear, why shouldn't I help him? If he is going to disappear, why should I settle for a mere fifty thousand? Kiral pictured the oversized crescent wrench hanging just inside the door of the engine room. He crept back down to the engine room and found Walt's back to him as he fooled with a deflated lightweight Zodiac. Kiral took hold of the crescent wrench.

It made a scraping noise as he took it off its hangar. He cringed. Walt froze.

Slowly, Walt started to turn around. Before Walt could see him, Kiral smashed the wrench across Walt's head and shoulders. The sound rang off the small room's walls.

Walt crumpled to the floor. Kiral pushed open the hatch to the short aft deck and dragged Walt's body across the swim deck. He shoved his former boss overboard and tossed the crescent wrench into the water behind him.

It had all been so easy. In only seconds, he'd repacked the Zodiac, stowed it in the ship's storage under the engines, and wiped down the engine room.

It'd been three weeks exactly since he left the ship. Since then, he'd spent money lavishly—the best hotels, the best food, and now the Lamborghini—never thinking about Walt. He poured another glass of fine wine.

He held back a chuckle. *And that crazy woman who worked for him was worried about if he was saved. What was her name? Oh, yeah. Mary Lou. Sweet little Mary Lou, I'd hate to shatter your illusions, but I'm pretty sure he wasn't saved from the sharks that night.* Kiral couldn't contain his laughter and spewed wine all over the white tablecloth.

He dabbed at his face with the white cloth napkin.

Then there was all that talk about Jesus forgiving murderers. Talk about naïveté. Where did she hear that? Oh, yeah, I think she said it was in the Bible. She looked like she really believed it. And she expected me to believe it, too. Sorry, Mary Lou—I'm too busy spending Walt's money to care.

After spending two hours at George's, mostly staring out at the ocean and watching the sunset, Kiral left the restaurant, strolled across the well-lit parking lot, and hopped in his red Lamborghini. He felt his heart race just a little as the engine roared to life. He couldn't help the smile that spread across his face. He went east on Prospect Street toward Roslyn Lane, negotiating the curb street to go on to La Jolla Parkway. He emerged onto I-5 toward downtown. After about six miles, he turned off on exit 20 and headed toward Rosecrans Street for less than a mile, then he turned onto Sports Arena Boulevard.

The lights of the Valley View Casino reflected off the hood of the Lamborghini.

Chapter Fifteen

Saturday, March 2
San Diego, California

Two o'clock in the morning found Kiral Nadeem behind the wheel of his favorite red Lamborghini, leaving the Valley View Casino after a night of heavy losses and heavy winnings. He felt lucky; his wins had outweighed his losses that night. He patted the thick pocket inside his dinner jacket and counted the balance in his head.

He straightened up in his seat and smiled. Yes, he was rich enough to gamble every night. He loved the thrill of winning. One of these nights, he would hit the jackpot and walk out of there with millions more.

That night had been weird. He couldn't shake the feeling that someone was watching him. He shrugged off the feeling again as he rounded the corner toward Hancock Street and drove on to Point Loma Boulevard.

The lights from the car behind him blinded him, and he nearly missed the curve in the road. Streetlights became scarce, and his headlights reflected off the pavement in front of him. The car stayed right on his tail. Kiral resisted the urge to brake to a full stop to force them to slow down. Still, he cursed out loud at the blinding rearview mirror.

The curve to the right slowed him down. The dark car moved up beside him. He could see only lights and the hood of a black SUV. The SUV pulled close to the Lamborghini, and Kiral leaned away and steered further toward the edge of the road.

His right wheels dropped off the pavement. The shock jolted him, and he pulled back onto the road. Instead of passing Kiral, the other vehicle fell back behind him, lights blazing in the rearview mirror once more.

Kiral sped up, cursing at the maniac behind him. *What kind of fool would do such a thing?*

He felt a shot of pain in his gut. *Who is behind me? Did someone see me pick up my winnings at the casino?* The lights in the rearview mirror pierced his pupils, and he stomped on the accelerator. He nearly missed a split in the road ahead; his tires squealed as he turned up Gatchell Road.

The oversized SUV bashed into his bumper. Kiral's head hit the steering wheel. Blood spewed from his nose, spraying the dash. A gash from his forehead dripped into his eyes.

Kiral roared up Gatchell Road toward the summit of Point Loma. He sped past a battery of large buildings. The dark SUV clung like glue to his tail end.

Seconds later, blinded by the lights behind him, Kiral missed the sharp curve and shot over the cliff at the top of Point Loma.

Some four hundred feet below, his precious red Lamborghini smashed into the boulders. Ocean waves quickly dragged pieces of the shiny red Lamborghini out to sea.

Tuesday evening, March 5
Longmont, Colorado

John Porter waited for his son to pick up the phone. They hadn't talked for a long time. John knew Bobby kept extremely busy in his new position as a detective in San Diego, so he didn't call often.

After the fourth ring, Bobby picked up. "Hullo." He sounded drowsy.

"Bobby, it's Dad. Are you all right?"

John heard bedding rustle as Bobby answered, "Oh, Dad, I'm all right. I just had a late project last night. I'm glad you called. I needed to get up anyway. Everything okay there?"

"We're all good. Just wanted to touch base with you."

Bobby chuckled. "I know. It's hard to get me, right? To tell you the truth, San Diego is more excitement than I bargained for, but I'm doing the job. You were on the force, so you know what I mean."

"Oh, yes. Those were the good old days." John relaxed in his recliner. "I have some news that you may find interesting, son. I've put off telling you anything about this until I was sure something was happening, but I think it's safe to tell you now. I've prayed about it, and the Lord didn't tell me to keep my mouth shut."

Bobby waited a full fifteen seconds. "Tell me, Dad."

"It's about Mary Lou. Remember when we talked about how much you cared for her? I told you that you should slow down with the relationship until you knew she was a Christian."

"I believe both you and Alex used the term 'equally yoked.' And I mistakenly used the same term when I tried to explain to her. Well, what's happened? Did you call to tell me that she's seeing someone?"

John chuckled. "No, son. I called to tell you that she's been attending our church services for over a month now."

Bobby choked out, "Hallelujah! You're not kidding me, are you?"

"No, son. She came in a month or so ago and spent the entire service at the altar. Next thing we knew, she was coming every Sunday. I didn't know who she was for a while—"

"She's attending Alma Temple? She's attending your church? If that's true, you know she's got to be growing spiritually."

Bobby's mother picked up the extension. "Mrs. Cunkell told me that she and Mary Lou have Bible study every Sunday after lunch up there on the hill. When Mrs. Cunkell told me her name was Mary Lou, I asked if her last name was Stots. Then Mrs. Cunkell asked if I knew her. I just said that you used to date her."

Bobby gave out a big, "Whoopee! She's studying with Mrs. Cunkell? That is far more than I even dared to pray for."

Friday, March 8
Northglenn, Colorado

Eileen sipped her mother's mild coffee. "Did you get new curtains?"

Mrs. Stots set out small dishes and placed a basket of muffins in the center of the table. "Oh, just the one over the sink. I saw it at Kohl's and couldn't pass it up. I like the yellow tassels. Just what I needed, to remind me that summer is on its way."

Eileen laughed. "I know what you mean. But really, we've had much worse winters. Remember when the snow covered the cars on the street? Now, *that* was a winter."

Mrs. Stots handed Eileen the butter. "Even so, every winter seems longer and colder to me. I wish I could talk your father into spending winters in Florida. I guess he's afraid if he leaves, he might miss something."

Eileen buttered her muffin. "Like what? He's retired. Isn't that what retirement is all about? You can come and go as you please, with no schedule."

It was Mrs. Stots's turn to laugh. "It's not like that, dear. But you will find out in due time."

Eileen took a bite. "Mom, your muffins are the best, especially when they're hot. Mm." She swallowed her bite. "But I came over to tell you something. I'm dating."

Mrs. Stots put her coffee cup down. "Well, I am happy for you, I think. Tell me about him."

Eileen bubbled. "I met him when Mary Lou and I went skiing at Winter Park. Mom, he is the nicest guy. It so nice to have someone to do things with and someone who really cares."

Mrs. Stots leaned back in her chair. "Someone who really cares? He must be something. You're glowing. Is this growing into something serious?"

Eileen drank the last of her coffee. "I wish Mary Lou would meet someone. She's been so down since Bobby left."

Mrs. Stots nodded. "It would be wonderful if my two daughters could be happy at the same time. Not that you need a man in your life to be happy, but Mary Lou has definitely been depressed since Bobby moved."

Eileen finished off her muffin. "And she's been acting so weird lately. Yesterday, we were going to dinner. She drove, so I had no control over what happened. We pulled up to a stop sign, and a panhandler asked her for money. She handed him a fifty-dollar bill."

Mrs. Stots frowned. "Our Mary Lou? That *is* strange."

"Mom, the guy looked like he needed another drink. I told her what I thought."

"What did you say to her?"

"That she'd just enabled an addict. No doubt he went off to buy drugs or booze with the money she gave him. And do you know what she had the nerve to tell me?"

Mrs. Stots's eyebrows went up. "I can't imagine."

"She told me—and I don't have any idea where this came from—she told me that God told her to give the man the money. She said that she did what God wanted her to do, and that what the man did with the money was between him and God."

Mrs. Stots smiled. "Well, dear, that does make some sense."

Eileen looked into her empty plate. "You could have knocked me over with a feather." She looked back up at her mother. "Such compassion from our little Mary Lou surprised me. Yes, she did make sense. It just seemed like I was with someone else for a minute. I guess I sometimes forget that God is always with us, always guiding us. Always amazing us!"

Sunday, March 10
Crown Point

Mary Lou parked her car outside Mrs. Cunkell's apartment after she and Mrs. Cunkell had attended the church service downtown at Alma Temple. She followed Mrs. Cunkell into her apartment. "Today's service spoke to me. How is it that every Sunday, I feel Dr. Dallenbach delivers a message meant just for me? I mean, does everyone feel like that?"

Mrs. Cunkell put two glasses of water on the table. "I don't believe everyone feels like that all the time. However, often the message seems quite on target."

Mary Lou placed her notepad and Bible on the table. "The message today spoke volumes to me. I have no difficulty in leaving some of my past behind, but some things simply will not go away."

Mrs. Cunkell sat across from her. "Some things are more difficult to release to the Lord than others. He wants you to make peace with the past so that He can use you in the future. He has plans for you, and old baggage sometimes gets in the way of progress."

Mary Lou leaned back in her chair. "How do you know that He has plans for me?"

Mrs. Cunkell opened her Bible. "Ephesians 2:10, 'For we are God's handiwork, created in Christ Jesus to do good works, which God prepared in advance for us to do.'"

Mary Lou opened her Bible to the same verse and reread it aloud, slowly.

Mrs. Cunkell nodded. "That's right. You know that God doesn't lie. He is truth. But in order to be truly effective for the good works He prepared in advance for us, we must claim our freedom from the past."

Mary Lou felt her eyes fill. "Oh, Mrs. Cunkell, I feel so guilty. I—I am so evil."

"Mary Lou, you are not evil. The evil one wants you to think that you're evil, but you are not evil. You belong to Jesus now."

Mary Lou looked up. "I have a confession to make." She let out a loud sob, then squeaked, "I don't know if I can do this."

Mrs. Cunkell leaned forward. "Take your time. It's going to be all right."

"It's too late to be all right. I hated Walt."

Mrs. Cunkell handed Mary Lou a tissue. "Listen, God understands and forgives us—"

"No—I prayed for him to die, and God answered my prayer. Now Walt is in hell." She burst into sobs. "How can I live with myself, knowing that I sent someone to hell?"

After a long moment of silence, Mrs. Cunkell said, "Oh, I see. Well, no wonder you're so upset. Dry your eyes. When you're ready to listen, we'll talk."

Mary Lou wiped her eyes and regained a bit of composure. "I'm ready now."

Mrs. Cunkell adjusted her glasses. "It is good that you believe God answers prayers. He most certainly does, and He loves for us to admit our anger and frustration to Him. However, He never does something outside of His declared will just because we ask Him for something." Mrs. Cunkell flipped to a well-worn chapter in her Bible. "Now read Second Peter chapter three, verse nine, and tell me what the Lord's will was for Walt."

After a few moments, Mary Lou said, "God did not want Walt to perish but wanted him to come to repentance. Oh, Mrs. Cunkell, that is what I really wanted, too—but instead, I asked for Walt to be gone, and now it's too late."

Mrs. Cunkell reassured Mary Lou, "I know if you had it to do over, that you would do whatever it took to save him."

Mrs. Cunkell turned to the book of Job, chapter thirty-eight. "You need to understand the sovereignty of God. Who do you think decides when we die?"

Mary Lou tilted her head. "God?"

"Exactly. God decides when we are born and when we leave this life. When we start deciding that we are responsible for someone's death, we are taking up God's territory. And my dear, He does not like that. Job thought he knew all the answers, and God corrected him. Now read this." She pointed at verse one. "And keep reading until I tell you to stop."

Mary Lou cleared her throat. "He said: Who is this that darkens my counsel with words without knowledge? Brace yourself like a man; I will question you, and you shall answer me. Where were you when I laid the earth's foundation? Tell me, if you understand. Who marked off its dimensions? Surely you know! Who stretched a measuring line across it? On what were its footings set, or who laid its cornerstone—while the morning stars sang together and all the angels shouted for joy? Who shut up the sea behind doors when it burst forth from the womb, when I made the clouds its garment and wrapped it in thick darkness, when I fixed limits for it and set its door and bars in place?"

Mrs. Cunkell raised her hand for Mary Lou to stop. "For the next three chapters, God explains to Job that He is God and that He is in control of all things. You are not mighty enough to have caused Walt's death. Only God can do that. As far as your hatred toward Walt, I believe you have released that to God already. If you haven't, pray about it and ask for forgiveness. He will forgive you. If Walt's in hell, that's between him and God, not you."

Mary Lou took a deep breath. "Of course. You're right."

Mrs. Cunkell closed her Bible. "If God wanted to use you to save Walt, He would have. That's our mission in life, bringing others to the foot of the cross. And you will bring the ones God plans for you to bring."

Monday, March 11
Denver, Colorado

It had been just over three weeks since the funeral. Mary Lou sat with Denny and Joe in a management meeting. Revenues for the next quarter headed the list of topics. Beth sat at the head of the table, listening to each report, stopping only to ask pertinent questions.

"I think everything's going quite well." Denny moved his chair closer to Beth's.

Moving in, Denny? Feels like you're going a little overboard making your point. Doesn't she see what's going on? This is a business meeting, for crying out loud.

Denny held another sheet filled with columns of numbers in front of Beth's face and pointed at figures on the page, scooting his chair even closer. Beth seemed oblivious.

Joe cleared his throat. He stood up and wrote on the whiteboard. "Let's look at where we were last year at this time. From all the information I had, we were ahead of the wave. The last report you gave me showed a huge deficit." He looked at Beth.

Beth's cheeks turned pink. "I—I know. The accountant knows what's going on. We had to make some adjustments for unexpected expenses. But if we look at the numbers for this year so far, we can take up the slack. I have every confidence in the sales and marketing force."

Joe grimaced. "Thanks to Mary Lou's team, the sales numbers have gone up." He paused. "From this report, revenues have increased, but company profits are significantly down. I don't understand, but we will do what we can to improve profits."

"This is new to me, too, guys," Beth said. "Please bear with me. I felt like the more you knew, the more we can understand what has to happen in order to turn things around."

Denny blurted, "It looks like International Enterprises has to stop spending…"

He shook his head and took his seat, pursing his lips. He looked deep into Beth's eyes. She glanced away.

His hand covered hers. "Beth, I promise I will do whatever you feel is necessary to make this company successful. If it takes more travel, more time, more investment—I'm with you. You can count on me."

Beth snatched her hand away. "The deficit is not your fault," she said, voice cracking. "That's true. We need to make up for it anyway, but it's not your fault. In fact, all of you all are doing a great job, and I appreciate your dedication and your willingness to go the extra mile in this unique phase of the business."

Beth gathered herself and stood. "This meeting is adjourned. Next Monday morning, perhaps we'll have a better handle on exactly what we need to do to make this company grow. I want International Enterprises to be more successful than ever. Make no mistake— expenditures will shrink."

She stepped toward the door. Both men jumped to their feet. Beth walked out.

Mary Lou sat scowling at the whiteboard. "Since when do you tell the CEO to stop spending? What is the matter with you guys?"

Joe folded his arms in front of him. "It's obvious that she needs our help. The company can't survive by losing money."

Mary Lou slapped her pen down on her page in front of her. "She's barely got a grip on coming to the office every day. Cut her some slack. I believe she's just beginning to get a full picture of what Walt's been doing every day for the past ten years."

Denny sat down and took another sip of coffee. "I don't think we were too hard on her. She gave us information. We didn't ask for it. She feels helpless right now. It's up to us to help her as much as we can and let her know we are here for her."

Joe picked up his notepad and briefcase. "She doesn't have a lot of family, so I expect she feels like we're the only people she can count on. And she's not sure of that because she really doesn't know any of us that well."

Mary Lou looked up at Joe. *This is certainly different from the way we worked with Walt. They seem to be as different as night and day.*

Denny finished his coffee. "Be careful how you judge. Beth was a part of the business before Walt was around. Things have changed, so she's now on unfamiliar ground, but it won't take her long to understand what's going on. I'm certainly going to help out as much as I can."

Mary Lou snickered. "Yeah, we got that, Denny. You practically slobbered that intention all over her."

He shot back. "Hey, I'm trying to be part of the solution here. I don't see either one of you consoling her."

Mary Lou blinked. "Everything is so weird. I keep remembering being on that yacht. *The Adventurer*—that's what he called it. I guess I'm still waiting for him to come in to work. Imagine how Beth feels."

Denny turned to leave. "I know what you mean. Did you guys hear about Kiral?"

Joe frowned. "Kiral? You mean the captain of *The Adventurer*?"

Mary Lou shrugged. "What about him? I talked to him a little bit after we got off the yacht. He seemed like a nice guy. So what's up with him?"

Denny stepped back and put his briefcase on the table. He opened it up and pulled out a newspaper. "Front-page news in the *San Diego Union Tribune*. Kiral was killed in an automobile accident."

Mary Lou sucked in a breath. "He was killed? Does Beth know?"

"Let me see that." Denny handed the paper over to Joe. He began reading the article. "'Kiral Nadeem died instantly in a tragic accident. His car missed a turn near the top of Point Loma near San Diego around three o'clock Saturday morning. The car was traveling at a rapid speed on Gatchell Road when it missed the curve at the top of the hill, near Point Loma Vista and plummeted over the cliff, hitting boulders four hundred feet below. The late-model Lamborghini burst into flames upon contact. It has not been determined what caused Nadeem to miss the curve.'"

Mary Lou read the words over Joe's shoulder. "How horrible!"

She hurried to Beth's office because she wondered how well Beth had known him. Beth was busily working on a small stack of papers.

Mary Lou smiled. "Do you have a minute?"

Beth welcomed her and returned her smile. "Sure. Come in and have a seat."

Mary Lou sat across from Beth. "Did you hear about what happened to Kiral?"

"Kiral?" Beth tilted her head. "You mean the captain of *The Adventurer*? I haven't heard anything about him. Is there something I should know?"

Mary Lou jumped up. "Wait a second. I need to get the article from Joe. Be right back."

Mary Lou hurried to Joe's office, where Joe and Denny were in a heavy discussion regarding a sales pitch in Saudi Arabia. "Give me that article about Kiral. I want to show it to Beth. She didn't know anything about it."

Joe handed Mary Lou the newspaper, and she dashed back to Beth's office. "Here's an article about the accident. Kiral was killed."

Mary Lou spread the article in front of Beth and sat quietly while Beth read.

Beth slowly looked up from the newspaper. "How tragic. It doesn't mention any family. And as far as I know, Kiral had no family here in America. To tell you the truth, I didn't even know his last name."

Mary Lou nodded. "Me either. I don't know anything about his family, but I do know Kiral was looking for a job after the—"

She didn't want to remind Beth about the awful night Walt disappeared from *The Adventurer*.

Beth rubbed her chin. She liked Mary Lou. She felt the woman's compassion. "It's all right, Mary Lou. We have to move on—*I* have to move on. Please don't feel bad about mentioning *The Adventurer*."

"I am so sorry. But for some reason Kiral's death seems significant or timely or whatever."

Beth looked thoughtful. "It does bring up some questions. I wonder if Kiral found another job. I know Walt didn't pay him that kind of money."

"What do you mean, 'that kind of money'?"

"It says here that he was driving a Lamborghini. I wonder if it was his. Aren't they four hundred thousand dollars or more? I know Walt didn't pay him that kind of money."

Mary Lou nodded. "I know they're very expensive. Kiral didn't seem like a rich man, but I have no idea what a ship captain makes for a salary." She leaned back in her chair. "But I have a friend in San Diego. He's a police officer. I haven't talked to him for a while. Perhaps I'll give him a call and find out if he knows anything about this accident or Kiral."

Chapter Sixteen

Saturday, March 16
Arvada, Colorado

Rain beat against the picture window in Mary Lou's living room. She was curled up on the sofa and staring at the telephone on the side table. *Should I call Bobby?* Their last conversation had left memory scars. He'd made her feel unworthy, and right then she'd decided they were through. Now she felt like the past two months had been an eternity. She missed him more than she wanted to admit.

Would he help me? Would he even speak to me? There was a time when I knew I could count on him. "As much as he hated to go"—she remembered those exact words. *Yes, he had said that as much as he hated to go, he felt he had more opportunity for quick advancement with the San Diego Police Department.* He had said he thought he was in love with her and hinted that he was having trouble staying pure. *What a bunch of bunk. Didn't Paul say if a man burned with desire he should marry? He could have proposed—I was even expecting it.* She could still feel the betrayal she had felt the night he said he was leaving.

Just before he broke the news about leaving, I had decided to do everything I could to get him to commit to me. What a joke. Why don't any of my schemes work? She looked at the rain beating against the window. *I get it, Lord. I guess I really don't want a man that doesn't want me. Manipulation comes so naturally to me. I know women who manipulated their way to the altar, and they aren't happy.*

It wasn't meant to be. So be it. But we were friends before. And now I have a reason to call him.

She realized how much she wanted to hear his voice again. She picked up the receiver and dialed the San Diego Police Department headquarters. After questioning a cold PBX operator, she was finally connected to his private office.

"Bobby Porter."

"Uh, hello. This is Mary Lou."

His voice brightened. "Mary Lou? It is you. It seems like it's been a long time."

Mary Lou's shoulders relaxed at the sound of his voice. *Should I ask if he's missed me? No, I don't want to know if he hasn't.*

"Is everything all right?" Concern swept across the miles.

She leaned back on the couch. "Everything's all right. I just had some questions that I thought you might be able to help me with."

Bobby cleared his throat. "Questions? How can I help you? I'll be happy to answer anything I can."

For a moment, she wondered if he was dating anyone in San Diego, but she stuck to the subject. "There was an accident in San Diego two weeks ago. I want to know if you have any information about the man that was killed. His name is Kiral Nadeem."

"What is this about? Did you know Mr. Nadeem?"

Mary Lou frowned. "Did you know that my boss was in a fatal boating accident a month ago? Oh—probably not. I doubt you have time for Denver news."

He sighed. "I follow the news in Denver. Yes, I did hear about Walt's death. How is everyone taking it? As I remember, he wasn't the most popular man around town."

Mary Lou picked up the notepad and pen from the space beside the phone. "He was my boss, and he did leave a distraught wife who is trying to take his place running the company."

"What's that got to do with Kiral Nadeem?"

Mary Lou scribbled little circles across the top of her notepad. "He was the captain of Walt's yacht, *The Adventurer*. The last time I saw it, it was in a slip on a Key West dock. I was actually on that yacht the night Walt disappeared. It's very disturbing to remember. But I thought it's an interesting coincidence that suddenly Kiral Nadeem is dead, too."

"I am familiar with the case."

Mary Lou heard paper shuffling on the other end of the line.

"In fact, I remember that case vividly for a few reasons. One, the accident took place on the road up to Point Loma. Two, the car involved was that very expensive Lamborghini. He paid cash for the car; he may have been a drug dealer. And then there were no skid marks on the road."

"What does that mean?"

"It means the driver didn't have time or wasn't aware of any danger and didn't slam on his brakes. The road up to Point Loma is winding and the place he went off is near the summit. As far as we could tell, he was driving up the road toward the top and would have had to accelerate purposely to get off the road and over the cliff."

She thought she heard a meow. "Did I just hear a cat in your office?"

"Uh, yes. They're fumigating my apartment building. I had to bring Hurricane with me today."

She pictured Bobby's beloved feline in his lap, purring while being gently stroked. Hurricane had never liked Mary Lou. One angering part of her relationship with Bobby that she never understood was why Hurricane got so much special consideration.

Mary Lou wanted to stay on the subject of her call. "So you're saying the accident is suspicious."

"I'm saying there were no skid marks. Don't make it any more than what I've already said. There was no family to contact, and I saw no mention of Pederson being his employer."

"Well, Walt was already dead, so he wouldn't be his employer anymore. But there has to be some connection. Don't you think it's weird that three weeks after Walt disappeared, Kiral is found dead?"

"No, I don't think it is weird. Don't make something out of a coincidence. Is there somebody else involved in this?"

"Walt's wife said Walt never paid Kiral enough money to buy a Lamborghini."

The phone fell silent.

Bobby took a deep breath. "You might be interested to know that I'm coming back to Denver. I've been offered the job I originally wanted—detective."

Her heart skipped a beat. "Detective? That's wonderful! That's what you wanted from the very beginning. You went to San Diego to become a detective, and now you got an offer from Denver?"

"Gosh, Mary Lou, I guess you never knew. When Denver found out I was working at the position here, they contacted me and offered me the same job back there. Of course, I can't wait to come back. You know I love Denver." He hesitated. "Hurricane loves Denver. We miss those Rocky Mountains."

Mary Lou felt a lump in her throat. She swallowed and felt tears welling up. *He can't say he missed me?* She steadied her voice. "Denver is a great place to live. I'm sure your buddies will be glad you're coming back."

I have a lot to tell Mrs. Cunkell. I hope she can give me some advice on how to handle my emotions. Right now, I'm hurt.

Tuesday, March 19
Lakewood, Colorado

The doorbell rang.

Beth jumped up off the couch. *Who would be coming over at this hour?* She glanced at the clock again. *Eight o'clock at night is too late for company.* She peeked through the little hole in the middle of the door and saw Denny Adams. She swung the door open. "Denny, what are you doing here?"

"I thought you might want some company this evening. Sometimes it's good to have someone to talk to."

Beth felt somewhere between indignant and found out. "It's eight o'clock at night, Denny."

"Oh, is it too late? I'm sorry; I just left the office and didn't notice the time. Grab your coat. At least we can go have coffee."

Coffee sounded good, and company sounded better. Beth stepped back and opened the door further.

Denny stepped in, leaving the door open. "I'll wait here."

She retrieved her jacket from the closet across the room, picked up her purse, and returned to the door. Denny stepped out onto the porch. She set the house alarm and closed the door behind her.

Denny took her by the elbow to help her down the curb and simultaneously opened his car door for her. She jerked, startled.

"Where would you like to go?"

"There's a Starbucks a few miles down the road. Is that all right?"

"Sounds like a great place for coffee." He closed the door after her and walked around to get in the driver side.

"You say you just left the office? You're putting in a lot of hours."

Denny started the car and pulled onto the street. "It's important that we get a grip on things as soon as possible. I do not want to leave any loose ends that might cause you problems later. So if it means staying later a few nights, it's no problem. But tonight, I kept thinking about you. I thought maybe you could use some company."

She watched out her window for a moment and turned toward him. "Company, huh? I suppose company might take my mind off International Enterprises. My father would be quite surprised at the turn of events, me running his business and all."

He turned on the wipers as a rain-snow mix started smacking the windshield. "Love Colorado weather. You never know how to plan. One day it's sixty degrees, and the next day it snows."

"Walt used to say if you don't like the weather, just wait." Denny pulled into the Starbucks parking lot. "So I was right. Of course you miss him, and it must be lonely at times. I get lonely, too. I don't think anyone ever really gets over losing someone they love."

Beth felt her eyes tearing up. She dug through her purse for a tissue and dabbed at her eyes. *Maybe it's just too soon for me to be going out with a man for coffee.* "I don't want to embarrass you by crying, but I can't seem to hold back the tears. And in some ways, I'm very angry at what happened to Walt."

Denny put the car in park and shut off the engine. He turned to her. "Let's forget all about that tonight. Let's talk about happy things. Let's talk about our childhood. When I was a kid, I couldn't wait till I was old enough to drink coffee. Come on. Help me celebrate." He laughed.

She couldn't suppress her grin. "You're a silly man. But you are old enough to drink coffee, so let's go."

After receiving their special custom-made concoctions, they found a booth in a corner where they could talk. Denny looked into her eyes. "Now tell me about your childhood. What was it you couldn't wait to do when you grew up?"

"I guess the biggest thing was that I couldn't wait to get my driver's license." She shivered at the remembrance "I just never thought I'd live to be sixteen."

They chuckled and talked about their childhoods for the next three hours.

Beth looked at her watch. "Now it's really late. And we both have to work in the morning. You need to take me home."

Denny stood up and held her coat open for her to slide her arms into. "It's been a wonderful evening. Better than sitting home in front of a TV dinner—in front of a TV."

She snickered. "What can I say? I have to admit I miss watching my daytime soap operas once in a while."

"Well, you've got a TV in your office. What's the problem?"

"I'm not watching soap operas at the office."

He followed her out to the car and opened the door for her. Once she settled in, he closed the door and walked around and got in the driver's seat. "Tonight meant a lot to me. I don't want you to ever feel uncomfortable around me. But I hope it's all right if we spend some time together."

Beth wondered exactly what spending some time together meant.

Friday, March 22
Arvada, Colorado

As far as Mary Lou was concerned, Friday night couldn't come fast enough. Her goal was to get home, dig a microwave dinner out of the freezer, and have dinner in front of the TV. Her second goal for that evening was to stay in front of the TV until she fell asleep.

She had driven far enough that the car was warm, but she pulled her new coat around her anyway. Soft fleece felt warm against her neck. *I think this is the best coat I've ever had. It's perfect for a day like today.* She glanced at dark clouds overhead. Mary Lou neared the last turn to her house. The stoplight forced her to stop beside the bus stop.

While she waited for the traffic light to change, she couldn't help but notice the tiny elderly woman sitting on the bench in front of the bus stop, hugging herself and shivering in the cold. She looked to be about the same height as Mary Lou, but she wore no gloves, hat, or coat, and she wore sandals without stockings.

Before she could think about it, Mary Lou threw the car into park, grabbed her boots from the floor of the back seat, and ran over to the woman. She tore her "best coat I ever had" coat off and put it around the woman's shoulders and flipped the hood over her bare head. Then she dropped the boots beside the woman. "Here—you take these."

Surprise still registered on the woman's face as Mary Lou drove off.

Oh, Lord. It's the least I could do for her. I pray that she has a good home to go to and that she has a good meal tonight. I am so blessed, Lord. I am truly thankful for all the blessings You pour out on me every day.

As soon as she got into the kitchen, her cell phone went off. Caller ID showed it was Eileen.

Mary Lou answered, "Where have you been? I haven't talked to you since you told me you couldn't go to Walt's funeral with me because you and Kurt had plans. All I get is texts that say 'Kurt this' and 'Kurt that.' Just so you know, the funeral went off fine. You should've been there. There was a casket and everything—they had us write good-bye notes to him to put in the casket, which were buried like he would've been. Is that not just wild?"

Eileen giggled. "I didn't call to talk about the funeral. I have something to tell you. Are you sitting down?"

"No, I'm not sitting down. But you're scaring me, now. What's going on?"

Eileen giggled again. "Tell me congratulations. Kurt and I are getting married."

Mary Lou walked into her living room and sat down on the couch. "Okay, now I'm sitting down. Tell me what's going on."

"I told you, Kurt and I are getting married."

"Eileen, is this some kind of joke?" *This can't be true. They haven't dated that long. Eileen's teasing me.*

"It's for real!" Eileen shrieked. "We are so happy!"

"Wait a minute—you cannot be marrying Kurt. You don't even know the guy. I was with you when you met him less than a month ago. You're kidding, right?"

"No, I am not kidding. And for your information, it's been two months since we met."

"Two months is nothing. What do you know about the man?"

Eileen's next remark cut Mary Lou to the core. "Well, I know he likes kids."

The connection went silent as Mary Lou contemplated her own biological clock. Finally Eileen said, "Are you still there?"

"Oh Eileen, I don't know what to think."

"Tonight Kurt and I decided to contact all our friends. So can I come over?"

Mary Lou got up, opened the freezer door, and scrutinized the frozen dinners at her command. "Would you be interested in going out to dinner?"

"I think that's a great idea! I have lots to tell you."

She'd better have a lot to tell me. I want to know how Kurt convinced my sister to marry him.

Eileen, still bubbling, said, "I'll pick you up. Three minutes, okay?"

Three minutes later, Mary Lou heard a short beep in front of her house. She grabbed her remote garage door opener and went out through the open garage.

Once inside Eileen's car, she pressed the button on the remote and closed the door as she turned to Eileen. "This had better be good."

"Where do you want to go? I'm not even get to say anything till we're sitting down with dinner in front of us. So tell me, where do you want to go?"

"Oh, anywhere. What's the closest place? Chili's—go to Chili's."

Eileen parked her Outback in front of Chili's. The brisk wind cut through Mary Lou's light jacket. She grasped it around her, and she hurried to the front door. Eileen got there first and held the door open. The hostess seated them, and they ordered before Eileen faced her interrogator.

"Now, I want you to tell me—Wipe that silly grin off your face."

Eileen grinned even bigger. "I want you to be my maid of honor."

"What? You—you want me to be your maid of honor? Are you nuts? You are not really going to marry this man. Seriously, you don't even know him."

Eileen thanked the waitress for pouring her cup of coffee, then turned to Mary Lou. "Kurt and I have been together constantly since I brought you home from Winter Park. I met his family. I have met all of his friends, including his old girlfriend. Oh, Mary Lou, he is the most wonderful man I've ever known."

Mary Lou slapped her forehead. *She's only known him for two months!* "You're losing it, girl. I am worried about you. What have you got yourself into? Do Mom and Dad know about this?"

Eileen's back straightened. "If anyone should be worried, it should be me, worrying about you. I'm getting married. We are going to have children. He loves me. I'm looking at the future I've always dreamed about. So don't give me this 'I'm worried about you' stuff. And as a matter of fact, Mom and Dad met him last night. They loved him."

All too aware of her own biological clock ticking, Mary Lou felt anger well up inside her. "So you're saying that I don't have a future? Well, my whole life isn't tied up in a man I met only a few months ago. I mean, you cannot have found out that much about Kurt in such a short time."

Eileen leaned back in the booth. She took a deep sigh. "He's good looking, isn't he?"

Mary Lou shrugged. "I'll give you that. He's good looking, and I'll give you that he's nice."

Eileen gave that silly grin again. "Oh, he is nice. He's a Christian. And he's rich."

Mary Lou crossed her arms and leaned back in her booth. "You know as well as I do that money isn't everything. Money isn't anything, sometimes—and sometimes it can be a real deal breaker. Tell me, how does he have money?"

"He started his own company when he was sixteen, delivering documents for attorneys throughout the city. Later he incorporated subpoenas and process serving. By the time he went to college, he was so familiar with the legal profession that he graduated a year early and passed the bar exam. At that time he was the youngest attorney in the state. He started his own law firm and his other business under a separate name, We Deliver. Two years later, he added partners to the firm—"

"You are kidding me!" Mary Lou put her hand to her mouth. "He's not—no, he's not Kurt Bell. Bell, Landis, and Hood is the most prestigious law firm in Denver."

Eileen slapped her hand on the table. "You got it! I'm going to marry Kurt Bell. And guess what? He told me I could quit my job and do anything I want to."

Jealousy washed over Mary Lou. *She's getting married and quitting her job?* "I thought Kurt Bell was married."

"Nope. Never been married. He told me he had been close before, but he has never asked anyone to marry him before. And here's the best part of it—he's a virgin."

Mary Lou wrinkled her nose. "Uh, time out. TMI. Puh-lee-z, I did not have to know that."

"Don't you see? It's answered prayer. I made certain that I would be a virgin when I married. I didn't know who God would bring into my life. And when Kurt told me he was a virgin, that sealed the deal. I know this is of God."

Mary Lou caved. In a depressed-sounding voice she didn't recognize, she asked, "So when's the wedding?"

"Does that mean you'll be my maid of honor?"

Mary Lou tried to buck up and smiled. "Of course I will be your maid of honor. What are sisters for?"

Eileen clapped her hands. "I'm thrilled. We can plan this wedding together. I'm going to need all of your expert advice. How many bridesmaids should I have? Where do you think we should have the wedding? What colors should I pick? We want to get married in the next few months. Would you help me pick out invitations?"

"Shouldn't your fiancé be helping you with this?"

"Oh, he told me he's not good at this kind of thing. He said I might enjoy doing this with you. That way I could make my choices and then run them by him. He said that he would probably go along with anything I chose, and because I have more time, I should run with it."

Mary Lou wrinkled her nose again. "That seems weird, but whatever."

"Don't be nasty. He's a wonderful man—and considerate—so stop being mean. You know very well he has a pristine reputation in this town. So knock it off."

Mary Lou sucked in a deep breath. *I am not jealous of my sister. I am happy for her. Lord, please help me change my attitude right now. Eileen is my sister, and I really want to be a part of her happiness. Show me how to do that, Lord. Thank you, Jesus.*

Mary Lou reached across the table and patted Eileen's hand. "I promise, I'll do anything you need me to do to make your wedding day unforgettable. I think it's going to be a lot of fun picking out colors, finding the proper venue, and—the very best part—testing cake recipes."

The waitress brought their food, and they started eating.

Mary Lou took a sip of water. "Did I tell you Bobby's moving back to town?"

Eileen swallowed a bite of her salad. "How did you find that out?"

"I called him. I had a question about someone in San Diego. We had a good conversation. Just before we hung up, he told me he had a job back in Denver."

Eileen wiped her mouth with the heavy cloth napkin. "Wow, that was fast. Interesting. Does that mean you'll be seeing him again?"

"Who knows? But I will tell you something funny. I happened to catch him at work, and while we were talking, I heard his cat meow."

Eileen's eyes widened. "He took Hurricane to work with him? He must be lonely."

"Yeah." Mary Lou laughed. "He said they were fumigating his apartment building, and whenever the exterminator comes, Hurricane goes to the precinct with him. Isn't that hilarious?"

Eileen giggled. "Hilarious? I don't know. Sick, maybe."

"That cat never liked me. I'm telling you, whenever I was at his place, Hurricane would run and hide. She wanted nothing to do with me. I was fine without her, but Bobby loves that cat. I suppose she's been a lot of company for him. That's sad, I mean I would have been happy to be company for him any day of the week." Mary Lou looked into her plate.

"Don't be sad. He's moving back. I know he's going to want to see you. You guys were great together. When I had nothing to do and you invited me to come along, you made me feel like one of the group, even though I know three's company. You never made me feel like the third wheel. I don't know if I ever told you how much I appreciated that."

Mary Lou looked up and smiled. "Hey, girl, you're my sister, and we were glad to have you along."

"Well, now you can hang out with me and Kurt if Bobby's not around. But I have a feeling that he will be. The Lord God said, 'It is not good for man to be alone'—Genesis 2:18."

Chapter Seventeen

Sunday, March 24
Palm Sunday, Denver, Colorado

Mary Lou sang "Hosanna to the Highest" with the congregation to finish the Palm Sunday service at Alma Temple.

After the closing prayer, she found Mrs. Cunkell gathering her things for the trip back to her apartment in Westminster.

Mary Lou picked up Mrs. Cunkell's books. "Let me carry these. Can you ride back with me?"

Mrs. Cunkell nodded. "That would be great. I have a new study book to show you. It's on the Book of James. I think you're going to like it."

The two of them got into Mary Lou's car. Mary Lou navigated out of the parking lot and headed down Lincoln Street toward 20th Avenue to catch the expressway. "I have something I need to ask you about. I'm not sure if I can wait until we get to your apartment."

Mrs. Cunkell turned toward Mary Lou. "Of course you can ask me now. Tell me what is on your mind."

They turned onto the expressway, and Mary Lou relaxed, not having to concentrate so much on traffic. "It's about the man I used to date. The police detective, Bobby Porter."

Mrs. Cunkell smiled. "Oh, yes. I remember you telling me about him. As I recall, he wasn't very nice to you."

Mary Lou grimaced. "I may have exaggerated that part of our relationship. Actually, he was pretty nice to me. I was so mad when he told me I needed to grow in my relationship with Christ that I couldn't see the forest for the trees, if you know what I mean."

Mrs. Cunkell nodded.

Mary Lou continued, "Anyway, now I think that he may have been correct. I was just too angry—I know, pride, but... Well, we dated for a few months, and I thought I was in love with him. I thought he was in love with me. I thought he was going to propose, and that was the night he told me he was leaving town. Oh, I'm leaving so much out. I don't know where to start."

"Slow down."

Mary Lou took her foot off the accelerator and checked her speed.

Mrs. Cunkell laughed. "No, not your driving speed. I mean your talking speed. We have all afternoon."

Mary Lou sighed. "I'm sorry to drop all this on you. Just tell me to shut up."

"You know I would never do that. Oops! Here's our turn." She pointed at the big red castle on the corner.

Mary Lou quickly got into the left lane to turn. "See, here I was talking and almost missed our turn. I can't even concentrate."

She parked the car in front of Mrs. Cunkell's apartment and helped Mrs. Cunkell out of the car. They went in. Mary Lou took off her jacket and hooked it on the coat tree. She took her normal Sunday afternoon seat across the table from Mrs. Cunkell.

Mary Lou resumed talking. "After he told me that I needed to grow spiritually, I wanted to get back at him by not ever seeing him again."

"Hum, sounds like that kind of retaliation hurt you more than him. He probably had no idea that you were being vindictive."

"I wasn't being vindictive. I was protecting myself." Mary Lou stopped and felt truth wash over her. "Yes, I was being vindictive. I'm so sorry about it now."

Mary Lou got her wits about her and told Mrs. Cunkell about how she and Bobby had dated and all the details of their breakup and about the last time she talked with him. "Now he says he will be moving back here. I'm thrilled that he's coming back, but I don't know if he's going to want to date me again. I mean, I'm so glad he's coming back. I've tried to forget about him, but the truth is that I have missed him so much, but... maybe he's dating someone else."

After Mary Lou had run out of things to say, Mrs. Cunkell said, "Dear child, please know this. God has already chosen the man for you."

Mary Lou's eyes widened. "He has? Who is it? Is it Bobby?"

"That's just it, child. It may not be Bobby. Whoever it is, God has not chosen to reveal it to you at this time for a reason."

"Oh, so God knows, and He won't tell me. That's not fair."

Mrs. Cunkell patted Mary Lou's hand. "You love God, right?"

"You know I do."

"Then you must trust His wisdom. He has not fully prepared you for this man, nor has He prepared the man for you. When these are done to God's satisfaction, your future husband will be revealed. Until then, you trust God and you wait on Him. And you remember when we studied how to wait on God?"

Mary Lou looked at the Bible in front of her. "Yes, I do. We work hard every day to be more like Him and do His will until the day He comes."

"Exactly."

Easter Sunday, March 31
Westminster, Colorado

Mary Lou picked Mrs. Cunkell up at her apartment to take her to church. As they drove off the Belleview Campus, Mary Lou decided to ask about some things Eileen had said.

She turned onto Federal Boulevard. "My sister told me that the big red castle is haunted."

Mrs. Cunkell's expression didn't change. "It is haunted, indeed. The Holy Spirit dwells there. You see, the Holy Spirit dwells in everyone who has accepted Jesus Christ as Lord and Savior. Everyone who works in the big red castle is Christian; therefore, the Holy Spirit is there. But I don't believe any other ghosts reside there.

"I came to the Pillar when I was ten years old. We had a program at Thanksgiving in the big red castle. None of us children were allowed to go upstairs in the building at the time. The older boys told us that there was a very scary man who lived upstairs. They said the man didn't have an ear and that he would come after us if we went up there. It scared us enough that we stayed where we were supposed to be. Years later, I met Samuel. He was a perfect gentleman who had lost his ear in a farming accident while serving God in Africa."

"My sister says that people she knows say they've seen ghosts there."

Mrs. Cunkell smiled. "I've heard those stories. There are many explanations for what people think they see, or what they choose to see."

Mary Lou merged onto the Boulder Turnpike. "Explanations like what?"

"For one thing, people say they've seen lights throughout the building at night. Well, that's certainly no mystery. The maintenance man lives on the property. At night he takes his flashlight and inspects the building from top to bottom. Does that answer your question?"

Mary Lou smiled at the woman's directness. "Almost. Eileen said that people have seen a woman in white on the balcony and walking around the castle."

Mrs. Cunkell laughed. "Oh, that was Carolyn. She lived in the castle for a while. She had long white hair and at night she wore a white nightgown. At night, if she walked to the window or out on the balcony or even around the building to get a breath of fresh air, people would say that she looked like a ghost."

Mary Lou merged onto I-25. "I guess no one got close enough to recognize her as a human being instead of a ghost. Perhaps she scared them."

Mrs. Cunkell nodded. "I suppose. Unfortunately, there's a lot of curiosity about the big red castle, the entire campus, and especially the graveyard."

"Eileen told me that the big red castle is haunted by the victim of a murder that took place there."

Mrs. Cunkell shook her head. "There was no murder there. People like to make up stories. I've also heard that the graveyard is haunted because they sometimes see a foggy mist there. We have misty days on the hill all the time."

Mary Lou smiled. "I guess some people are good at making up stories. They must not have enough to do."

Mrs. Cunkell laughed. "If you make up a story, it should at least have a point. If the big red castle is haunted—so what? What's the point? If the graveyard is haunted—so what? I don't believe any of it."

Mary Lou parked in front of Alma Temple. She and Mrs. Cunkell climbed the stairs to the opened front doors. As they walked into the sanctuary, Mary Lou's eyes immediately fixed on the stained glass window depicting Jesus holding the lamb while other lambs surrounded him.

She walked down the aisle beside Mrs. Cunkell, who greeted longtime friends until they got to their usual pew. Mary Lou sat on the end, with Mrs. Cunkell and another older couple down the row.

The service began. The worship leader stepped to the pulpit. "He is risen."

The congregation responded, "He is risen, indeed."

The invocation was given. Then the first hymn of the morning, "He Lives," started the service.

Dr. Dallenbach gave the message, talking about how much God loved the people He created. "God loves us so much that He was willing to send His one and only son to die on a cross for us. Can you imagine how painful it would be to watch your one and only child die the horrible death of crucifixion? But someone had to pay the price for the fall of man, for the sins of all people throughout eternity. Only One was worthy. That was Jesus Christ."

Mary Lou stared at the stained glass window, at the depiction of Jesus who had appeared to her. He had started the process of changing her into the woman He'd created her to be.

At the end of his message, Dr. Dallenbach said, "No one else in all of humanity was worthy to die for our sins. It had to be Jesus, because only Jesus lived a sinless life. Any one of you could have volunteered to die for the sins of the world, but none of us are worthy. We are all blemished. And even in the day of animal sacrifices, the lamb had to be perfect and without blemish."

Mary Lou felt tears in her eyes. *Dear Lord, teach me how to make a true commitment to You. You died for me, and I am so very thankful. I don't know how to pray about how I feel right now. I guess I'm asking You to give me a pure, unblemished heart—a heart that can be truly committed to You and Your desires, instead of my own.*

After the service, Mary Lou helped Mrs. Cunkell into the car and headed back to the hill. Dr. Dallenbach's final words about a sacrifice without blemish rang in her ears. She remembered studying a passage about believers making themselves a living sacrifice.

As they pulled in front of Mrs. Cunkell's apartment, Mary Lou asked, "In a world like we live in today, just how are we to live our lives without blemish? I mean, nearly every day, I find myself regretting something I've said or done."

Mrs. Cunkell smiled. "It's no different in this day and age than it was in the past. Even in Biblical times, the constant battle existed between the old nature and the redeemed nature. It will always be with us. Paul teaches us how to defeat the old nature. Look here." She opened her Bible. "Here it is in Romans, chapter seven. Look at verse fourteen. You read it."

Mary Lou took the Bible and read, "'We know that the law is spiritual; but I am unspiritual, sold as a slave to sin. I do not understand what I do. For what I want to do I do not do, but what I hate I do. And if I do what I do not want to do, I agree that the law is good. As it is, it is no longer I myself who do it, but it is sin living in me. I know that nothing good lives in me, that is, in my sinful nature.'" Mary Lou looked up. "Wow, that is deep. Nothing in my sinful nature is good."

Mrs. Cunkell nodded. "Read on."

Mary Lou continued, "'For I have the desire to do what is good, but I cannot carry it out. For what I do is not the good I want to do; no the evil I do not want to do—this I keep on doing. Now if I do what I do not want to do, it is no longer I who do it, but it is sin living in me that does it' ...Oh, Mrs. Cunkell, how can I ever get rid of this sin within? If the apostle Paul couldn't do it, how can I?"

Mrs. Cunkell patted Mary Lou's hand. "My dear, we have many advantages that Paul did not have. We not only have Paul's teaching on a better way, but we also have the testimonies of people since, who have defeated sin daily and lived holy lives that pleased God. Read just a bit further, and we'll talk."

Mary Lou picked up the Bible again. "'So I find this law at work: when I want to do good, evil is right there with me. For in my inner being I delight in God's law; but I see another law at work in the members of my body, waging war against the law of my mind and

making me a prisoner of the law of sin at work within my members.'
Are we always going to have this inner battle? Am I always going to
be fighting myself in order to do the right thing?"

Mrs. Cunkell pointed at her apartment. "Now that we've
confronted the issue in Romans seven, we should take some Bible
study time right now. Come in, and we'll look at Romans eight, where
you will find that we are controlled not by the sinful nature but by
the Spirit of Christ. As we submit to the Holy Spirit, we choose to
triumph over the old nature. And the more we choose to live God's
way, the less appealing sin appears."

Mary Lou followed Mrs. Cunkell into the apartment and took a
seat at the kitchen table.

Mrs. Cunkell pulled her own worn Bible out of her bag. "At this
point in Romans seven, things look pretty bleak, don't they? But
remember—Paul's Bible at the time consisted of the Torah and the
prophets—what we call the Old Testament. Today we have the New
Testament and much more."

Mary Lou looked at her with a question in her eyes. "More?"

"Well, of course we do. We have Jesus and the Holy Spirit." Mrs.
Cunkell flipped open her Bible to Romans, chapter eight, and handed
it to Mary Lou. "This will answer your questions. Read it to me."

Mary Lou read, "'Therefore, there is now no condemnation for
those who are in Christ Jesus, because through Christ Jesus the law
of the Spirit who gives life has set you free from the law of sin and
death. For what the law was powerless to do because it was weakened
by the flesh, God did by sending his own Son in the likeness of sinful
flesh to be a sin offering. And so he condemned sin in the flesh, in
order that the righteous requirement of the law might be fully met
in us, who do not live according to the flesh but according to the
Spirit.'"

Mrs. Cunkell closed the Bible. "Now you tell me, in your own
words, what you just read."

Saturday, April 20
Lakewood, Colorado

Denny stood at the front door of Beth's house. He had rung the
doorbell twice. What was taking so long? It was time for their first

official date—and it had not been easy convincing her that it was all right. *Maybe she changed her mind.*

Feeling rejected, he turned toward the street and was about to step down off the porch when he heard the door open behind him. He spun around.

There she stood, wearing a green velvet dress with emerald earrings that complemented her dark-red hair. Denny stared, speechless.

"Sorry it took me so long to get to the door. I guess I'm a little nervous. I wanted everything to be just right."

Denny gulped. "Everything is more than just right. You look absolutely stunning." He held out his hand.

She wrapped the matching shawl around her and pulled the door closed behind her. She took his hand, and they stepped down to the sidewalk. They held hands until they got to Denny's red Corvette. He opened the door for her, made sure her shawl was safely inside, and closed the door. As he walked around to his side of the car, he looked up into the heavens and breathed a "Thank You."

Once in the car, he turned toward her, taking in the face he had dreamed about for so many years. "I've been looking forward to this evening."

She smiled. "I never thought I would ever date again. You're a hard man to turn down."

"Well, I hope so, because I have a great evening planned. First, dinner down on Larimer Street downtown. Then to the Denver Symphony. After that, dessert at Voodoo Donut, then I take you home."

"That sounds wonderful. How did you know I love going to Larimer Street? And how did you know I love the Denver Symphony? Denny Adams, it sounds like you've done some research."

"Don't put it like that. I haven't done research. I just pay attention. I try to remember what you like."

Beth thought of Denny fixing her coffee on her first day as CEO. She'd been so impressed when he knew exactly how she liked her coffee—it had been the amount of cream and sugar. And she was picky about her coffee.

She watched his profile as he started the car and drove down the street toward I-25. "I believe you do pay attention, Denny.

I've noticed in several of the reports, you caught some seemingly insignificant details that turned out to be extremely important."

Denny mock-pouted. "We aren't going to talk about work tonight, are we?"

She laughed. "The last few weeks, it's all I've talked about. You're right. We need a break. Okay, no talk about work. Let's talk about our favorite movies."

Denny turned onto the I-25 ramp. "Movies? Did you want to go to a movie tonight?"

"No, I just suggested we talk about movies instead of work. What's your favorite movie?"

"My favorite movie? Now? Or for all time?"

"Let's say for all time."

"That would be hard because there's a lot of time. Let's see… I think it was *Silence of the Lambs*." He held back a laugh.

Beth frowned. "Are you kidding me?"

He let the laugh escape. "Yes, I'm kidding. That movie scared me to death." He turned onto the Park Avenue West exit to go past Coors Stadium on to Larimer Street. He parked near the front of the Bistro Vendome, got out, opened Beth's door, and helped her out. They entered, and the hostess immediately seated them at a window near the street.

Denny commented, "The food here has a reputation for being good. I checked the reviews. You can't go wrong on anything you order."

The waiter appeared and handed them menus. After spending a few minutes studying what was offered, they were ready to order and their waiter reappeared with glasses of ice water.

Beth ordered the pan-roasted scallops, apple-thyme panisse, braised red cabbage, and persimmon purée, with pickled persimmon relish. Denny chose the pan-seared Idaho trout, with butter-poached red bliss potatoes and mushroom sauce. Both of them decided not to have an appetizer. The waiter left with their order, and they turned to look out the window.

Some spring flowers lined the street, a bit early for Denver. Twinkling lights dotted the windows of the building across the street. A wreath made of pine branches still hung on one of the light posts. Fluffy snowflakes began to fall.

"Oh look, Denny. It's starting to snow. The big flakes, so fluffy—they look like they should bounce when they hit the streets. I love it when it snows in April. It won't stick."

The dim lighting in the restaurant, the nearby fireplace crackling with flames, and sitting across from the love of his life had already intoxicated Denny. His heart bursting with joy, he reached across the table and took hold of Beth's hand. He looked into her eyes. What he had been waiting for all these years was within reach at last.

Fear constricted his heart, and he dropped her hand quickly. He looked out the window and casually asked, "It is beautiful, isn't it?"

Beth seemed oblivious—but then, how could she know how much he loved her? And how long could he stay at arm's length?

Their dinners arrived, and they chatted about the weather, about how wonderful it was to live in Colorado and enjoy the four seasons. The busboy cleared away their dishes.

The waiter reappeared. "Have you decided if you would like to consider dessert this evening?"

Denny smiled at Beth. "I promised dessert after the concert, but if you see something you like—but oh, look at this."

He really didn't want dessert, but the warm atmosphere of their surroundings made him want to stay longer. He ordered the Death by Chocolate.

Beth said she would have a cup of decaf.

The waiter placed the Death by Chocolate plate in the center of the table, presenting a fork on each side of the dessert. It was a colossal warm pastry, covered with caramel and chocolate icing and topped with frozen custard.

Beth covered her mouth with her hand and giggled. "That is huge."

Denny smiled, charmed. He gazed down at the mountain of chocolate and laughed. "I'm glad they gave us two forks. You know you've got to help me out."

Still laughing, she picked up her fork and took a little helping off the edge. She put the bite in her mouth and rolled her eyes. She laughed. "Mm-mm. This is absolutely evil."

Denny took a bite. "Incredible! How do they do this?"

Beth took a second bite. "Mm—Centuries of practice—that's the only way they could create something like this."

They laughed and ate half of the mountain of chocolate before both of them confessed that if they ate another bite they would get sick.

"We don't want that." Beth pushed the plate away.

Denny motioned to the waiter. "Check, please." He turned to Beth. "Are you ready for the symphony?"

"Yes! I used to go to the symphony all the time, but I can't remember the last time I was here. I'm really looking forward to this."

They walked outside into the light snow. It was melting as it hit the ground, and none of it had stuck to the car. Denny made his way across town and parked the car in the attached parking garage. They strolled into a packed house. The musicians were all in place and busily tuning their instruments.

They found their seats five rows from the front, center stage. *Perfect,* Denny thought.

After an evening of music, beautiful and relaxing, it was time to leave. The evening was about over, and as Denny started the car, he realized that he didn't want this night to end.

"I'm assuming dessert at Voodoo's is out of the question, but they do make a good cup of coffee."

Beth stifled a yawn. "Oh, excuse me. I'm usually in bed by this time. Death by Chocolate was over the top. This has been a wonderful evening. Thank you so much. It's late, and I should probably get home."

Denny turned toward the freeway. "I'm so glad you enjoyed it. It was my pleasure, and I look forward to when we can do it again."

Thirty minutes later, he pulled up in front of her house, shut the engine off, and turned toward her. "You'll never know how much tonight meant to me. Some good food, good music, and the company of a beautiful woman—that's about all a man could ask for. Let me walk you to the door. Stay there. I'll be around to help you out."

She waited, and after he opened the door, she stepped out and took his hand for help up the curb. She held onto his hand as they walked up to the front door.

When they reached it, Denny wanted to put his arms around her and pull her close. He wanted to smell her hair. He wanted to kiss her on the lips. But if he tried that tonight, she might never see him again. The minute things got complicated, it would be over.

He resisted his urges and tried to smile easily. Yes, he loved what he'd gotten tonight. And he would hang onto that until the time was right, until Beth was ready for more.

Denny leaned down for Beth to give him a peck on the cheek. "Thank you for a wonderful evening."

She stepped back. "I enjoyed it, and I hope we can do it again sometime."

He backed away and gave her a little wave. "See ya Monday morning."

She opened the door, punched in the security code, closed the door, and peeked out the window to watch Denny drive away as tiny snowflakes decorated the scene.

It was ten thirty, and Beth wasn't tired. In fact, she felt energized. She went in and put on her pajamas. She wanted someone to talk to. But who could she call at ten thirty at night, just to chat?

Ten minutes later, her phone rang. She checked the caller ID: Denny Adams. *What?*

She smiled and picked up the phone. "Did I leave something in your car?"

He laughed. "No, nothing like that. I got home and ready for bed, and I wasn't tired. So I thought I'd give you a call and see if you wanted to chat."

She snuggled into her bed. "You called to chat with me at this hour? You must be psychic. I'm not tired, either, and I was just trying to think of someone to call. Usually I choose someone on the west coast because of the time change."

"I'm not psychic, but I just seem to have a lot of energy tonight. After a day of work, I'm usually ready for bed."

"I know what you mean. I'm the same way. We've both been spending long days at the office. I think I'm ready for a vacation."

"That sounds like fun. Are you inviting me for a vacation?"

Beth giggled. "What would people think if we went on a vacation together?"

Denny laughed. "What do we care what people think? Aren't we in charge of our own lives?"

Beth felt high. She giggled again, sounding like a teenaged airhead. "I don't think anyone's really in charge of anything. You know how the old saying goes—we plan; God laughs."

Denny sobered up. "I think God has a great sense of humor. I'm sure he's laughed at me many times. But in spite of that, where would you want to go on vacation?"

"I would choose somewhere warm, but not too far. I've done enough of the tourist stuff all over the world. There are a lot of options when you're just looking for a quiet place to land."

"Are you thinking Las Vegas?"

"Oh, Lord, no. That's the last place I would want to go for vacation."

"Well there's always Phoenix, San Diego, Key West, Ft. Lauderdale—Oh. I'm sorry."

"Don't be sorry. You can say Ft. Lauderdale. It's not going to bring anything up. All that's over, thank God. Now those other cities are all large. Name a small city that's warm in the winter."

"You mean a small city that's warm in winter that's not far from Denver, right?"

"Exactly."

He paused for a full two minutes. "Santa Fe."

She laughed. "I said someplace warm in winter."

"You tell me. You name one—a small town that's warm in winter and not far from Denver."

She laughed again. "Galveston, Texas."

He chuckled. "Galveston, Texas. I thought you meant someplace within driving distance. Galveston is a long way. Maybe you could drive it, but it's certainly not a day trip."

"It does sound like a long way, but it's not very big, and I bet it's warm there all winter. I don't really know—never been there in the winter. But it's a small town, someplace you could go and just be."

"So that's the objective—to go and just be." Denny sighed. In a quiet voice, he said, "It sounds wonderful. When do we leave?"

Beth giggled again. "We could leave tonight."

"I'm on my way."

Alarm filled Beth. "No, no, no—you know I'm only joking. I mean I'm not joking, but I'm only half serious."

The pitch of his voice lowered. "You know I would do it, don't you? I could be there in ten minutes. You could escape. I would take you anywhere you want to go. And if you wanted me to, I would leave you alone."

Taken aback by the seriousness in his tone, she whispered, "I know you would."

Chapter Eighteen

Monday, April 22
Lakewood, Colorado

Feeling nervous, Beth sat at the vanity in her dressing room. Admonishing the face in the mirror, she said to herself, *Having a date with Denny Adams Friday night was the dumbest thing you've done in a long time. How could you be so stupid?*

And then the phone call... She sighed. *That was just incredible. I think we talked for three hours.*

But you're the boss. How can you walk in and treat Denny Adams like any other employee? You've known him since college, but that's no excuse. He was Walt's roommate, for heaven's sake. That was over twenty-four years ago, she silently argued with the reflection.

I have to say, I've always thought he was cute, but I haven't seen him for twenty-four years. He was Walt's friend.

She grabbed her head with both hands. *What have I done? Walt's not been gone quite three months, and I'm already dating. What are people going to think?*

She wore her gray suit with a purple scarf and matching purple shoes. She went down to the kitchen, pushed the button on her deluxe Keurig, and chose the Mountain Man Nantucket blend. She dug an energy bar out of the cupboard.

She stuck the bar in the front flap of her purse and waited for her travel mug to fill. After adding cream and sugar, Beth grabbed her briefcase and headed out. She pressed the garage door opener, got in the car, and took a sip of her coffee before she put her Lexus SUV in reverse.

Once on the street, she pressed the button to close the garage door and took her regular route to the office.

Her phone rang, and the speaker announced, "You are receiving an incoming call from Sweet Estates rehabilitation center."

She pressed the answer button. "Uncle Ralph, is that you?"

"Of course it's me. You sound like you're talking in a well."

She laughed. "Oh, Uncle Ralph, I'm on my way to work. I'm in the car."

"Oh, I'm sorry. I should let you go to work. I forgot you took over that company."

"It's okay, Uncle Ralph. I have about half an hour before I get there. What's been going on there?"

"The same old thing. Hey, I did want to fill you in. Have you been watching *On the Horizon*?"

"I have not been able to watch one episode since I started going to the office. I guess I'm going to have to count on you to keep me up to date."

"Well, it's just as frustrating as it's always been."

Beth braked for the rush-hour traffic in front of her. "The last I heard, they exhumed the body, and the casket was empty. Then what happened?"

Ralph went on for a while before he got to some advancement in the plot. "They found old Victor. It was the craziest thing. His ex-wife from twenty years ago—turns out she'd been stalking him. And that's the reason he disappeared. They're still testing to find out if this is true, but they think she poisoned him. They found his body in the freezer in her basement. Now isn't that something?"

"She must be a new character. How did they find out about her?"

"Some new detective got on the case. He decided to research Victor's history. Turns out, Victor's been married six times. Every time he married an older woman, she would die suspiciously, but nobody could ever prove he was to blame."

Beth couldn't believe she was getting sucked into the ridiculous story. "Well, she survived. He didn't kill her."

"They're saying he did try to, and that was why she divorced him. She never went to the law, because she was afraid he'd get away with it and come after her again."

Beth was approaching the International Enterprises building. "I'm here at the office. Let me call you tonight when I get home."

"Shoot. You can call me anytime."

Friday, April 26
Broomfield, Colorado

Bobby pulled into the parking lot near the entrance of the Runway Grill at Rocky Mountain Metropolitan Airport. Alex parked next to him, and the two of them took the elevator to the second floor, where the hostess seated them right away.

Their waiter appeared within seconds. Bobby ordered the BLT with fries and a Pepsi. Alex chose the burrito supreme with iced tea.

Bobby folded his arms on the table and leaned forward. "This is my first day back. I haven't even opened my suitcase. It's good to see you. You picked a good place for lunch."

Alex looked out the glass wall toward the tarmac. "I like to watch the planes come and go. Also, the food is good, and they're usually not too busy. A good place to talk."

Bobby followed Alex's gaze out the window. "I got a lot of good experience in San Diego. I kept pretty busy, didn't have much down time."

Alex turned toward Bobby. "Did you find a church?"

Bobby brightened. "One of the first things I did was check out churches. I found a great one: Citywalk in downtown San Diego. It was perfect for me, close to my apartment and to work. Met a great bunch of guys who held a Bible study on Wednesday nights."

Alex thanked the waiter for arriving with their drinks. "Did you meet anyone?"

Bobby took a sip of his Pepsi. "I didn't go to San Diego to date. You know how I feel about Mary Lou."

"Have you seen her?"

Bobby toyed with the corner of his napkin. "I'm afraid I blew it. She called me once with a question about a case I had worked on, but she seemed more interested in her questions than me. Our last date turned into something out of a Freddie Kruger movie. I still shudder when I think of how stupid I was. I can't get her off my mind. I don't know how to fix it. She was not impressed when I told her we were 'unequally yoked.'"

Alex put his hand over his eyes. "You did not come right out and say it like that!"

Bobby grimaced. "I'm afraid I did."

Their food arrived, and after Alex said a short prayer of thanks for God's provision in all things, he asked, "Does she know you're back in town?"

Bobby picked up a French fry. "No, like I said, I just got here. I don't know what to do. I really think she's the one for me. No one else interests me in the least."

Alex swallowed his first bite of burrito. "Call her."

Bobby picked up his sandwich. "What if she doesn't want to talk to me?"

"She called you about that case, right? She will talk to you for that reason, if nothing else. I think she does want to talk to you. I think she misses you. I could be wrong, but I've got a feeling about you two."

"I'll wait until I get settled and give her a call. I have to think about what I say. I mean I did hurt her feelings. I probably owe her an apology for that."

Alex slapped his forehead. "Now that's exactly what you don't want to do. Don't dig up old business. Ask her out and suggest that the two of you start over."

Bobby wiped mayonnaise off his lip. "I'll think about it."

Saturday, April 27
Arvada, Colorado

All Eileen's jibber-jabber about where she should have her wedding was making Mary Lou crazy. So far she'd been dragged all over the surrounding mountain venues, to every mega-church in the metro area, and even to several outdoor venues.

They were sitting on Eileen's living room floor, magazines spread all around them.

Mary Lou tried to convince Eileen not to have an outside wedding. "Listen, if you guys are getting married in just a few months, I don't think it would be wise to have it outside. You know it often snows in Denver in May and June."

Eileen half listened as she thumbed through the latest bridal magazine. "I know, I know. I just can't decide what I want. Maybe I should tone it down a little bit. We don't have much family, but Kurt has a huge one—and he told me that a lot of his clients will want to attend. I don't want to disappoint anybody."

Mary Lou mumbled, "And you want to impress everybody."

"I did *not* hear you say that. But what's wrong if I do want to? I'm only having one wedding. And I'm marrying a man that can give me as big a wedding as I want. He'll go along with a small wedding, if that's what I insist on. But I am not going to go with a small wedding."

Mary Lou shrugged. "Obviously. I haven't been to one venue that would accommodate less than a thousand people. Exactly how many do you expect to invite?"

"We'll invite around two thousand people. But they say only half will attend. So that's not to be a problem. It's just that we don't have an exact date, and Kurt and I are supposed to decide that by the end of the week. We have been trying to work with his schedule, and he is a busy man."

Mary Lou nodded. "He's a busy man, all right. It's a good thing you found that out now. No surprises, right?"

Eileen frowned at Mary Lou. "I didn't want to tell you this yet, but right now we're down to two dates, and we'll probably decide which one tonight."

Mary Lou's ears pricked up. "What two dates? Can't you tell me what two dates?"

Eileen shook her head. "No, I can't tell you, because that's just between me and my fiancé right now. I feel like we need some things just between us."

Mary Lou slapped her forehead. "Oh, please. You're asking me to help you with wedding planning, and you won't even tell me the dates you're considering?"

Eileen shot her a weary look. "I'm going to tell you, as soon as we decide. So you can hang on another day or maybe two."

"Ay yai yai, you are making me crazy. How can I help you if you won't give me information? Are you sure you still want my help—I mean, is there any way I can get out of this?"

Eileen popped her on the head. "No, there isn't. You're my sister and you're stuck with me. 'Therefore, as God's chosen people, holy and dearly loved, clothe yourselves with compassion, kindness, humility, gentleness and *patience*'—Colossians 3:12. You need to be patient with me."

Mary Lou stood. "I really don't have that much time to myself. Maybe I should come back when you have more information. I'm going home. It's been a long week at work, and I'm not complaining, but I've spent nearly every free minute going over wedding planning. I have a life. Call me when you have a date."

Eileen jumped up. "We can go pick out my dress. You know you're the only one I can trust to go with me to do that—you'll tell me the truth, whether I like it or not."

"You're right about that. Do you want to buy something locally? Or something out of, say, New York?"

Eileen put her magazine down. "I don't have time to travel."

Mary Lou shook her head. "Eileen, Eileen, Eileen. It is 2013. Get out your laptop. We can shop online."

Eileen frowned.

"It's a start. It'll give you an idea of what you might want to look like on your wedding day. We don't have to buy it online, but at least we'll know what you're looking for."

"That would save us a lot of time. Good idea." Eileen went into her cubbyhole of an office and retrieved the laptop. She set it up on the kitchen table so they both could see the screen.

Mary Lou looked out the kitchen window at the foot of snow on the ground. "I know you don't have a date yet, but it's going to make a difference on your dress. Are you going to have a winter wedding, or are you going to have a summer wedding?"

Eileen grimaced at the snow. "I could see myself in a white dress trimmed in a white faux fur. It would be beautiful to be married on Lookout Mountain in the winter. But then if I chose that kind of dress and it didn't snow, I would be disappointed."

"I think it can be difficult for two thousand people to wrap up in their winter duds, covering all their wedding finery, to enjoy your wedding. People like to be comfortable, and an outdoor winter wedding does not sound like fun. Are you going to wear snow boots under your dress?"

Eileen snickered. "I've seen some pretty cool white furry boots. Now I know what they're for." She laughed. "I wonder if they make them in platform heels."

Mary Lou's cell phone vibrated in her pocket. She took it out and checked the text message. *I am officially back in town. We should go to coffee and catch up. I'm heading over to our old Starbucks now. If you can stop by, I'd love to see you. Bobby.*

Mary Lou captured the number and added Bobby Porter to her list of contacts. She stood and picked up her purse. "I really need to get going. We can go look at dresses tomorrow."

Eileen squinted at the computer screen in front of her. "That's okay. I'm going to keep looking at what they have to offer online. That was a good idea. By tomorrow I should have a better idea of what kind of dress I really want."

Eileen stood up and gave Mary Lou a hug. "Thanks for hanging in there with me. I really don't mean to be a bridezilla, but I know that's how I come off sometimes. I'm not really nervous about getting married, but I am nervous about everything that has to get done soon."

"We'll get it together. No worries. Ah… 'Be anxious for nothing'… ah…Philippians four something."

Eileen walked Mary Lou to the door. "I certainly hope so. Kurt wants to get married in the next few months, I think it's going to be hard to put off him much longer. That means no winter wedding, but in the meantime, I've got a lot of work to do. And it's Philippians 4:6. 'Do not be anxious about anything, but in everything, by prayer and petition, with thanksgiving, present your requests to God.'"

Later the same day

Heart racing, Mary Lou got in her car and roared to Starbucks. She couldn't wait to see Bobby again. It'd been almost four months, and she now understood what he'd said about them being unequally yoked. *I wonder if he's a virgin, like Eileen and Kurt. Curious.*

Nonetheless, to keep from being vulnerable, she attempted to let go of any expectations other than seeing him and sharing a cup of coffee. She used to see his car out front whenever she pulled up. This time, she had no clue as to what he could be driving.

She searched a few license plates to see if she could spot a California tag, but she didn't see anything from out of state. She hopped out of her car and walked in, and she looked around the room. It took her a moment before she spotted a somewhat familiar man sitting at a table next to a glass wall across from where she had parked her car.

She didn't fully recognize him until he stood. *It's the beard. How distinguishing. And I didn't think you could get better looking.*

She walked over, and they hugged. He pulled a chair out for her and made sure she was seated comfortably, then he sat across from her.

He leaned forward, his arms on the table. "It's been a long time. How do you keep getting younger?"

She pulled the scarf from around her neck. "You sweet talker, you. It hasn't been *that* long."

The sparkle vanished from his eyes. His mouth in a straight line, he looked directly into her eyes. "I've missed you."

She wanted to jump into his arms and kiss him. But anger rose up—anger at him for leaving, for not keeping in contact, for making her feel like she wasn't good enough for him. Then she remembered that the last few weeks, she and Mrs. Cunkell had been working on forgiveness.

She felt her back stiffen. "I don't know if you understand how much you hurt me when you left. I've been praying for you. And I've been praying to forgive you."

He reached across the table and took her hand. "I didn't mean to hurt you. I only knew that I wanted to be one hundred percent honest with you. I knew if I called you, I'd be back in Denver before achieving what I needed to do. I didn't dare risk calling you and hearing your voice. I'm sorry—I never meant to hurt you in any way. Please forgive me."

She unbuttoned her coat and hung it about her shoulders. "I forgave you. It's the forgetting that's hard. I thought about you all the time. I figured you'd moved on, and that was why I hadn't heard from you."

Bobby put his other hand around hers. "Did you move on?"

"I tried as best I could. I kept busy with work. And then there was all that business with Walt's accident. I finally just accepted that you were over me."

"But I never did get over you. I threw myself into *my* work so that I could be the best detective I could. I knew once I got that confidence, I could come back to Denver when something opened up. Everything happened much quicker than I thought it would."

Mary Lou blinked wetness from her eye. "So I was supposed to be waiting for you? How come I didn't know this? Don't you think this is something we could have discussed? Or was I supposed to read your mind? Because last time we talked, we were 'unequally yoked,' and I had some spiritual growth to do before I could be acceptable for you. And now, believe it or not, I kind of understand where you were coming from."

He smiled. "You knew how I felt about you."

She looked at their hands. "How was I supposed to know? I don't know. How do you feel about me now? Why are you here? Why did you call me to meet you? You see, Bobby, all I have are questions—questions about you and our relationship. And when I say 'our relationship,' I'm talking present time—like today, like now."

Bobby let go of her hands. "I certainly didn't mean for our first meeting to get so serious. I thought we would have a cup of coffee and reconnect. A little small talk, a little laughter, the way we used to, and just get to know each other all over again. But obviously God had other plans."

Mary Lou found a tissue in her purse and dabbed at her left eye. "God is definitely in charge. I know that more than I ever did before. But it seems like you were never gone. I guess I've had so many mental conversations with you that I feel like I've been talking to you the whole time you've been gone."

He chuckled. "Mental conversations? You've been talking to me in your head? It's interesting that you've had imaginary conversations with me. I've had a few with you, too."

She looked him directly in the eyes. "I've been praying for you, too. Especially for your safety."

"I'm always thankful for prayers. One can never get enough of those. I had a mental conversation, telling you that I was going to San Diego—except you agreed to come with me. Of course we know that was a dream. That would never happen, because you would never leave your job with International Enterprises."

"Bobby Porter, that's one option you never gave me. It wasn't fair for you to decide what my decision would be. No one should think for someone else."

He folded the napkin in front of him into quarters. "I couldn't agree with you more. You decided that I thought my job was more important than you were. I never told you that. Did you ever consider that you might have had something to do with the reason I left?"

Mary Lou looked out the window. "I know I was the reason. You told me as much. I needed to grow spiritually for us to continue our relationship."

Bobby knit his fingers together behind his head. "You called me."

Mary Lou folded her arms to her chest. "I called you because Kiral Nadeem was killed in a car accident. I found that interesting because he was the captain of Walt's yacht, and you said you found it suspicious."

He rubbed his forehead. "No, I said there were no skid marks. You said it was suspicious. You keep jumping to conclusions. That's something you can't do when you're a detective on the police force. I found out there was alcohol involved. We spoke to the casino personnel, and they remembered him. They said he had been drinking all night before he left." Bobby grimaced. "I guess in a matter of speaking, the alcohol did kill him."

Mary Lou's eyebrows shot up. "So what was his blood alcohol level?"

Bobby straightened his chair. "His body was never recovered. His car crashed into the ocean, remember? Those currents are treacherous. He'll turn up somewhere. They didn't even find all the parts to the car. We know he was driving. There was a lot of blood in the car as a result of the crash. Enough for a DNA test to be sure it was Kiral. I'm telling you this to satisfy any curiosity you might have about whether or not he was driving the car."

Mary Lou leaned forward, "I'm suspicious because I was there when Walt disappeared, had an accident, or whatever. And now, suddenly out of nowhere the captain of the yacht dies in a freak accident. Don't you see red flags all over the place?"

Bobby stood. "Let me get us some coffee. Are you still drinking those vanilla lattes?"

She nodded and smiled.

He went to the counter and placed their order.

Just when I thought I was going to find something out, he switched the subject to Kiral Nadeem. It's funny. He left because Jesus meant everything to him, but tonight he hasn't mentioned Jesus once. And what was that remark about me not going with him? It's not like we were engaged.

She watched him as he waited at the counter and checked her attitude. *Thank You, Lord, for this evening. I'm so glad he's not wearing a uniform. That would make him irresistible, and I have to keep my wits about me.*

He texted me. He didn't have to do that.

Bobby returned to the table and handed her a grande vanilla latte. "Just the way you like it."

Mary Lou thanked him and took a short sip as he sat. "This hits the spot. I'm glad you're back. I've really missed you."

He took her hand. "I missed you, too. I'm sorry if I did anything to cause you pain. Forgive me?"

She felt her eyes filling even more and wiped away some moisture. "I already forgave you."

He squeezed her hand and brushed a drop from the corner of her eye. "Would you consider today a new start?"

"I will."

Chapter Nineteen

Monday, April 29
Denver, Colorado

Beth parked her car in the familiar CEO parking spot. She got out, carrying her handbag on a shoulder and balancing her briefcase in one hand and a cup of coffee in the other.

"Hey there. Let me help you."

She turned to see Denny Adams walking up behind her. He reached for her briefcase.

She pulled it close to her. "No, no. I've got it. Thanks anyway."

"All right. If you're sure." He pulled the door to the building open for her.

She walked in, passed a security guard, and waved Denny off with a quick "See you later" and turned to go to her office. Once on the carpeted hallway to her office, she tried to listen for footsteps behind her, hoping against hope that he was not following her. Hoping against hope that he was going to his own office.

Just as she reached the door to her own office, she peeked behind her. The hallway was empty.

She rushed into her office, took off her coat, and hung it on the coat tree in the corner of her expensive cherry wood-trimmed office. She took a seat behind her desk and began perusing the pile of mail in front of her.

The return address on the thick white envelope identified the sender. Executive Yacht Leasing, Inc., from an address in Ft. Lauderdale. It was postmarked January 31, 2013. *This must have gotten lost in the mail.*

Mary Lou pulled out the three-page contents. The cover letter began, "Dear Mr. Pederson, it is come to our attention that the lease on your mega yacht has expired. Enclosed, please find the necessary documents to renew your lease."

Beth was taken aback. *When did Walt lease a yacht? Is this talking about* The Adventurer*? No, it can't be, Walt often said he paid twenty-two million for it.*

Walt, another lie. How many am I going to find before this is over?

You were never really a husband to me. The only reason I stayed with you so long is that I didn't want to disgrace the church. For twenty-four years I was faithful in a loveless marriage, believing that one day you would be saved if I kept praying.

Look at me now. I've been so lonely in our marriage that the first man who gives me some attention after you're gone has my heart. I'm afraid to love again. I blame you for breaking me. You weren't much of a husband. You were never a businessman, either. I can't decide whether to celebrate or mourn your death.

She looked at the contract and noted that the date for renewal had passed over a month ago. *I'm sure it was Walt's intention to renew, but I don't care. I have no use for a mega yacht. I can't even claim to have any good memories there.*

Someone knocked on her office door. Beth looked up.

Mary Lou carried a manila folder in and sat across from Beth. "Good morning, Beth. I have reports from last week. Denny was very helpful in closing this particular equipment sale to Kuwait. The shipment goes out next week. The sale was in excess of two hundred million."

"I'm impressed and pleased. Do you have a minute? You've worked with Walt for long time. In fact, you were around Walt more hours a day than I was. I think you may be able to help me understand."

Mary Lou held up her hand. "Whoa. I was here in the office with him, but most of the time he worked with Joe and the other agents. I was only in on general meetings. Besides, he spent a lot of time out of the office. You know, business travel, and all."

Beth tapped an envelope against her other hand. "Of course he did. In any case, you may have heard something, so let me run something by you. Did you know that Walt was leasing *The Adventurer?*"

Mary Lou tilted her head. "Leasing? I thought you owned it. Well, no—I thought International Enterprises owned it."

Beth held up the envelope, her thumb pointing to the return address. "I just got another little surprise from Walt. Turns out he's been leasing *The Adventurer* since, uh... Has it been three years?"

Mary Lou slowly answered. "I believe it was three years ago when he announced the purchase. He kept saying it was twenty-two million. I couldn't imagine…"

Beth rubbed her forehead. "I really didn't know what was going on most of the time. I guess it's been pretty obvious the last few weeks. I want to thank you for all the help. Without you, Joe, and Denny, I probably would've given up by now. So another piece of news, another piece of the puzzle, of what my husband was. Who was the real Walt Pederson?"

Mary Lou got up and went over to Beth. "Can I give you a hug?"

Beth burst into tears and nodded. She stood up, and the women hugged.

Beth nodded toward the door, and Mary Lou closed it. Beth retrieved a tissue from the corner of her desk, dried her eyes, and blew her nose.

Beth tossed the tissue in her trash. "I'm so sorry, Mary Lou. I'm having a hard time keeping it together this morning."

"Don't you dare apologize. I want you to know I'm here for you. You can call me anytime. You can ask me to do anything. I want to help you any way I can. Nobody gets over something like this in a few weeks—or months, or years. Things like this, we just learn to live with, and we only get better at it over time."

Beth suddenly had a whole new respect for Mary Lou—her director of sales and marketing, her new friend.

A knock at the door interrupted their conversation. Mary Lou opened the door a crack.

Beth's secretary looked a bit disgruntled. "I had to sign for this." She handed Mary Lou an envelope. "It's from Executive Yacht Leasing, Inc., in Ft. Lauderdale Florida for Mr. Pederson. I didn't open it; I thought it might be personal." She watched to make sure Mary Lou gave the letter to Beth before returning to her desk.

Mary Lou handed the letter to Beth.

Beth read out loud, "To Walt Pederson, International Enterprises, Denver Colorado—it has been brought to our attention that you have opted not to renew the lease on the 2010 prestige mega yacht. Because we have had no contact with you and you have not returned our calls, we felt we had no other option than to put all of the items left on the yacht in storage. You will receive an invoice from Harbor Storage, Ft. Lauderdale, for storage on these items beginning March 1, 2013.

"Please be advised the name of the yacht will be changed according to the desires of the new lessee. It has been our pleasure doing business with you. We hope to be at your disposal when you desire a first-class yachting experience."

Mary Lou's curiosity was off the scale, but she didn't want to say anything because it was Beth's company—it was Beth's tragedy—and she wanted to be Beth's friend. She didn't want to be nosy; she just wanted to be helpful.

"What else can happen?" Beth asked then shook her head. "It doesn't do any good to speculate. We need to get back to work. It's time for the weekly update meeting."

Mary Lou followed Beth to the conference room, where Denny and Joe waited. Beth went to the head of the table and led the meeting.

After an hour of analyzing sales and expectations, Denny raised his hand. "I have an idea to make our product even more desirable to the people we're selling to."

Beth sat down as he approached the whiteboard.

He drew a horizontal line across the board. "This is our base group, the customers we've served for years. This is the foundation of the company, what we must build on to get new clients. However, our base clients have not been enticed to share what we do for them for a reason. As long as they deliver more of a better product than their competition does, they flourish. They don't even think of us— that our products and equipment help them make their goals."

Joe said, "Get to the point, Denny. Tell us something we don't already know."

"All right. Here's what I recommend. Let's talk to our best clients and see if they would put a tagline under their copyrighted name. Something like, 'Noble Oil,' and then in small print 'Supported by International Enterprises equipment.'"

Joe snickered. "Like any of our clients would consider that."

Denny shrugged. "We're living in a new age, Joe. I'm just saying that everything is about community these days. It wouldn't hurt to ask. Once they make that type of statement, we've cemented our relationship with them. They won't order equipment from anybody else. Their competitors will want to find out what's so good about us that we earned a line on their logo. And other clients may approach us to get us to allow them to use us on their logo. Everyone knows that we provide the best customer support in the industry."

"Okay." Joe rubbed his chin. "Let's say a company asked us to do that. We would want a thorough investigation of their product and business practices before we would consider such a thing. We have a reputation to protect."

Beth said, "It's true, but this would get our name out to the right people. Let's look into it. Denny, it's your idea, so I'm handing this project to you. Find the right people to talk with and get back to me."

Denny's smiled brightened the entire room. "Thanks. I will."

Beth felt heat rise in her face. She gathered up her notes and stood. "Meeting adjourned. Have a good week, everybody." She left the conference room.

Denny caught up with her before she could make it to her office. "Beth, wait up. Are you mad at me? Did I do something wrong?"

She held herself tall. "No, Denny, this is the business Beth."

He grinned. "Okay, I understand, totally. I'm going to call that other Beth tonight." He turned to go, then he turned back and whispered, "Would you give her a message for me? Tell her I can't wait to talk to her again." He quickly left.

She felt herself smile as she entered her office. *That man is too much.*

Friday, May 3
Westminster, Colorado

Bobby Porter signed off on the last items the movers had brought into his new residence, happy they were leaving. He wasn't particularly fond of the house, but it was in the right neighborhood, only a short drive to work. The price was in his range.

At least all his things were inside. He inspected his new property. It was a brick ranch, probably twenty years old. It had an established yard with a blue spruce on either side of the double driveway. The double garage included a small workshop toward the back.

He parked his vintage 1937 Graham on the far side of the spacious garage. He covered the restored vehicle with a chalk-white tarp. The car had taken many hours of concentration and work to restore. He had named the project Destiny because it represented his hope for finding true love. Recently he had changed her name to Mary Lou. Destiny had been his obsession for the past three years. She was a beauty—a beauty to be saved for just the right time. His obsession now bore the correct name.

He inspected the back covered patio, which was what he liked the most about the property. The blue-carpeted slab ran the entire length of the back of the house. The roof extended the full fifteen-foot depth. He imagined spending a lot of time out here.

He opened the lid to the grill that had just been delivered. He couldn't wait to get settled in and have his first day grilling and enjoying the backyard.

Bobby looked around, trying to picture what he wanted for furniture on the patio. *There is so much room. I could get a patio set and something like my aunt in Missouri had. A comfy old wicker couch and chair would work out here. Yeah, that's the ticket. Well, I have a few months before the weather's right.* He walked back through the sliding glass door into his kitchen.

He checked his cell for messages. There were none, so he punched "Mary Lou" and waited until the third ring.

That same day

Mary Lou answered, breathless. "Hi, Bobby. What's up?"

"You sound like you're busy. Is this a bad time?"

Mary Lou stopped. "Oh, I'm just lugging a box of files down for filing."

"The movers just left. Want to come over and see my new house? I know for sure I'm going to need a woman's touch around here."

"Who helped with the woman's touch while you were in San Diego?" *Oh, I did not say that. Mary Lou, stop it. He will hang up on you.*

"I didn't buy a house in San Diego, so it wasn't important," he said firmly. "Get it, Mary Lou? I wasn't planning on staying there. Now can you come over or not?"

Her voice became diminutive. "I can come on my lunch break."

He laughed. "See you in a few hours." He hung up.

Mary Lou dropped the box of files at the shared secretary pool. She signed in the documents.

The young girl began sifting through the box. "Looks like you've been busy this morning."

Mary Lou nodded. "Old files take up too much space. I have a small office."

She headed back to her office, and her cell buzzed. She didn't check the caller ID, so she answered with, "This is Mary Lou."

"Well aren't we formal? It's Eileen."

"Oh, hi. It's just been crazy busy here, and I just got a call from—"

"Can you come with me to look at dresses and cakes tonight? I finally got an appointment with Terry Ault, the wedding cake guru."

Mary Lou picked up speed. "What time and where?"

"I'll pick you up at your house around five thirty?"

Mary Lou was practically running into her office. "Okay, but that means I must leave here no later than four thirty, because I at least want time to change into something a little more casual."

"Don't worry about what you wear. Just be comfortable and ready to look at dresses and eat cake. I've narrowed it down to eight dresses, so it really shouldn't take that long to get those all tried on for you to inspect. Now the bridesmaids' dresses may take longer, but we don't have to make a final decision on those tonight."

All of a sudden, Mary Lou felt overwhelmed by Eileen's unexpected infringement on her free time. "When is the cake appointment?"

"I want to do the cake first. That's at six o'clock downtown. We can't be late—I've been told that punctuality is very important with Terry Ault."

Mary Lou, resigned to spending the evening preparing for Eileen's wedding, said flatly, "We certainly wouldn't want to disappoint Terry

Ault." *I have to change my attitude. I said I would help.* She changed to a lighter tone. "I'll be ready, but I have to go now. I have a job. Aren't you still working?"

Eileen giggled. "No, Kurt told me I should quit so that I can get all this wedding planning done. I've got to go—that's him on the other line. See you tonight."

She quit her job! What does she need me for? Mary Lou jammed her cell phone into her pocket. As soon as she got to her office, she brought her computer up to check emails and put out client fires before they erupted into volcanic explosions.

It was noon before she knew it. She grabbed her purse out of the bottom right-hand drawer of her desk, threw on her jacket, and raced down the hall and out the door to her car. Mary Lou headed over to Bobby Porter's new address. When she pulled up in front of the house, she saw him standing out in the drive, his arms folded, inspecting the massive blue spruce tree between the drive and his neighbor's property line.

Mary Lou parked at the curb. She got out and waved. "So this is the new house? Nice. I like that huge tree."

"Thanks for coming. I was just thinking—that tree needs to be trimmed. It hangs two feet over the driveway. Luckily, I don't park on that side, but still."

"It's such a beautiful tree. Whatever you do, don't cut it down."

He motioned for her to follow him. "Come on and let me show you what we have to work with."

We? What does "we" mean? No, I'm not saying anything.

He opened the door for her. She stepped into a wide-open living area extending to the kitchen at the other end of the house. To the left end of the house was a beautiful full-walled fireplace. To the left of the kitchen was a sliding glass door, and she could see onto the spacious patio.

She walked to the patio doors and looked outside. "This is beautiful." A tall hedge enclosed the entire backyard.

Bobby smiled. "That's what finally made the sale. The backyard is just the way they described it—perfect. And, by the way, none of that yard art you collect is coming over here."

She laughed. "Oh, so now you're making fun of my yard art collection. For your information, I haven't had time to work on my own yard yet this spring. With Eileen and all her demands... Oh, I don't want to go there. That's a gorgeous patio."

He opened the glass door. "I love this patio."

Mary Lou nodded her head. "Who wouldn't? You could screen it in or glass it in and have a sun room. But then that would take away from the outdoor feeling."

He took her elbow. "Let me show you the rest of the house."

He led her down the hall to what appeared to be an office space, two small bedrooms with bath between them, and a master bedroom with bath attached.

"This is perfect for you," she said. "Why do you need my input?"

"I have to confess. I wanted you to keep me company while I unpack."

She looked for a place to put her purse down. "I'll help you. Just show me what boxes you want open and let's do it. But I can only work for an hour."

He stepped back. "No, no. Let me take you to lunch."

She dropped the purse on the floor. "We can get a lot done together in an hour. Let's tackle some of these boxes." She tore open the one next to her. It was full of books. "Okay, now. We'd better make sure you know where you want your bookcase."

They started working. First they set up the bookcase. Then they opened boxes of books and started unloading.

Mary Lou started handing him books. "I can't get Kiral out of my mind. Is there something that you haven't told me?"

Bobby arranged books on the shelf. "Well, yes. I probably didn't tell you that when we were looking for who to notify of his death, such as next of kin, we went to Kiral's apartment in La Jolla. Somebody had ransacked it. We never found any next of kin."

It was one fifteen, and Mary Lou needed to get back to work. "Bobby Porter, you just now remembered to tell me this? Don't you think something like this is important?"

Mary Lou set the books she'd been holding on the floor. "I mean, think about it. A man is captain on a yacht. The owner of the yacht dies while the captain is on board. Three weeks later, the captain of the yacht dies in a mysterious car crash, and then you find out someone ransacked his apartment. None of this makes sense, but I have a feeling it's all tied together."

She looked at her cell phone. "I'm late. Sorry, Bobby, I've got to get back to work."

Chapter Twenty

Later the same day
Arvada, Colorado

Eileen picked Mary Lou up at five thirty on the dot. "I'm so glad we could do this tonight. I just spoke to Terry Ault, and he has seventeen cakes for us to try. Which of them will I choose for my wedding cake's layers? I think I'm going to have a five-layer cake—then we can have sheet cakes of different flavors, too. A thousand people can eat a lot of cake."

Mary Lou cringed. "And here I've been trying to cut down on sugar. This is going to wreck me, but what are sisters for? Have you decided a range of flavors you might prefer?" Mary Lou laughed at her own question.

"You mean, like, chocolate or strawberry or... No, I think I'm going to have to try them all. It's a dirty job, but somebody's got to do it." Eileen laughed at her own remark.

She parked at Terry Ault's Bakery. They got out, and Eileen rang the doorbell.

A tall blond man with a big smile answered the door. His gaze met Eileen's. "You must be Eileen, the bride to be."

Eileen turned to Mary Lou, who was standing behind her. "Yes, and this is my sister Mary Lou. She's come along to help me decide."

"Come in, come in."

They followed him through a foyer into what looked like a formal dining room.

"Have a seat here, and I will begin serving you the different cakes. Now, as I serve them, I will explain the ingredients and what's available as far as fillings for which cakes."

Eileen squealed with delight. "This is going to be so much fun. Too bad for Kurt, but lucky for Mary Lou."

Mary Lou rolled her eyes inwardly. *Forget trying to cut down on sugar. My sweet tooth is ready to jump into this full force.* They tasted cakes and tasted cakes until Mary Lou felt full and lightheaded. One more cake filled with something as disgusting as chocolate raspberry truffle or lemon cream was going to make her sick.

Terry Ault was reading his notepad. "Let me see. Is this correct? You're going to have five layers. The top layer, you want to be a white cake, with blueberry filling. The layer under that, you want a chocolate cake with chocolate raspberry filling. The layer under that, you want lemon cake with caramel filling. The layer under that—"

Mary Lou put her hand on her throat. "Where is your bathroom?"

Terry Ault pointed down the hall, and Mary Lou ran toward the open door. She slammed the door behind her, but it didn't block the sounds of her throwing up in the commode. She gasped, came up for air, and threw up again.

She flushed the disgusting scene and unrolled paper to wipe her face and hands. Then she went to the basin and washed her hands and face with the soap from the dispenser.

Mary Lou returned to the table. "I'm so sorry. I haven't had anything to eat today, and I think my stomach's just not used to that much sugar. I am so sorry."

Eileen jumped up and put her arm around her. "I didn't know you hadn't eaten lunch. Now I'm the one that's sorry."

Cake baker Terry Ault looked down his nose at his notepad. "I believe we have the wedding cake plans completed. Now about those sheet cakes?"

"That, we can do later. As soon as I get a number of attendees, I will call you with the number of flat cakes and the flavors." Eileen was putting on her coat. "I think my sister needs to leave. Thank you so much for seeing us tonight."

Mary Lou followed Eileen out the door, and they got in the car.

Eileen asked, "Are you all right?"

Mary Lou groaned. "I feel so much better since I barfed. It had nothing to do with the cakes. They were all wonderful. But I'm still on a sugar high."

"It's almost eight thirty, and they're expecting us at the bridal shop. Are you going to be okay with that?"

"I told you, I'm fine. Let's go find the perfect dress for the perfect bride."

Twenty minutes later, Eileen parked in front of David's Bridal.

A woman saw them walk up to the door and unlocked it for them to enter. "Please come in, Miss Stots. Follow me back to the dressing rooms." She looked at Mary Lou. "You can sit in the observation chairs, and she can model for you on the stage."

"I'm her sister, sitting in for her groom, Kurt Bell." A little name-dropping never hurt. *Surely the woman knows who Kurt Bell is.*

The woman gave her a blank stare. "The groom seldom comes to help choose the wedding dress."

Eileen had already chosen three dresses. She shouted through the dressing room door, "I love the ruffles on this one! I can't wait for you to see this." She burst through the doors toward the stage.

Mary Lou groaned inwardly. *The dress makes her look fat! It's going to be a long evening.*

Saturday, June 9
Arvada, Colorado

Mary Lou pulled on her gardening gloves. *Today is the first day all year that I've been able to get out here and pull a few weeds.*

She surveyed the menagerie of art in the backyard. *Man, I haven't bought one thing for my yard art collection this year. All I've done is go to possible wedding venues, shops for wedding attire, shops for wedding decorations. Shop, shop, shop. I am sick of it. This will be good for me.*

She pulled up the black wire ant eating a piece of watermelon. *You should be over by the fence.* She moved him and then went for the small flock of pink flamingoes. *You guys have faded. Nothing a little spray paint can't fix.* She took them to the garage.

Next she inspected the large metal pinwheel sunflowers, the husky dog, and the rusty tin cat. *I've just got to get some new stuff. These guys look lonely.* She lined them up along the fence.

Mary Lou unpacked the Eiffel Tower Joe had bought her as a thank-you gift for going to Alaska for him. *This will make the perfect centerpiece.* She took it to the center of the yard, where the windmill stood. Mary Lou pounded the Eiffel Tower into the ground and moved the windmill back to the fence.

She pulled the weeds from around the two oversized wagon wheels up against the deck. She started humming a familiar tune from church. When she came to the chorus, she realized the song was "How Great Thou Art."

Oh, Lord, how great You are! You are my God and my King. You are the Master. They call You Wonderful, Counselor, Almighty God. Thank You for finding me again. Of all the things that have happened to me this year, You being in my life is the best. You are teaching me so much about how to live a victorious life. Thank You for the Bible. Thank You for Your Word.

Sunday, July 14
Galveston, Texas

Beth and Denny meandered out of Island Church after having enjoyed a lovely worship time, followed by a moving message by the young pastor.

Beth got in the rental car, and Denny drove them both back to their hotel. Beth had been pleased when Denny insisted they have separate rooms as they planned their secret getaway. Of course, if he hadn't insisted, she would have.

Denny let Beth out at the front door of the hotel and went to park the car while she hurried to her room and changed into her modest swimsuit with a long skirt cover-up and pink flip-flops.

As quickly as she could, she made her way down to the beach to find the perfect place to watch the waves roll onto the sand. She found a spot between tall sea oats and the beach.

She stopped and found Denny standing right behind her. She started laughing. "How did you get down here so fast?"

He grabbed her around the waist. "I'm Superman. Didn't you know?"

She reveled in the wind and laughed, exuding joy from her very being. "You really are Superman. Do you know that?"

He let her go and spread a blanket on the sand. "I think you're a super woman." He plopped down on the blanket and held a hand out to her, and she sat beside him. They watched the waves and the birds for a few minutes.

Beth lay back on the blanket and stared at the sky. "This is absolutely heavenly."

Denny looked at her. "I'm glad you think so. It was your idea, after all."

She smiled at him. "Are you in the business of making my daydreams come true?"

He leaned over her. "Would you like to make one of my daydreams come true?"

She laughed. "I suppose I owe you one. All right, I'll do my best. What is it?"

From out of nowhere, a small black box appeared in his extended hand. "Beth Pederson, will you marry me?"

Friday, August 2
Lakewood, Colorado

Beth had been engaged almost three weeks. In the six months since Denny arrived, her life had changed completely. *Denny treats me better than Walt ever did. He listens to every word I say. He pays attention. I can hardly believe he's stayed single so long.*

Beth and Denny decided to have a quiet wedding in a small church in Poudre Canyon, north of Fort Collins. It was summer and a beautiful Colorado day. Denny had made all the arrangements and picked her up promptly at nine o'clock that morning. Once she was settled into the passenger seat, he reached in the backseat of the car and produced a white box.

"Open it," he said. "I hope you like it."

She pulled the lid off the white box to find a beautiful bouquet of white and yellow roses.

He kissed her nose. "Your wedding bouquet."

She held the flowers to her nose and smiled. "These are absolutely beautiful. You are so thoughtful. Thank you so much."

It took them over an hour to get to the little church in the country by the river. The pastor greeted them at the front door. "This is my wife Bella. She could be a witness for your signatures on the wedding license. You do have a wedding license?"

Denny fumbled in the lapel of his suit. "Oh yes, here it is." He handed it to the pastor.

The pastor inspected the document and handed it to his wife, who took a step back. "My wife can play the piano, if you would like some music. That way Beth could walk down the aisle to you."

Denny smiled. "What do you want to do, Beth? It's up to you."

He's never been married before. I will walk down the aisle toward him—I think he would like that. "I want 'The Wedding March.'" She turned toward the pastor's wife. "You know 'The Wedding March'?"

The pastor's wife began to play the familiar music. Beth smiled, nodded, and walked back to the front doors. The pastor's wife stopped playing then began again and nodded toward Beth. Beth stepped carefully to the music until she stood beside Denny, standing in front of the altar.

The pastor held the open Bible. "The step which you are about to take is sacred. It is a union of two people founded upon mutual respect and affection. It is a lifetime promise. Your lives will change, your responsibilities will increase, but your joy will be multiplied if you are sincere and earnest with your pledge to one another. Denny Adams, will you have this woman to be your wedded wife, to love her, comfort her, honor and keep her, and forsaking all others, keep you only unto her, for so long as you both shall live?"

Denny's smiled lit the room. "I do."

"Beth Pederson, will you have this man to be your wedded husband, to love him, comfort him, honor and keep him, forsaking all others, keep you only unto him, so long as you both shall live?"

Beth reflected Denny's smile. "I do."

"Take each other's hands and repeat after me: 'I, Denny Adams, take you, Beth Pederson, to be my wedded wife, to have and to hold, for better for worse, for richer for poorer, to love and to cherish, from this day forward.'"

Denny did so, and Beth repeated her own vows.

"Do you have a ring for the bride? Please place the ring on the bride's finger and say: 'With this ring, I thee wed.'"

Denny placed the ring on Beth's finger. He looked into her eyes. "With this ring, I thee wed."

The pastor asked, "Is there a ring for the groom?"

Beth placed the ring on Denny's finger. "With this ring, I thee wed."

The pastor announced, "Let these rings be given and received as a token of honor, affection, sincerity, and fidelity to one another. By the authority vested in me by the state of Colorado, I now pronounce you husband and wife. You may kiss your bride."

The pastor's wife played "The Wedding March" again as they walked out of the church. Beth held the flowers high. *Mrs. Denny Adams.*

Denny grabbed her and kissed her passionately, and he put his arm around her waist as they walked to the car. "It's about time. I've waited for this day for so long." *My whole being is filled with peace. I know this is right.*

They stopped at the car. She leaned her back against the car, and he faced her.

"I've never told you this, but I fell in love with you the first day I saw you. When I found out you were dating Walt—well, he was my roommate, so I didn't think it would be right for me to ask you out."

"Oh, Denny, I can't believe you're telling me this now. I was fascinated by you, even then. But Walt and I were dating, so I put you out of my mind. When Walt proposed, I had no idea that you were interested in me. But you are probably right. You did the right thing. Because I'm sure if you had asked me out, I would have turned you down out of loyalty to Walt, even though we were not engaged yet."

Denny whispered to her, "I believe there are times when we have to wait for the best things in life. And when they happen later, they're even better than they would've been before."

She reached up and kissed him. "I believe that, wholeheartedly."

They had taken a long weekend so they could honeymoon at a remote bed and breakfast in northern Wyoming.

Denny drove through Wyoming with a contentment he had not felt in years. Beth was his wife, finally. She really was sitting beside him and they were on their honeymoon.

They arrived at Shane's Bed and Breakfast after the sun had gone down. As he carried their bags to the room, he could hear coyotes howling in the distance, piercing the quiet. Their eerie cry caused him to look up. The night sky looked beautiful, stars standing bright against the dark sky.

Beth opened the door for him. Denny put the bags down, picked her up, and carried her over the threshold. "Mrs. Adams, welcome to our cozy nest for the next two nights."

He put her down. She turned around and put her arms around him.

Monday, August 5
Denver, Colorado

Beth and Denny went to the office together. They got in a little before eight o'clock so they could prepare a memo to all employees to inform them of their marriage.

To all employees of International Enterprises: Please celebrate our happiness by stopping by the break room sometime during the day to enjoy wedding cake. Beth Pederson and Denny Adams were married Friday afternoon.

After it was finished, they both reviewed it. Denny's finger hovered over the send key. "Are you ready?"

Beth reached over and punched the key. "I am so ready. Today is going to be the best Monday I've spent in this office. Come on—we need to get down to the break room and start serving cake."

Denny and Beth walked into the break room just as the cake arrived. Beth signed for the cake, and Denny tipped the young man who put the cake in the center of the center table. Several early-arriving employees stood outside the break room.

Beth motioned to them. "Come in, come in. You haven't seen the memo yet. We're celebrating. We just got married."

Denny handed one of the agents a cup of coffee. "Hope you like cake for breakfast."

The agent grinned. "Congratulations."

Beth pulled the cake out of the box. "Now everybody find a seat. Denny, the paper plates are in the cupboard above the microwave.

The agent laughed. "She's bossing you around already."

Denny picked up a stack of paper plates off the shelf. "She can boss me around any time she wants."

Before long, Beth and Denny were working together, serving as employees drifted in and out.

Mary Lou approached the break room and wondered at the gathering. She had not seen the memo, and she joined the others to see what was going on. When she saw Denny and Beth serving cake, she didn't understand… until she saw the little plastic bride and groom in the middle of the cake.

Her hand went to her mouth, and she looked at Beth. "Did you?"

Beth beamed and reached for Denny's hand. "Yes. We tied the knot Friday."

Mary Lou gulped. "Uh. Congratulations. Rather sudden, wasn't it?"

Denny laughed. "Oh, come on now. You can't say you're surprised."

Beth went over and hugged Mary Lou. "I wish you could've been there. It was lovely. We got married in the chapel in Poudre Canyon."

"That's a beautiful place. Did anyone go with you?"

Beth answered, "It was just us, and the pastor, and the pastor's wife. The pastor's wife played the piano, and with the sound of the nearby Poudre River and the birds singing, it was just about as good as it gets."

Joe walked in. He was still carrying his briefcase and had his jacket on. He obviously had not seen the memo yet, either, and his eyes fell on the wedding cake.

"D-did someone get married?" he asked, looking at Mary Lou. Mary Lou stepped out of the way, and he saw Beth and Denny sitting at the table.

His gaze met Denny's. "Denny?"

Denny stood up and held out his hand. "Congratulate me, buddy. Beth and I got married on Friday."

After Joe recovered from shock, he congratulated them, and they told him all about the wedding. He accepted a plate of cake and took it to his office to enjoy while he checked his email and planned his day.

Mary Lou stopped by his office on her way to hers. "Well, it happened. I'm a little surprised that it happened so soon, aren't you?"

Joe munched on the cake. "You know what they say. Love is blind."

"They know what they're doing. It's not like they're both kids. I think both of them have been lonely for a long time."

Joe finished off his cake. "I'm certainly not judging them. They're adults. I just happen to work for International Enterprises, that's all. They get married. I get cake. I wish them well."

Mary Lou noticed that Beth had gone into her office. "Excuse me, Joe. I want to talk to Beth."

She strolled to Beth's office and stuck her head in the door. "Congratulations. You sure surprised us. I am very happy for you."

Beth met her at the door. "Thank you so much. Come in."

She did, and Beth closed the door behind her.

"I want to talk to you about something," Beth said. "I really appreciate all you've done to help me since Walt's death. I feel like we've grown close the last few months."

Mary Lou nodded. "I feel that way, too. I appreciate the fact that you've trusted me enough to confide in me in the past. Now you have Denny. I am very happy for you. I hope your future is full of happy years."

Beth smiled. "I'm sure it will be. He is a wonderful man. I feel blessed. He's been the perfect gentleman."

Mary Lou added, "When Walt first hired him, I felt threatened because they were old college buddies. Then I figured Walt just hired someone he wanted to play with all the time. In a way I was glad, because it took the focus off me and how I was doing my job. Then again, he had become my competition as a fellow agent."

"You never had anything to worry about. You were always top in sales. Besides, since Walt died, Denny hasn't been an agent. He's been consulting for me, helping me on the business and finance side that Walt never took care of. Denny's been able to make the company more efficient, saving us lots of money. He's also helped attract large oil companies to the firm. Making him my right-hand man," she smiled at the correlation, "in more ways than one—it's the best decision I've ever made."

Mary Lou grinned. "Yeah, I have to admit that I was wrong about him at first. He's a great guy."

Beth's cell phone rang. She looked at the caller ID. "I have to take this. I haven't told my Uncle Ralph yet. I hope he takes it well."

Mary Lou closed the office door as she left.

Beth answered and told her uncle that she had married Denny last Friday.

Ralph roared over the phone, "I haven't met this guy. You need to bring him over so I can get a look at him. How long have you known him?"

Beth gazed at the world map on the wall across from her. "I knew him in college."

"He couldn't be any worse than the bum you just buried."

Beth cringed. "Uncle Ralph, that's no way to talk about Walt. He did the best he could do."

"That's what they all say. Have you been watching *On the Horizon?*"

Beth laughed. "I've been sort of busy."

"Well, the old gal hid the guy in the freezer. I told you that, didn't I?"

Beth listened as the old man shared details of the soap opera and his opinion of the characters and writers.

Friday, August 9
Denver, Colorado

Mary Lou looked at the clock on her office wall. It was three o'clock, and Eileen had made appointments for the bridesmaids' final fittings.

Mary Lou's cell phone buzzed. She took a quick glance to see that it was a text from Eileen. It read, *We are waiting for you. What is the holdup?*

Mary Lou tried to squelch the jealousy. *What's the holdup? You may not have to work anymore, but I still do. I've spent nearly every waking moment either here at work or out with you—looking at dresses, looking at venues, looking at invitations, looking at decorations, looking at centerpieces, looking at menus, picking out bridesmaids' dresses that I can't stand... I could go on, but what can I do? She's my sister. Lord, give me an attitude adjustment. I love my sister. Only two weeks until the wedding. I will be so glad when these two are married. I just pray it lasts forever.*

Mary Lou picked up her purse and closed her office door. She rushed out to the parking lot and roared over to David's bridal shop. It took her fifteen minutes to find a parking place.

She hurried into the store to find a ticked off Eileen with her fists on her waist. "It's about time you got here."

Mary Lou resisted the urge to choke her. "I have a job. Traffic was horrible, and this place has no parking. I'm here now."

Several of Eileen's twelve bridesmaids stood around her in their bridesmaid dresses. Eileen shouted at them and the ones who were milling about the store, "Everyone come over here, now. I want you to form a line and walk past so Mary Lou can inspect each one of you individually."

Allison snickered. "Who's going to inspect her?"

Eileen burst out laughing. "That would be me."

Relieved at the quick mood change, everyone joined her in the laugh. Mary Lou took a seat outside the dressing room doors so she could watch them as they walked by. *I will be so happy when this charade is over. Everyone looks absolutely beautiful. The only thing I would change is the dresses. But that was Eileen's choice, and it is her wedding. I can't wait to wear it and get rid of it. I'm glad I left mine hanging in the closet.*

After Mary Lou approved the bridesmaids' dresses, Eileen sent them all back to the dressing rooms to change so they could all go to dinner.

Mary Lou's cell phone vibrated. She looked down and saw that it was Bobby. She answered and was delighted to hear him invite her for dinner that night. "I'd love to go to dinner."

Eileen walked over and took the cell phone out of Mary Lou's hand. "Sorry, Mary Lou is having dinner tonight with my bridesmaids and me. You will just have to find another night. This is important, Bobby."

Mary Lou snatched her phone back and glared at Eileen. "How dare you." Then she put the phone up to her ear. "I'm sorry, Bobby. I have to apologize for my sister. Talk about a bridezilla. She's gone a little crazy."

She heard Bobby laughing. "It's obviously important to her. We can meet later. I have to go home and feed the cat anyway. Why don't you go ahead and have dinner with the girls, and we can go out for pie and coffee afterward? You can just text me when you're ready, and I'll pick you up at your place."

Mary Lou felt torn between Bobby and Eileen's agendas for the evening. She inwardly sighed in relief. "That would be great. Thanks for helping me out on this one. I will be so glad when this wedding's over."

He laughed again. "That makes two of us. But you're there for your sister, and that's what matters. I'll see you later."

Eileen was instructing the women where to meet them for dinner. "I've made reservations at the Brown Palace, and we're supposed to be there in fifteen minutes. Take your dresses—now, don't get them dirty. Be careful. I'll meet you over there."

She walked over to Mary Lou. "Do you want to ride with me?"

Mary Lou rejected the idea of being dependent upon Eileen. She would take her own car. "No thanks. I'll meet you there."

Eileen frowned. "You never did bring your dress in for alterations. Did you bring it tonight?"

"No, it fits fine. I didn't need alterations. Remember, they gave me the sample dress. Those are always small, so it fit me perfectly."

Eileen wrinkled her nose. "All right. But I don't want you to take any chances. It has to be ready for the wedding. After all, you are the maid of honor. Next to the bride, you're the most important woman there."

Mary Lou managed a smile. "You sure that wouldn't be the caterer?" She headed out the door to her car.

It seemed like forever before all of the women showed up and got seated around the large table. Mary Lou just wanted to order, get her food, snarf it down, and get out of the Brown Palace Hotel. She wanted to be with Bobby. And yet she wanted to support Eileen. *Why can't I be in two places at once? I should clone myself. Wait a minute—then I'd have to keep track of two of us. That would never work. It reminds me of an old joke: You want to clone yourself? Now wouldn't that be just like you?*

Thirty minutes after the lengthy process of ordering, the meal arrived. Before they started eating, Eileen tapped on her glass to get everyone's attention. "Let's bow our heads and ask the Lord to bless our meal and our time together."

Everyone bowed their heads, and she said a short prayer. Afterward, the table got noisy as the women chatted over a fabulous dinner in beautiful surroundings.

As soon as Mary Lou finished her meal, she nudged Eileen, who was talking to Allison. Mary Lou waited a good five minutes for their conversation to pause, but obviously that wasn't going to happen. "Excuse me, Eileen. I need to leave. Thank you. It's been a wonderful evening."

"You can't leave before dessert," Eileen protested. "It's cherries jubilee. I know that's one of your favorites. That's why I ordered it. You have to stay."

"Please enjoy it for me. Now I have a date." She got up and left the table.

As she hurried out the door, she took a quick glance back and was relieved to see Eileen had already resumed her conversation with the woman next to her.

She got to her car and texted Bobby Porter. *I'm free! I'm free! I'm on my way home.*

He texted back, *I'm bringing coconut cream pie and your favorite decaf latte. I'm only bringing decaf because it's late.*

She laughed with glee as she started the car.

Later the same day

Bobby got there ten minutes after she had arrived. He held up the bag. "Wednesday's Pie at Larimer Street. They make the best pie."

Mary Lou took the bag to the kitchen and found her mother's blue china to serve it on. "This cannot be served on a paper plate." She put her nose down and took a deep sniff. "Oh, that smells so good. I love coconut."

"I knew that. Hurricane loves it, too. She's the only cat I've ever known that will eat coconut. Is that just nuts?"

Mary Lou sighed. "Hurricane is a unique cat. I think it has something to do with her daddy."

They sat at the kitchen table and savored the pie.

Bobby finished his piece and sat back in his chair. "I'm thinking about planting a garden next year. I staked out a little area in the backyard."

"That sounds like fun and lots of work. What do you plan to grow there?"

Bobby scratched his head. "Maybe some tomatoes, some corn, green beans, and cucumbers. Those things grow pretty easily around here."

She laughed. "I tried a garden one time. It didn't work very well. I had a hard time keeping up with the weeds. And then when everything got ripe, I had to be out of town for one thing or another. It was sad, because most of my vegetables rotted on the vine."

He winked at her. "If you had a garden, and you were out of town at harvest, I could come over and harvest it for you so nothing would rot. I could even help with the weeds."

She put her fists on her hips. "Are you asking me to help take care of your garden? There's no need to be sneaky about it. You can come right out and ask me. The answer is no. I'm through with gardening. However, I would be happy to help you eat some of that good produce."

Bobby shook his head. "I'll bet you would. I haven't made a final decision yet. Part of the reason the garden idea came into play is because it's been a long time since I had a home of my own. You know, I could plant a garden if I wanted to."

"I understand. To tell you the truth, having a garden seems like a luxury to me. It just takes so much time."

"But harvest time—that's the payoff. There's nothing like a homegrown tomato."

Mary Lou laughed. "Coconut pie comes close."

They chatted until the living room clock chimed eleven o'clock, and Bobby said it was time to go. She walked him to the door.

He turned and gave her a peck on the cheek. "Will I see you tomorrow?"

"Give me a call. I should be here, but if Eileen calls me, I will have to go. I promised her I would see her through this wedding, and there's only two weeks to go. I will never have a big wedding. It's way too much work."

Bobby opened the door looked out onto the street. "You never know. You might change your mind. You always have that option."

Chapter Twenty-One

Tuesday, August 13
Westminster, Colorado

Mary Lou had not heard from Bobby for four days, even though they'd made plans for him to call her the day after he brought coconut cream pie to her house. She'd thought about him a few times during the day but got busy between business and Eileen's wedding.

It's been four days. He must be on some important case.

She took a swing by his house just to check on him. His car was in the drive, and she decided to find out what was going on. She knocked at the door.

Bobby answered. His face looked ashen, and he had dark circles around his eyes. His shoulders were slumped. "I didn't expect you."

"I haven't heard from you. I just stopped by to check on you to make sure everything's okay."

He opened the door wider to let her in, then he sank down in the chair across from the couch. He covered his face with both hands. "Everything is not okay."

Mary Lou knelt in front of the chair. She had never seen him like this. "What happened?"

He took her hands. "It's Hurricane. She's been gone for three days. I have no idea how she got out of the house. I have checked every place." He straightened in the chair. "She can't fend for herself out there." He nodded toward the window. "She's never even been outside before. She had been declawed when I adopted her."

Inside, Mary Lou heaved a sigh of relief. *It's only the cat. Good grief! I thought his mother died.* "Where have you looked?"

"First I thought she might be hiding in the house. You know how she gets when I'm not home at night. She was really mad when I got home from your house. I think she could smell you on my clothes."

The hair on the back of Mary Lou's neck stiffened. "It's no secret Hurricane and I are not friends."

"When I got home that night, I sat down and she jumped in my lap. She snuggled up against me, and I started to pet her. Then she bit me." He held up his little finger. "Right here on the end of my finger."

Mary Lou took his finger. "Did you put something on that?"

He brought his hand back and rubbed at it. "I'm fine. Then she ran away. She jumped down from my lap and went and hid. I was tired, so I went to bed. The next morning, I got up to feed her, and she didn't come when I put food in her bowl. It doesn't matter how mad she gets at me. She always comes for her breakfast. I haven't seen her."

He rubbed his temples. "What am I going to do? I've looked all through the house. I didn't find her, so then I started looking all through the house for places where she might've gotten out. This place is solid. There's no way."

Mary Lou sat on the couch across from him. "I don't know much about cats, but I've heard they can get through very small places. It's not important how she got out. It's important that we find her."

"I looked through the garage, in the shed out back, all through the yard."

Mary Lou shook her head. "If she got out, she's not going to hang around here. Did you call the animal shelter?"

"No, I didn't call the shelter. They won't have her. They'd never be able to capture her."

Mary Lou was already getting the number from Google. "I'm calling the pound."

After a few rings, a woman answered, and Mary Lou explained about the missing cat. After she gave the woman the best description she could think of, the woman took Bobby's number and promised to call back in a few minutes.

After she hung up, Bobby said, "I knew they wouldn't have her."

"They didn't say they didn't have her. They said they were going to look. She also asked me if you had a chip in the kitty."

Guilt registered on Bobby's face. "She never went outside; she didn't need a chip."

Mary Lou's eyes widened. "Are you kidding me? Everybody's pet should have a chip. It's like buying insurance for a car accident. You don't ever want to have one, but it just might happen. Besides that, it's the law. We are going to find her. But if they have Hurricane at the pound and she doesn't have a chip, you're going to get in trouble."

The phone on Bobby's kitchen counter rang. "This is Bobby Porter," he answered. "Yes. Yes." He looked at Mary Lou and raised his eyebrows. "Yes, ma'am. Yes, we'll be there in ten minutes. Good-bye."

Mary Lou could not believe her good fortune.

Bobby was ecstatic. Tears came to his eyes. "They have her. Let's go get her right now." He went to get her traveling cage. "They've had her for three days. They must have gotten her right after she left here. She hasn't had a thing to eat. They said she wasn't injured, but they did have a hard time catching her." He chuckled to himself. "I didn't think anybody could catch her."

While Bobby kept talking, Mary Lou thanked God that Hurricane had been found.

Monday, August 19
Arvada, Colorado

The Eileen Stots and Kurt Bell nuptials were to take place in less than a week. Mary Lou had worked with the wedding planner to double-check that all plans were in place and that all systems were ready to go, down to the hotel rooms out-of-town guests would occupy.

Mary Lou pulled her bridesmaid dress out. *I will wear it one time and make Eileen happy. Then I believe it's going to go to the Salvation Army and make someone else happy. I'll never wear this thing again.*

She called the caterers and the florists to make sure delivery would be made to the proper church at the proper time. She had put in a long night and wandered upstairs to go to bed.

It was three in the morning when she was wakened by the doorbell. *Who could that be at this hour?* She peeked through the drapes down to the curb and saw a strange car. She squinted and finally made out a white Lexus. Then she saw Eileen and Kurt waving up at her window.

She grabbed her fleece robe and made her way downstairs. When she opened the door, they pushed their way inside.

Eileen hugged her. Then Kurt hugged her. Eileen stuck her hand in front of Mary Lou's face, displaying not just her engagement ring but the engagement ring attached to a wedding band.

"I'm so excited to tell you—we did it! Kurt and I are married. Mary Lou, tell us congratulations!"

Mary Lou blinked. *Surely this is a dream. Or is this a nightmare?* "You—you're married? You eloped? You *did not elope!*"

"Isn't it romantic?" Eileen gushed.

"I—I'm in shock. I don't know what to think." Anger welled up, and Mary Lou fought it back. *What about all those wedding plans? What about all those arrangements, late nights, and hating the fact that everyone is getting married except me?* She felt heat rising to her head. *Lord, help me. Please breathe Your peace into me.*

Kurt put his arm around Eileen. "I think it was just all getting to be too much pressure. We decided to just do what we wanted to instead of what everyone else wanted."

Remembering the hours she had spent trying to please Eileen, Mary Lou came dangerously close to exposing her real feelings. She bit her lip. *Thank You, Lord. Hold my tongue.*

She summoned a smile. "You are right. I suppose congratulations *are* in order. Congratulations. It's three o'clock in the morning. Don't you have someplace to go?"

Eileen giggled. "We wanted you to be the first to know." She turned and kissed her new husband. "We are so happy. We'll let you go back to bed. We are going to Hawaii for our honeymoon. I'll call you next week when we get back. Now give me a good-bye hug."

Mary Lou stepped close so Eileen could put her arms around her. "Good night, Eileen. Good night, Kurt. You have my best wishes. Have a safe trip. Enjoy Hawaii." They backed out, and she closed the door.

A quick knock had Mary Lou opening the door a crack.

Eileen smiled sheepishly. "I hope you don't mind notifying everyone. The caterers, the bridesmaids, the—well, you know.

Everyone who was supposed to come. Especially Mom. I think she was looking forward to the big wedding. I'll try to call her from the airport."

Mary Lou slumped into the door. "Don't worry about a thing. Go."

She watched out the window as their car started and went down the street. She went up to bed but couldn't go back to sleep. *Eileen's married. They'll probably have children in the first year. Beth's married. She found her soul mate.*

I can't believe that, after all the work we put in, Eileen eloped. I wish I could stay in the shocked stage, but I'm drifting into anger. I have a lot of cancellations to make. She didn't even tell Mom. Help me, Lord. Mrs. Cunkell and I have worked hard on how to love others. How could she do this to me?

Thank You, Lord, that there is a bright side. At least no one will see me in that hideous dress.

And, Lord, what's wrong with me? Why is everyone getting married except me?

Later the same day
Denver, Colorado

When Beth got to work, she found a man dressed in a business suit waiting to see her. He came into her office and set his briefcase on the floor. "I am Barry Hamilton. I'm here on behalf of your late husband's insurance company. I believe I sent you a letter some time ago."

Beth remembered the nightmare she'd had the night she received that letter. "Oh, yes. I believe the letter mentioned that you would do an investigation before settling."

"Exactly. That was the purpose of the letter. I'm here to assure you that after our investigation into the death of your husband, we are prepared to present you with full payment of the policy."

"Of course," Beth said absently, thinking about her schedule for the day.

The man stood and approached her desk, check held out. "This is a rather large sum, but given the position your husband held in the business, it seems justified."

Beth accepted the check and held it in front of her. "Ten million dollars. I remember when I received your letter. I had no idea Walt had this much insurance."

She knew she didn't have to explain but felt compelled to do so. "There was a time when I wasn't involved with business or finances. But since Walt passed, I am very much aware of financial details."

Mr. Hamilton turned to go. "The fact that he had purchased that policy so long ago made it easier for us to release the funds after our investigation. We spoke to the judge who declared Walt dead, and it seems there is no question that he is gone."

"No question," Beth repeated.

"If you ever have additional insurance needs, please feel free to call us." He placed his business card on the corner of her desk. "Now that you've assumed Walt's position, you might consider doing something similar."

They stood, and Beth shook his hand. "I have no intention of taking out such a policy. Thank you for delivering the check. Have a good day."

Beth closed her office door behind him, still holding the check. *Ten million dollars. Ten million dollars to go directly into my personal account. I don't mean to be bitter, but I feel like I earned every bit of it.*

A knock at her door snapped her back to reality.

Denny opened the door a crack and peeked in. "Are you busy?"

"Come in. Did you see that man leaving my office? He was from the insurance company." She held up the check. "They just paid me the full amount of Walt's insurance policy. Ten million dollars. I consider it Walt's good-bye gift to us."

Denny took a seat across from her. "I detect a hint of bitterness."

She laughed, and her eyes widened. "Me? Not really. I got over that a while back. However, now that I reflect on it, it's the least he could do."

Denny leaned back in his chair and folded his ankle across his other knee. "What are you going to do with it?"

"I'm putting it in my personal account today. Later, I'll probably put it away somewhere."

Denny pursed his lips. "Yes, put it away. We don't need it. We've got what we need." He grinned.

He stood as she approached him. She put her arms around him and pulled him close, and she kissed him passionately. "I'm so glad you came back to Denver."

"I am, too. And I'm glad we could be together."

Tuesday, September 3, Denver, Colorado

Beth sorted through the mail on her desk. *What's this from Harbor Storage in Ft. Lauderdale?* Remembering the last time she had seen that company name, she tore open the envelope.

After reading the contents, she called Denny. "Can you come to my office? I just got an invoice from that storage company in Florida that has everything the leasing company took off *The Adventurer.* Two thousand dollars for six months of storage. I am not paying another dime for stuff I don't even want. We're going to go to Ft. Lauderdale."

He arrived in seconds, smiling. "Hey, babe, I'd like to take you to Ft. Lauderdale any day of the week." He kissed her on the cheek.

She brushed him off. "This won't be fun. This letter reminded me that all the junk from *The Adventurer* has been there six months. Let's go down and see what we have to do to get rid of it. I know there's a lot of fishing equipment. You could help get rid of stuff like that, couldn't you?"

He sat across from her. "I'm curious about what all could be in there. Is there furniture? That dining room was amazing. I wonder if those fancy dishes were his? Anyway, we should contact an auctioneer to take it, then all we have to do is wait for our check."

Beth shrugged. "An auctioneer. Brilliant! But I have no clue what was his and what was rented, but I know who paid for all of it. Me. So I want to see every bit of what's in that locker. Are you with me on this?"

"You know I'm with you. I'd go to the moon with you. How soon do you want to leave?"

Friday, September 6
Westminster, Colorado

Bobby parked his car in the garage and headed into the house. *TGIF. I'm ready for the weekend.* He hung his jacket on the hook in the laundry room and stopped at the kitchen sink to wash his hands.

He glanced into the living room. "Hurricane! Get off the mantel. You know that's a bad cat."

Hurricane jumped down and ran over to rub against Bobby's leg. She was already purring loudly. Bobby picked her up. He massaged her between the ears as she pushed her head into his fingers.

He carried her to his recliner and sat. "You're a good cat now. Listen to you purring."

Hurricane nuzzled into Bobby's armpit. Bobby ran his hand down her back. "You're my sweet kitty, but we need to talk. You need to understand that Mary Lou is going to be around here a lot more than she used to be. That is, if I have anything to do with it."

Still purring, the cat rubbed her head on Bobby's chest. "Sometimes you're not very nice to her. Now, Hurricane, that's going to have to change. You need to be nice to Mary Lou. After all, she's the one who found you."

Bobby pulled the cat's face up to his. "You know that, don't you? It was Mary Lou who called the shelter. Otherwise, who knows where you would be today."

He hugged Hurricane. "Mary Lou is nice. Mary Lou is really a very sweet girl." He started talking softer. "She's a wonderful... woman. The fact is, Hurricane, I'm in love with her. She's got so many beautiful qualities. That's just it. She doesn't realize how beautiful she is. She's sweet and compassionate."

Hurricane looked up at Bobby and meowed.

"That's right. I'm in love with her, but I'm afraid she doesn't feel the way she used to about me. I hope I didn't make a mistake by leaving. Maybe I should have stayed after she told me she was a Christian. She got so angry at me that night. I'll never forget. She said she's forgiven me, but I don't feel like she's really forgiven me. Maybe it's the 'I can forgive, but I can't forget' thing. Maybe she doesn't trust me to stay in her life now."

"Meow."

"That's just the thing, Hurricane. She doesn't need a man. That's one of the things I love about her. On top of all that, she really cares for other people. And she loves Jesus. I've seen so much spiritual growth. Her great desire is to live a life pleasing to Jesus. I love her so much."

Hurricane pawed at his chest. He closed his hand around her paws and she nipped at his face. "Stop that—don't bite, Hurricane. You have to start being nice to Mary Lou. You know I love you, too."

Monday, September 9
Ft. Lauderdale, Florida

Beth and Denny left the office of Harbor Storage with keys in their possession for unit 666.

Beth spotted it first. "Over there, on the left."

Denny opened the padlock and rolled up the garage-like door. "This is their largest storage unit, and it's full, top to bottom. Look, Beth, there's the dining table."

She pointed past the table to the far wall. "A file cabinet. That's what I want to see. Maybe some answers."

Denny pulled a few chairs into the large hallway. "It may take some time to get to it. The guys from the auction house I hired should be here in a few hours. They will haul everything to their facility."

"I will want to see everything in that file cabinet, so let's start working to get to it. I can see that it's almost impossible to get to, but I know you can do it. I'll start here." Beth opened a large box of fine china. "Dishes. Who knows what could be wrapped in here with them? I know it sounds crazy, but I'm going through every wrapped dish."

Denny put his arm around her shoulders. "I understand."

She wore a cotton shirt with light denim jeans, ready to get dirty if it was necessary. "Oh, I definitely want to go through everything."

Denny handed her a pair of gloves. "I brought these because they wear them on *Storage Wars*, and they're always glad they have them."

Chairs stacked upon each other needed to be moved before she could get to another box. She started moving chairs. "*Storage Wars* would love to get this unit."

Denny stopped her. "I'll do the moving. Did you get through the box?"

Beth nodded. "Nothing in that one except dishes. Let's get as much done as we can before the haulers get here."

Denny began pulling furniture out into the hallway. Beth sat on one chair and dug through the box of dishes. Denny placed another box in front of her, and another, and another. It was going to be an all-day job.

Denny rescheduled the haulers for late in the afternoon.

All morning, Beth searched boxes of dishes, silverware, goblets, bedding, and kitchen utensils.

Denny brought a heavy box labeled "Wine" down from the top of a dresser. He set it down in the hallway. After opening it, he pulled out a bottle. "There was a heck of a lot of wine on that boat. There must be a dozen here, and there's a crate twice this size under the table. What do you want to do with all this?"

"Well, I certainly don't want it. Just have your guys dump it."

Denny laughed. "I'll tell them, but you can be sure they would not dump this wine. Seriously, they can auction it, no problem."

She wrinkled her nose. "Let them have it. I don't want anything but answers."

He rubbed his forehead. "I know it. I hope we find what you're looking for."

Beth looked around. A nightstand was in reach. She pulled open the drawer.

She caught her breath then screamed. "Denny, there's a gun in here! I don't want to touch it."

He shoved his way through items between them. "Here, let me look at it." He picked up the 9mm Glock pistol and checked the magazine. "Yes, it's loaded. I'll take the magazine out." He checked the barrel. "Relax. There's no bullet in the chamber." He handed it to her.

She threw up her hands. "Don't give it to me. I don't want it near me."

Denny shoved it into his back pocket and went back to sorting.

Within minutes, he set a trunk marked "master suite" in front of Beth. "You were the last person in the room. I don't think you'll find anything here."

She tore into the box. "I didn't inspect everything when I was there, that's for sure."

Walt's bathrobe was on top. She threw it aside. His suitcase was next. She opened it and riffled through his clothing and toiletries. Nothing.

She stopped. *I have no feelings whatsoever about going through Walt's things.* She smiled. *I think I'm free of you and a lot of bad memories, Walt.*

Denny was getting to the back corner and let out a "Whoa! Look at all this fishing gear."

Beth wiped the hair out of her eyes. "You can't have it. I don't want anything that was on the boat."

"I don't want it. I'm just amazed." He held up a huge harpoon. "This is for big fish, like whales. I've never seen one of these close up. Look, Beth—here's that mounted mackerel that was in the dining room."

"Ugh. I hate that thing. I think it's barbaric to hang dead bodies of what used to be a living thing on a wall. That's just disgusting."

Denny tried to lighten the room. "I'm getting to know a lot about you, Mrs. Adams."

She smiled and pushed the trunk aside. "That's done. How close are you to the filing cabinet?"

He extended his hand. "You can get to it. Let me help you over these tools."

Once in the back of the room, Beth yanked the top drawer of the filing cabinet open. "Empty!"

She jerked the next three drawers open. All were empty. She scowled and sat on the floor. "I just knew there would be something. I don't know what, but something."

Her eye caught a box marked 'captain's quarters.' "What's that one?" She pointed. Denny lifted the box. "It's from Kiral's quarters. Now come back here and sit in the chair. I'll open it for you."

"Well, look here. These must be Kiral's clothes and toiletries. This looks like a prayer rug. He must have left in a hurry. He even left his razor and toothbrush. Eww."

Chapter Twenty Two

Friday, September 13
Denver, Colorado

Bobby Porter decided to take a long lunch. He walked over to the Sixteenth Street Mall and entered the William Crow Jewelry Store on impulse. He scrutinized the rings in the glass case at the back of the store. *Did my heart just skip a beat? No doubt. Which one of these diamonds would Mary Lou pick?*

The young lady behind the counter asked, "May I help you?"

He looked up. "I'm just looking today. I like to plan ahead, and I thought I'd just stop by and look at the engagement rings."

"When are you getting engaged?"

He felt himself blush. "I'm not getting engaged."

The woman tilted her head.

Bobby swallowed. "I mean, I don't know if I'm getting engaged."

She smiled.

He couldn't stop himself from talking. "I mean, I am getting engaged, but I don't know when. I'm just looking at rings today."

The clerk opened the case from her side. "Tell me about her. Does she like a lot of glitz? Which one do you like?"

He pointed at the Eberly brand circle of diamonds. "That one is nice."

She pulled it out and set in on the jewelry case. "Oh, yes. This is one of our finest. Eberly has been creating unique engagement and wedding rings for us for many years. This one is exquisite."

He took the ring between his fingers and studied it. Bright red fire flashed from the ring's facets in the store lighting. He handed it back to her. "It's not her. I don't think she'd want so many stones."

The clerk pulled a ring with a single diamond from the case. "How about this one? It's lovely, and many of the women prefer it to a ring with numerous stones."

Bobby held the ring up so sunlight from the window pierced the facets. It exploded with color.

The clerk reached over and turned the small tag toward her. "This is a one-carat princess cut. It's eighty-five hundred."

He handed the ring back to her. "It is a beautiful ring." He backed away from the jewelry case. "Thanks for your help." He turned and walked out of the store.

Whew! I need to call Dad.

Monday, September 16
Denver, Colorado

Mary Lou scrolled through her emails. She returned a note to Feldman in Zedlav, who had just purchased another rig from International Enterprises. He had written, "Too bad you didn't come for the signing of this contract. Weather has been very nice. You would love it here today."

She smiled and wrote back, "I'm sure it is. Thanks for the return order. I'll never forget my time in Alaska! Maybe they will send me next time."

She shivered at the remembrance of freezing in her room at the Moose Run Hotel.

Beth entered Mary Lou's office and closed the door. "We went to Ft. Lauderdale to see what the leasing company took off *The Adventurer.*"

Mary Lou sat straight. "Oh, my. What'd you find?"

Beth plopped into the chair across from Mary Lou. "You would not believe all that was in storage. It was the largest unit they had, and it was full, top to bottom."

Mary Lou frowned. "How could that be? There was just some luggage, right?"

"Oh, no, not right. Walt had bought all the furnishings on that humongous boat. There was so much to go through that both Denny and I knocked ourselves out for a full day. We worked at full speed, right up until the auctioneer's people came to haul the stuff away. I'm still exhausted."

Mary Lou leaned forward. "Find anything interesting?"

Beth sighed. "Where do I begin? Let's see. Remember all the gorgeous china? That was there. I unwrapped every piece and inspected it. Everything was in like-new condition, even the cookware."

"Didn't you keep anything?"

Disgust flashed through her eyes. "I didn't want anything off that boat. Too many bad memories—and I don't mean of *The Adventurer*. I mean of Walt."

Mary Lou looked down. "I understand. I don't blame you."

Beth shook her head. "There was enough fishing equipment for a national contest. I tell you, the man liked to buy stuff. We found a harpoon." She laughed. "That's Walt. His ego was as big as the whale I guess he thought he was going to bag."

Mary Lou, thankful for the humor break, laughed with Beth. "A harpoon. Men."

Beth changed to serious. "I found a gun, and it was loaded."

Mary Lou cringed. "Yikes! A loaded gun sitting around. That sounds dangerous. And to think, I was right there on *The Adventurer*."

Beth nodded. "I wouldn't touch it. Denny picked it up and told me it was loaded. I'm so glad I didn't pick it up. I'm such a klutz; it probably would have fired. I'm so glad Denny came with me. You know, I considered asking you to come along instead. And I would have if Denny had given any signs of being uncomfortable with it, but he was fine with it. I think he was as anxious as I was to put all this behind us."

Mary Lou perked up. "I would have gone with you in a New York minute."

Beth smiled. "Denny had to do a lot of heavy lifting. Some of that furniture was very heavy."

"The furniture? You mean everything on *The Adventurer* was Walt's?"

"Sure was."

Mary Lou rolled her eyes. "He personally furnished that yacht? I guess he did like to shop. And you let them take it to be auctioned off? Oh, I loved that settee in the salon." She saw Beth's expression change again and added, "But I wouldn't want anything that Walt had on that boat, either."

Beth leaned forward. "Besides all that, we found a box with everything from Kiral's room in it."

"What did he leave?"

Beth frowned. "Lots of things. One thing he left, I can't get out of my head. Now this is really silly, but he left his toothbrush."

"His toothbrush? Ick."

"When I first opened the box, I found a prayer rug. I was kind of surprised. I guess he must have more than one of those. Then I found his clothes. There were three uniforms, six pairs of pants, and three pairs of knee pants. Also, probably a dozen or more shirts and undershirts along with his unmentionables. And why would he leave four pairs of shoes? It seemed like all of his toiletries were left behind."

Mary Lou reflected on the last time she had seen Kiral. "When I left the boat, Kiral was leaving at the same time. In fact, I had hoped he would help me with my bag, but he was carrying a large duffel bag. It seemed heavy, because when I stopped him, he set it on the pavement for just a minute."

Beth rubbed her forehead. "He left a lot."

Mary Lou frowned. "If he left his clothes and his toiletries, just what was he carrying in that heavy duffel bag?"

Beth's hand covered her mouth. "I felt like this was private, but..."

"It's okay. I don't need to know."

Beth wet her lips. "I think Kiral was carrying cash off that boat."

Mary Lou smacked herself on the forehead. "Oh, boy, cash? That would have to be a *lot* of cash. I mean, it was no small duffel."

Beth nodded. "What I haven't told you is that the first week I came back to work, the accountant took me on a full audit of the books. At that time we found an account called the Eastern Surface CAP Expense fund."

Mary Lou fixed her eyes on Beth's. "What on earth is that?"

"This is hard, Mary Lou." Beth eyes narrowed. "I realized that it was an acronym for the word *escape*, and I couldn't help but think it was Walt's little nest egg to escape from me. I'll be right back. I want to get a file."

Beth was gone less than thirty seconds. She slapped a folder labeled "Eastern Surface CAP Expense" on Mary Lou's desk.

Mary Lou examined the label. "I see where you got the word *escape*. Are you telling me it was an account with no money in it?"

"Oh, it had money in it. Only it had been withdrawn two days before we left for Ft. Lauderdale."

Mary Lou picked up the folder. "How much was it?"

"Five million dollars."

Mary Lou dropped the folder. "Wait a minute. Are you saying Kiral was walking off the boat with a duffel bag full of money—five million dollars' worth of money?"

Beth rubbed her chin. "It sounds crazy, I know. But what if Walt was planning to run away with five million dollars?"

Mary Lou shook her head. "Do you think Kiral was in on it?"

Beth shrugged. "*The Adventurer* was Walt's favorite toy. He could have planned to run away on it with Kiral captaining the ship. It sounds like something Walt might do. But why would he run away with all of us on board? That makes no sense."

After a few seconds of silence, Beth continued, "I just don't know. Maybe he's escaped to somewhere. Probably a tropical island, where he will never be found. I can't believe I'm saying this, but sometimes… Sometimes, I feel like he's still alive."

Mary Lou jumped to Beth's defense. "Don't be so hard on yourself. Run away from what? He had everything a man could want—a beautiful wife, all the money he could spend, and plenty of free time because everyone around here kept the business going. What else could he want?"

Beth sighed. "Maybe there was another woman."

Mary Lou shot back, "That's ridiculous. He wasn't interested in anyone but Walt. He loved playing, but he was too busy playing the big shot to romance anyone."

Beth sarcastically asked, "Do you really think so?"

Mary Lou frowned. "So if Kiral's clothing and his toothbrush were back on the boat, what was in his huge duffel bag? That's what I want to know."

Beth's fists went to her waist. "I think we both know. But what can we do? It's all speculation. We have no proof. And, even if we did, what good would it do us? Let's just put it to bed. I don't want anyone else to know anything about this conversation."

Mary Lou stood. "But why?"

Beth whispered, "Walt's dead. Kiral's dead. We don't know where the money went. Forget it. It's not worth the embarrassment."

Mary Lou's eyes widened. "Wow. Five million dollars is a lot of money. Are you sure?"

Beth stood. "Absolutely, because this is speculation. Please do not make me look like a fool." She walked out of the office.

Mary Lou's mouth fell open. "But…"

Monday, October 7
Denver, Colorado

Since getting married, Denny had traveled for the company sometimes, but only when he could return the same day. That morning, a longtime client had requested a two-day consultation at their site in Houston, Texas. He went to Beth's office. "This will be our first night apart since we married. I'm going to miss you."

Beth kissed him. "It's just one night. I'm going to miss you, too, but I'll see you tomorrow."

Denny drove to the airport and parked his car in USAirport parking. He caught the shuttle to the United terminal. He grabbed his carry-on bag and made his way to check in, then through security. Going through security took him longer than most, because he forgot to take his computer out of the attaché case.

Then he forgot to empty the change out of his pockets. He took off his shoes and walked through the scanner. The guard held up a hand as the buzzer alerted her that Denny had unclaimed metal in his pockets.

He went back and emptied his pockets of change and keys. Denny walked through the gate to pick his belongings up off the conveyor belt. He finally grabbed his shoes, found a place to sit on the provided bench, he began putting them back on.

He looked up to see a familiar figure duck into the crowd of people. He knew the back of that head—but Walt Pederson was dead.

Denny finished getting his shoes on and ran to catch up to the man, but he never saw him again.

That was weird. Walt must have a twin somewhere. I would have bet money that was him. He was still feeling uneasy when he got to the gate just as they were boarding his flight. He found his assigned seat by the window. As he looked out the window, watching airline personnel on the tarmac, he felt as though someone was watching him. He tried to shake off the feeling, but he studied every person he could see on the plane. He stayed in his seat the entire flight.

When he arrived at his destination, Cooper Oil Corporation, he went directly to the office of the general manager to meet with his client. They had a good discussion regarding the corporation's drilling needs and then went to lunch. After lunch they continued their discussion, which included planning and negotiations. Denny left feeling as if he had accomplished his mission for the day. He went to the hotel.

He went down to the lobby to find the hotel restaurant, where he enjoyed steak and potatoes, with cheesecake for dessert. He turned in early so he could be fresh for the continued meetings with Cooper Oil in the morning.

Tuesday, October 8
Houston, Texas

The resounding thud of heavy footsteps woke Denny in the middle of the night. He turned on the light.

Walt Pederson was standing before him.

Denny frowned and rubbed his eyes.

"It's me, Denny. It's been a long time, old friend."

He looked around the room to make sure he wasn't dreaming. "Walt? How can it be you? You... You are..."

"I'm dead? Does it look like I'm dead? I'm very much alive. And I think we have a lot to talk about."

Denny sat up in the bed. "It really is you?"

The man shook his head. "Denny, Denny, Denny, I thought we already settled that. I'm alive. I'm here. And we have to talk."

Denny blinked, trying to process what was happening. "All—all right. Sure. Let's talk."

"I want a little justice. And you're going to help me get it. You see, you married my wife, you're running my company, you just collected ten million dollars of my life insurance, and you don't deserve any of it."

"What are you talking about? You're alive. The money goes back to the insurance company. And, as far as Beth goes, we'll all have to work that out somehow."

Walt let out a laugh that sounded more like a howl. "You think I want to go back? No, that's not the plan."

Denny threw the covers off and sat on the edge of the bed. "Everyone thinks you're dead." He rubbed his temples and then he realized... He looked up at Walt. "That's what you wanted them to think, isn't it? You faked your death."

Walt pulled the chair from the desk and sat. "Now you're beginning to get the picture. It's true. I had a plan, but—well. The cold water brought me back to consciousness before I could drown. Kiral didn't plan for that. You were long gone by the time I got my bearings. If it hadn't been for that old hermit of a fisherman, I would be dead."

Denny's eyes narrowed. "That sounds like a scheme to me, right now. You have a lot of explaining to do."

Walt looked at the ceiling and dramatically threw up his hands. "When I started this little adventure, I had a plan. I had money. Then everything blew up in my face when I ran into someone as greedy as I was, the captain of my ship."

"Kiral?" Denny asked, taken aback.

"The fool thought I was dead when he threw me in the ocean. But now that I'm dead, I want to stay that way. So no worries—I won't be breaking in on you and Beth. The only thing I want is money. The way I see it, you've broken the law seven ways to Sunday. First of all, you accepted insurance money when I'm not dead. Second, you married my wife—and again, I'm still alive. I could go on, but you get the drift."

Denny's anger kicked in. "How could you do this to Beth? She stood by you your whole married life. And since you died, she's had a very difficult time getting over it."

Walt laughed. "Don't give me that. She's glad I'm gone, and I'm sure you're just as happy."

"I never wished you dead. You know me better than that."

Walt smirked. "Fact is, my dear friend, I do know you well. You will do just about anything to protect Beth. If you want to keep me from ever coming back into her life, you're going to have to take care of me in a lavish way. I need money, and I need it now."

Denny stood. "Of course I want to protect Beth. I'm not sure why you faked your death, but if you came back into Beth's life, I would do whatever it takes to make her happy. If it meant I had to go, I would do it."

Walt stared Denny directly in the eyes. "Oh, let me get out my violin," he said sarcastically. "You always rise to the occasion. I'm telling you right now that I'll stay out of Beth's life. It will save her a lot of pain, and it will save you a lot of pain. It's simply going to cost you. You can continue to run International Enterprises and stay married to the lovely Beth."

Denny smiled. "I'm not running International Enterprises. Beth is, and she's doing a superb job."

Walt laughed. "Beth doesn't have the brains or the guts to run the business. Don't give me that garbage. You're pulling the strings."

Denny couldn't help but show his pride in Beth. "No, Walt. She's running the company, and I have very little to say about it. She's also holding all the purse strings. I don't have your ten million dollars. Beth has tucked it away in some account."

Walt growled. "I can make more trouble for you than you can think or imagine. If you don't believe me, ask Kiral Nadeem. You'll find a way to get the money. If you don't, something terrible is going to happen—and it's going to happen to both of you, not just Beth."

Denny's hands closed into fists. "You're threatening me? Us?"

Walt raised an eyebrow. "You bet your life—and Beth's—I am."

Denny sighed, his shoulders slumping. "What do you want? Just spit it out."

"To begin with, keep my secret. As far as the world is concerned, Walt Pederson is dead. And then I want five million dollars."

Denny gasped. "Five million dollars. You know I can't get that kind of money. There's no way."

Walt snarled. "You'll figure it out. I don't care where you get the money. I want five million dollars next Wednesday."

"Next Wednesday? That's only a week. I can't do it, Walt."

Walt set his jaw. "Fine. If I don't get that money Wednesday morning, I'll be paying Beth a visit that afternoon. And it won't be a social visit. It will be business."

Denny tried to reason with Walt. "Are you sure you want to add this to your list of crimes?"

Walt shrugged. "What crimes? All I've done is survive a boating accident. You're the ones who broke the law."

"Beth told me she found indications of embezzlement when she returned from California."

Walt sneered. "Go to court and prove it. If you don't get me five million dollars by Wednesday, Beth's life is over." He backed toward the door.

Denny choked out the words, "I'll get it."

"I'll contact you on Tuesday with where to meet me."

The not-dead Walt Pederson walked out the door.

Denny collapsed onto the bed. He took a deep breath to steady himself. *That wasn't a dream. How am I going to get five million dollars by Wednesday?*

Chapter Twenty-Three

Wednesday, October 9
Denver, Colorado

Denny knew Walt was capable of carrying out his threat to kill Beth. Denny had every intention of following Walt's instructions to the minutest detail. He would not alert the authorities. He would pay Walt off. Beth would be safe. She didn't have to know about any of this. She had already been through enough heartache because of Walt.

He told Beth he wanted to get to the office early, so he left without her. He went to his office and began to try and figure out how he was going to come up with five million dollars that week. Denny had to get to the books

The day before, he had stopped and purchased a post office box near the office. He faked an invoice and authorized a five million-dollar payment to Ellison Equipment, a company he made up. He made a note to Accounting that the check was to be immediately submitted to the attached address. He filled in the post office box number and felt his heart racing.

It's not going to be easy keeping anything from Beth. We have no secrets. But I can't let Walt hurt her. Walt Pederson is a monster.

I love her so much. I want to protect her. Is deceiving someone because you love them right? If she ever finds out that I lied to her—or even worse, stole from her—it would be the end of us, but what choice do I have?

I hope Walt uses this money to get out of our lives forever.

Saturday, October 12
Denver, Colorado

Bobby wanted to do something special for Mary Lou since she'd helped him find Hurricane. He took her for brunch at Ellyngton's at the Brown Palace.

He held up a glass of orange juice. "Here's to my favorite little detective. To Mary Lou, who found my beloved Hurricane."

She tipped her cup of coffee to clink against his glass. "Here's to Hurricane. May she live long and be happy."

He took a sip of the orange juice. "You stepped up when I was helpless. I had done everything I knew to do and had given up. Then you came up with such a simple idea. And not only that, when I told you I thought it was ridiculous, you acted on it and called the pound. I still can't believe it was that easy. And Hurricane was there. You are a brilliant woman."

Mary Lou laughed. "You're so silly. You would've thought of it eventually. You were just upset."

"Hurricane and I are a team. We moved back and forth from San Diego and survived—and let me tell you, there were days when she was the only one I spoke to. The only disagreements we ever had were when I had to go out of town. She would pee all over my bed. I used to get so angry, but I knew it was because she missed me."

That's exactly why I don't have a cat, Mary Lou thought. "That just sounds disgusting."

"Oh, it was. I could smell it the minute I came in the house. I'd be tired from traveling, but I would have to wash all the blankets and sheets and bedspreads, steam off the mattress, and sleep on the couch till everything dried. Hurricane would watch the entire time."

"You are a lot more patient than I would be. I'm afraid one little kitty would've found herself left at the kennel. You've heard of kennels, right? I mean, that's a good place to leave your pet when you go out of town."

Bobby took a bite of his hash browns, then cleared his throat. "Kennels are not nice places to stay. They're like nasty little jail cells. I'm not ever taking Hurricane to a kennel."

Mary Lou held up her hand to stop him. "All right, all right. It's not my place to decide. Hurricane is your kitty. Not to change the subject, did you ever figure out why Kiral's apartment was ransacked?"

"No. And now that I'm no longer on the San Diego Police Department, I don't care—unless, of course, you've solved the case."

Mary Lou shook her head. Beth had begged her not to tell about the five million dollars. "I don't know why I just can't get that out of my head. It just seems like there's got to be a connection between Walt's disappearance and Kiral's death. It's just too… It's just too… I have a gut feeling."

"Oh, no, I don't like the sound of this. Gut feelings are hard to get over. What do I have to do to prove to you that they had nothing to do with each other?"

"For one thing, help me find what they were looking for."

Bobby rolled his eyes. "All right. Let me call some of my friends back in San Diego. I don't think there's any more in that file, but I'll check it out."

For the first time that morning, Mary Lou gave a real smile. "That would be wonderful."

Later the same day

Eileen and Kurt went hiking for the weekend. It was their first free weekend since Hawaii. Eileen was wearing her cutest jeans and top, hiking boots, and a bright scarf.

Kurt packed the backpack with snacks, first aid kit, jackets, and lightweight sleeping bags, with his new featherweight tent. "The weather's been so nice, I can't wait to get out and see the fall colors. I love it when the leaves are falling and the colors are changing. It's going to be cold up there. Be sure to wear an extra sweater."

Eileen gave him a little hug. "Why don't you leave the tent? We can sleep out on the ground. That would be so cool, just out under the stars."

He gave her a peck on the cheek. "And if it rains or snows? I don't think you would like that."

She pecked him back. "I didn't see rain or snow in the forecast."

He laughed. "You trust the weatherman more than me? They don't know what can happen in the mountains. Trust me, we'll need the tent. Let's get going. We're burning daylight."

Kurt took Highway 119 to Rollinsville, turned right, and parked the car about a mile into the wilderness. Eileen and Kurt followed the trail up the mountain. They walked about an hour, enjoying the beautiful red and gold leaves from the aspen trees, then stopped for lunch. While the two of them were eating, they found themselves staring across the valley at a remote cabin.

Eileen observed a black SUV pulling into the drive. A familiar-looking man got out and walked up onto the porch and went inside.

Eileen grabbed Kurt's arm. "I can't believe it. That looks like Walt Pederson. His walk even looks like Walt Pederson's."

Kurt started packing up trash from lunch. He looked across the valley and squinted. "I'm not sure I could identify anyone from this distance."

"But I'm farsighted. And I'm telling you, that looks like Walt Pederson. I know he's dead. I'm just saying."

Kurt paused. "Do we need to check it out? We can go over there."

She shook her head. "It couldn't be him. But that was just weird. Wait until I tell Mary Lou."

Kurt packed up, and he and Eileen headed on up the trail. He wanted to reach the peak by sundown. Eileen wanted to see the beauty of the stars viewed from the top of the mountain on a clear fall night.

Monday, October 14
Arvada, Colorado

As soon as Kurt left for work, Eileen called Mary Lou. She wanted to tell her what she had seen when she and Kurt were on their hike in the mountains.

Eileen gushed, "Mary Lou, you will never believe what happened this weekend on our camping trip."

"Slow down," Mary Lou said, sounding impatient. "I can't understand a word you're saying."

"We went up to Rollinsville. Remember, I told you we were going camping last weekend—"

"Yes, yes, I remember. I assume you had a wonderful time, you naughty newlyweds."

"Oh, stop it. Listen, Mary Lou. We were hiking up the peak from Rollinsville and stopped and had lunch. There's a large, beautiful cabin up there in the middle of nowhere. It was right across the draw from where we ate. And while we were lunching, a black SUV drove up. A man got out and went into the house."

Mary Lou was looking at her computer. "That's nice, Eileen. I'm glad you had a good time."

"No, no! The man who got out of the car looked exactly like Walt Pederson."

Mary Lou froze. "Are you saying you saw Walt Pederson? I mean, he's dead."

Eileen said, "I know, but I'm telling you, this guy looks exactly like him. It was creepy."

Suspicions clouded Mary Lou's mind. "What did Kurt say? Did he say it was Walt?"

"He said it was a long way across the draw and he couldn't really see. But I'm farsighted, and I know I saw someone who looked just like Walt Pederson. And he lives in a secluded mountain home in the woods."

Mary Lou's mind raced. *This is all getting to be too coincidental. After what Beth just told me, I'm even more suspicious.*

Mary Lou wanted to ease her sister's excitement and imagination, so she relaxed her voice and spoke with confidence. She tried to give an attitude of discounting what Eileen had just said. "They say everybody has a twin."

Eileen backed off. "I guess they say that. I wonder what mine is doing."

Mary Lou giggled. "She couldn't be having more fun than you are."

Mary Lou couldn't wait to get off the phone so she could call Bobby Porter.

Later that same morning
Denver, Colorado

His answering machine asked for her message.

"Bobby, this is Mary Lou. Come to my house tonight. I'm fixing your favorite spaghetti dinner." She was setting him up, but she needed his full attention that night. Walt Pederson could indeed be alive.

She wasn't about to mention it to Beth. *Beth is living her dream. Married to the man who adores the ground she walks on. He would do anything at her beck and call. No, I am not going to mention any of this to her. There is no reason to trouble her if this is all just coincidence.*

Mary Lou stopped at the Blue Parrot on the way home and picked up Bobby Porter's favorite, spaghetti and meatballs. After she got home, she set out the good china and lit two candles in the middle of the dining room table to soften the lighting.

Bobby showed up right on time. When he walked in and spied the candles and the beautifully set the table, he gave the proper response. "Wow! This is very… romantic."

She smiled. "Romantic, yes. But even more so, it's very relaxing. I thought I'd add a little ambience to dinner."

Red flags waved fiercely in Bobby's mind. "A little ambience, all right. All right, now I'm suspicious. What do you want?" He sat in the chair she had pulled out for him.

"Golly, can't a girl do something nice for someone? Maybe I just want to serve you a nice meal with candlelight."

His tone lightened. "I smell spaghetti and meatballs."

She went in the kitchen and brought the meatballs, which had been warming on the stove. She spooned the food into their plates.

Bobby inspected his plate of food. "This looks exactly like the Blue Parrot."

She wrinkled her brow. "You thought I came home and spent all afternoon fixing this?"

He started laughing. "I caught you. You admit it. If I hadn't said that it was from the Blue Parrot, you would've let me believe that you did cook this."

She smiled. "Maybe. Now I guess you'll never know for sure. You want me to take it back?"

"Never."

After enjoying dinner and light conversation, Mary Lou brought out coconut pie.

Coconut cream pie! Now Bobby knew. Mary Lou was up to something. "All right, out with it. What are you doing?"

"Eat your pie, then we'll talk."

"Out with it, Mary Lou."

"Oh, all right. I have some information you might be interested in."

Bobby stared at the pie in front of him. "This wouldn't be about Walt Pederson, would it? Or is it about Kiral Nadeem?"

Mary Lou leaned forward. "Now hear me out. Beth and I have discovered several interesting facts, but she doesn't want any of this to get out. She says it would embarrass her. She doesn't want the police involved, and I don't want to go against her wishes."

Bobby held up his hand to stop her. "Don't tell me anything you don't want me to know. I am an officer of the court."

"But couldn't you just listen as a friend?"

Bobby picked up his fork and scraped at the piecrust. "I have been listening as a friend. You haven't crossed the line, but I'm afraid you're going to have to back off on this Kiral thing before you do."

Mary Lou gulped. "Beth said that when she first started back at the company, she went through all the finances with the accountants. She found an account that had five million dollars in it, and all of the money had been taken out two days before we all went to Florida." She stopped to take a breath.

Bobby said, "Okay, so the company paid some bills."

Mary Lou held up her hand. "I said I wanted you to hear me out. I'm not finished. Beth went to Florida last month to dispose of what was in storage from *The Adventurer*. She found all of Kiral's personal belongings, including his toiletries and his prayer rug."

Mary Lou took a deep breath. "The day Walt died, or disappeared, or whatever, everyone was ordered to leave the boat. I walked off the pier with Kiral. And he was carrying a large duffel bag. I thought he had his personal belongings in the bag, but obviously not. I think Walt and Kiral were in this thing together. First I thought Kiral killed

Walt for the money. Something else has come up recently. I was thinking about Kiral's apartment being ransacked. What if Walt and Kiral were supposed to meet up later and Kiral didn't keep his end of the bargain? What if Walt killed Kiral? What if Walt went to Kiral's apartment to find the money?"

"What money? You can't connect the missing money to Walt or Kiral. You have no proof. What if Mary Lou Stots would stop questioning everything that happens?" Bobby Porter threw his napkin on the table.

Mary Lou shouted, "Now, stop it, Bobby! I'm not finished! You need to hear me out."

Bobby responded in a quiet voice. "Why would Walt Pederson do such a thing?"

"Beth said that they had a miserable marriage. And that she thinks he tried to steal five million dollars from the company."

Bobby responded with, "He could get a divorce."

"And leave all that money behind? I don't think so. One more thing. I heard from Eileen today. She and Kurt went camping up in the mountains. They were in a very remote spot, but they could see a house across the gorge. Eileen said she saw a black SUV pull into the driveway. A man that looked a lot like Walt got out of it. He went right into the house, so she only got a short glance. But she said it sure looked like Walt Pederson."

Bobby looked interested now. "What did Kurt say? Did he think it looked like Walt?"

"He couldn't see that well. Eileen's farsighted. She said she could see."

"Have you been filling Eileen's head with these ideas of yours?"

Mary Lou frowned. "That's just it, Bobby. I haven't mentioned any of this to Eileen. Eileen's been busy with her wedding and being married. I haven't shared any of this. Besides, anything Beth and I talked about had to be confidential."

Bobby took his first bite of the pie. "Where is it that they saw Walt? I'll check it out."

"It was somewhere around Rollinsville. I'll have to check with Eileen to find out exactly where it was. So you believe me now?"

Bobby shook his head. "I'll look into it. But don't expect anything. It seems very far-fetched to me."

Chapter Twenty-Four

Tuesday, October 15
Denver, Colorado

Beth entered Denny's office and closed the door.

He looked up from his work and saw that she was frowning. "What's wrong?"

"I think you know what's wrong."

He stared blankly.

She smacked the invoice in her hand down on his desk. "Do you mind explaining this to me?"

He picked up the invoice and pretended to scrutinize it. "Well, it looks like an invoice from Ellison Equipment for a very expensive piece of equipment."

"Yes, Denny, that's exactly what it is. Only that company does not exist. And we never bought that piece of equipment from them."

Denny looked bewildered. "How did you know?"

She sat across from him and struggled to keep from crying. "Why would you do this? Are you just like Walt? You're stealing from the company? If you're doing it just to escape from me, let me help you. You can go. I'll give you money or whatever you need."

He came around to stand in front of Beth. He sat on the edge of his desk. "No, I don't want to go. It's—this is not about me."

The tears spilled onto her cheeks. "If it's not about you, what is this?"

Denny shook his head and held his face in his hands. He muttered, "I told him I couldn't do it. I knew I couldn't lie to you. But he threatened..."

"Who are you talking about? Who threatened what?" She stood. "Tell me what is going on."

He sucked in a breath. "It's Walt."

Her face went ashen. She wiped tears off her cheeks, and her voice turned to metal. "Walt is dead. You're going to have to come up with something better than that."

Denny took her hands in his. "That's just it. Walt's not dead. He came to my hotel in Houston. He threatened to kill you. And he told me if I didn't pay him five million dollars, he would reappear in Denver. I have until Wednesday to come up with the money."

Beth blinked. "I suspected as much, but what possible reason would he come back here, after taking five million dollars with him?"

Denny searched her eyes. "You knew about that?"

Beth pulled her hands away. "I knew five million dollars had been embezzled. I was pretty sure Walt took it."

Denny reached for her again. "Walt told me he had money when he left. He said he hadn't planned it very well. He said someone stole it from him. When he went to find it, the money was gone. Something about Kiral gambling it all away."

Beth tilted her head as she took his hands. "That doesn't make sense. Why would he do this when he could divorce me and get money? And so now he comes back, and he's blackmailing you. This makes no sense."

Denny stepped closer. "He may not be in his right mind. He just kept saying he needed money, and I was going to get it for him. I told him I couldn't do it. And he said if I didn't, he would be back in our lives. He kept repeating, 'All I did was survive a boating accident. That's all I did.'"

Beth looked up at him. "If that's all he did, why doesn't he just come forward? So his little scheme failed. It's not the first one. I guess you never knew he tried to take the company away from Daddy right after I married him. He accused my father being incompetent and actually had the nerve to try to get him committed so he could get his job. Of course, he got the job eventually, because Father died. I wouldn't be surprised at anything Walt does."

Denny put his arms around her. "What are we going to do?"

Beth's spine straightened. "We're not giving him any money. So forget that. By the way, explain to me how you were going to cash this check written to Ellison Equipment?"

Denny sounded sheepish. "I told him I didn't know how to do this. I had to do everything quickly. I never really had time to plan it out. I got a post office box to use for an address. I made up a company name. I came back and made up the invoice and gave it to Accounting. I told them I wanted it paid right away."

She smiled. "That's why they alerted me. Nothing goes out of this office without my approval. I immediately knew the company was bogus, but I gave you the benefit of the doubt and did some research."

He buried his face in her hair. "And you found there was no company. I had planned to go to the bank and sign as the company owner, get the cash, and take it to Walt."

She laughed. "And you didn't think they were going to call me? Oh, Denny." She held his face in her hands. "I am so glad you don't know how to be a crook."

"I don't know. Maybe somewhere deep inside, I wanted you to catch it so that all of this could be out in the open. But still, I don't want you to get hurt."

A slight grin crossed Beth's mouth. "I'm fine. I think we need to make Walt think his plan worked."

Denny frowned. "Why would we do that?"

Beth stepped back and rubbed her chin. "If he thinks you're bringing the money, and he actually accepts it from you, we can get him for extortion. We need to find some way to record it or even video it—"

Denny protested, "But he's married to you."

Beth felt strength flow into her soul. "It's much easier now that I know he's alive. I can fight that. It was the not knowing that made me feel helpless. I'm not going to die like a crumpled rose. I'm going to fight him. And we're going to win."

Denny held her again. "I think he's out of his mind. But I'm with you all the way. I don't want to endanger your life. We need to be smart about this. We should call the authorities."

Beth shook her head. "I really don't want to do that just yet. Let's talk to Mary Lou. She's been in on a lot of information since the night Walt disappeared. I trust her, and she may have an idea on how to pull this off. After all, she's dating a police detective."

Denny released her and looked into her eyes. "Do we want another person to know that Walt is alive? I mean, he threatened me."

Beth's shoulders relaxed. "Everyone's going to know it, pretty soon."

"I don't want anyone to get hurt, especially you. If you think Mary Lou can help and you want to talk to her, then call her in."

Ten minutes later, Mary Lou knocked at Denny's office door. Beth opened the door and discreetly closed it behind Mary Lou before a word was spoken.

Mary Lou studied their faces. "What's going on here? Beth, have you been crying?" She glared at Denny.

Beth indicated the chair next to her. "Maybe you better sit. There's something we need to discuss."

Mary Lou felt her defenses go up. "Did—did I do something?"

"No," Beth said. "It's about Walt."

Mary Lou fixed her eyes on Beth. "What about Walt?"

"He's alive." Beth couldn't believe she said it. "Walt Pederson is alive."

Mary Lou gasped. "For sure? You know this? Oh, no! I guess I may have known this."

Beth and Denny simultaneously asked, "You knew?"

"My sister and her husband were hiking in the hills up around Rollinsville. My sister thought she saw Walt drive up in a black SUV and go inside a cabin—a very remote cabin. She saw him from across a gulch. It wasn't real close, but she said it was someone who looked a lot like Walt."

Beth glanced at Denny. "I wonder how long he's been in the area."

Mary Lou rapidly flung a string of questions at Beth. "How do you know it's him? How did you find out? Did you see him?"

Beth looked at Denny. "He contacted Denny last week when Denny was in Houston. I assume Walt followed him there. He demanded that Denny give him money so that he could disappear again."

Mary Lou tried to process the new information. "So Walt contacted Denny and wanted money?" She looked at Beth. "I thought he had money. Didn't you tell me..."

Beth answered, "I guess his partner in crime, Kiral, wasn't as trustworthy as he thought."

Denny added, "He told me that when he went to find Kiral's money, there was nothing there."

Mary Lou sucked in a breath. "Kiral's ransacked apartment! Walt ransacked Kiral's apartment in La Jolla." Her eyes widened. "Did he kill Kiral?"

"Could Walt kill someone?" Beth rubbed her eyes. "I don't know this Walt Pederson. I wonder. Maybe that's why he doesn't want to come out in the open." She looked at Denny. "He lied to you when he said he hadn't broken any laws. I know it sounds awful to accuse him of murder, but I think he could do it."

Mary Lou blanched. "It has all seemed so distant and unreal until now. What shall we do? What are you going to do?"

Beth took a deep breath. "Relax. We're going to come up with a plan. I want Denny to deliver the money Walt demanded. Here's my idea. We continue to act as though Walt is dead. But once we get some evidence on tape, we can press charges for extortion."

Mary Lou's pulse quickened. "You want to catch him in the act."

Beth nodded. "That's why we asked you to come in. You and I have talked about this off and on for months. You've been suspicious, just as I have. Who knows what the man is capable of? He used to listen in on my phone conversations at home. Sometimes that was the most irritating of all his bad habits. Anyway, because you've been dating a police officer, I thought you might have ideas on how we could get this little upcoming meeting on tape, audio, or video."

Mary Lou grimaced. "He's a detective. But Bobby will never go along with anything like this. Especially if we're going to do it without involving the proper authorities."

Beth shook her head. "I am not getting the police involved. I can talk to Walt. I believe we can settle this ourselves."

Mary Lou turned to Denny. "Where are you meeting Walt?"

"He's supposed to let me know this morning."

Later that evening

Mrs. Cunkell answered the door. "Mary Lou, I'm so glad we could do this tonight. Now why was it that you couldn't come on our regular night?"

Mary Lou set her Bible and notebook on the kitchen table. "I had an unexpected event come up."

Mrs. Cunkell sat across from her. "Well, these things happen. Anyway, I am so glad we could have our study tonight. Let's pray before we begin." She bowed her head. "Father in Heaven, we come to You this evening to study Your Word. We ask for Your guidance and direction in this. Please join us here and lead our study tonight. We thank You for this and for Your many blessings. In Jesus' name, Amen."

Mary Lou opened her Bible. "I've been trying to memorize the love chapter, First Corinthians, chapter thirteen. 'If I speak in the tongues of men and of angels, but have not love, I am only a resounding gong or a clanging cymbal. If I have the gift of prophecy and can fathom all mysteries and all knowledge, and if I have a faith that can move mountains, but have not love, I am nothing. If I give all I possess to the poor and surrender my body to the flames, but have not love, I gain nothing.'"

Mrs. Cunkell smiled. "That's wonderful."

Mary Lou held up her hand. "Oh, there's more. I just have to think. 'Love is patient, love is kind. It does not envy, it does not boast, it is not proud. It is not rude, it is not self-seeking...' Wait a minute. 'It is not self-seeking, it is not easily angered, it keeps no record of wrongs.' Oh, there's more."

Mrs. Cunkell waited almost a full minute, then said, "You are doing quite well with the verse memorization. Why did you pick this whole chapter?"

Mary Lou surrendered to the fact that she could get no farther in her recitation. "It's just that we've studied so much about how God loves us. I wanted to have His definition of love in my head and heart. I'm going to get all of it. I just need more time."

"You will get it. Don't rush it. Now let's talk about how God loves us. Turn to the Book of John, chapter fifteen. You see here that John is talking about Jesus being the true vine. He says that God the Father is the gardener that cuts off the branches that do not bear fruit. And the branches that do bear fruit get pruned so they will bear more fruit."

Mary Lou looked in her notes. "Fruit is more than just witnessing and bringing others to Christ. It's about all kinds of things, like serving and comforting other believers, and praying, and more."

Mrs. Cunkell added, "It's how we love our neighbor. The fruit can be how you live out your Christian life."

Mary Lou nodded. "I remember our first lesson about the fruit of the Spirit. It is love, joy, peace, patience, goodness, kindness, gentleness, faithfulness, and self-control. But I want to know more about what true love is all about, from Jesus' perspective."

"Oh, my, yes. We are learning a lot."

Wednesday, October 16
Westminster, Colorado

Bobby sat in his SUV in front of Mrs. Cunkell's apartment. He was early for the Wednesday night Bible study, but he knew Mary Lou would be there as soon as she could leave work.

Bobby felt content. Hurricane was home. Mary Lou had settled into a routine where he could call her a few times a week, and they saw each other on weekends. He had started attending Alma Temple with her. Wednesday evenings were special because, if he wasn't working, he joined Mary Lou and Mrs. Cunkell for Bible Study. Tonight was one of those nights.

He checked the time again. Five fifteen. He opened his cell phone calendar to review his schedule for the next week.

He looked up to see Mrs. Cunkell standing at the front door, motioning for him to come in. He got out of the SUV and walked up to the door. "How are you this evening?"

Mrs. Cunkell stepped back to let him enter. "I'm blessed. Come in."

Bobby went in and sat at the kitchen table. "I guess I'm a little early."

Mrs. Cunkell stood across from him. "We can start now. Mary Lou can't make it tonight. We had a study last night."

Bobby put his Bible on the table. "Did she say why she couldn't make it?"

"No, she just said she had an unexpected event come up. Can I get you some water?"

Bobby stood. "No, thanks. Is it all right if we wait until next week when Mary Lou will join us? I thought she would be here, and I'd really like to study with her here."

Mrs. Cunkell walked him to the door. "It's quite all right. I thought you knew. In fact, I was surprised when I saw you drive up."

"Thanks, Mrs. Cunkell. I'll see you next week."

He strode to his SUV and waved good-bye to Mrs. Cunkell as he drove off. After going a few blocks down the street, he pulled over to the side of the street and dialed Mary Lou.

Mary Lou picked up. "It's really strange that you would call me right now."

Bobby shifted the SUV into park. "I missed you at Bible study. You forgot to tell me that you weren't going to be there. What's going on? Mrs. Cunkell said that you had an unexpected event come up."

From her position, Mary Lou saw Walt walk around the corner of the block and into Beth's backyard. "Oh, no. It's Walt."

Bobby sat straight up. "Are you back on the Walt kick again?"

"No! It's him. I'm looking at him right now. Beth and Denny told me he was going to kill Beth. He's alive, and I am looking at him. He just went in the back door."

"Where are you?"

"I'm at Sandy's house. Beth's next-door neighbor. We're setting up video to catch him in the act of extorting money for Beth's life."

Bobby's voice cracked. "You are what?"

Mary Lou shot back, "We're going to catch him breaking the law, and you can't stop us."

"Where's Beth and Denny?"

Mary Lou looked down on the street. "They're on their way. I can't talk. I gotta go."

Bobby yelled into the dead phone. "Mary Lou, wait for me. Do not let them go in there. Do you hear me?"

En Route to Lakewood, Colorado

Beth adjusted the tiny camera in the brooch on her sweater. "I hope this works. I told James in the audio-visual department that I needed it to record a seminar on flower arranging."

Denny rounded the corner. "The nerve of the man, wanting to meet in our living room. I hope he doesn't freak out when he sees you. He told me to come alone."

Beth polished the camera lens with a tissue. "I should have taken you up on the offer to build a house of our own. At the time, I just couldn't face all the upheaval it would have meant. You were right; it would have been worth it."

Denny patted her knee. "It's not too late. After you divorce Walt, and we get married again, we are certainly going to build our own home."

She grinned in spite of herself. "Divorce? You have been planning ahead. Of course Walt's getting a divorce."

They pulled up in the driveway of their home.

Beth pulled a large satchel from the seat behind Denny. "Here's the decoy. Like we would actually bring money to him."

Denny looked into the camera and spoke into Beth's brooch. "Mary Lou, are you there? Is everything a go?"

From inside Sandy's house next door, Mary Lou answered, "I can hear and I can see everything that's going on. That would be a 'go.' He's inside."

Beth took a deep breath. "Let's do this."

Beth and Denny entered the house. Not a sound came from the living room. Beth stepped into the kitchen. Empty. Denny looked in the family room. Empty.

Beth called out, "Walt, are you here?"

Silence.

Her shoulders relaxed. "Let's check upstairs." She headed up the stairs to their bedroom.

Denny, the satchel still in his hand, followed her. "I want to keep you in sight."

They rounded the corner at the top of the stairs and stepped into the bedroom.

Beth turned to Denny. "Don't worry. Walt's a paper tiger."

She turned back around and found herself face to face with Walt. She struggled for a breath.

Walt bellowed, "I told you to come alone!"

Denny dropped the satchel. "She insisted."

Beth took a step toward Walt. "You're alive."

Walt paused and took a step back. "I'm about to start living again. Where's the money?"

Beth walked toward Walt, and he backed into the master bedroom. "Walt, what are you doing? This makes no sense."

All three of them were standing in the bedroom.

Walt backed up to the windows. He sneered at Beth. "You couldn't stay away. He told you, and you had to see for yourself. I hope you're happy."

"Happy? How could I be happy when you faked your death? I'm concerned. I'm not happy about this." Nervous tears began to fall. *This is the man I was married to for twenty-four years, yet I have no idea who he is. He's gone mad.*

Walt screamed, "*I hate* that. Stop crying, *now.*" He pulled a pistol from behind him. "You just couldn't give it up. Now you have to pay."

Beth's tears evaporated. She stared at the gun pointing at her. "I—I don't know what you're talking about."

He turned and pointed the gun at Denny while still talking to Beth. "You had to have the body exhumed. I'm sure they found the poison. Why do you think I had to disappear?"

Beth's brow wrinkled. "Body? What. Are. You. Talking. About? There was no body. Here you are in front of me. You're standing right here in front of me. What poison? They found what? You did what? I don't understand."

Walt turned the gun back to her. "Don't play games with me. I heard all about your plan. You should be more careful what you talk about with Uncle Ralph on the phone. I just happened to pick up the extension, and *I heard* you say they were going to dig your father up."

Beth's hand went to her paling face. She whispered, "I never said such a thing." Her mind raced. *Is Walt talking about Father? He thinks I had Father dug up, but why would I?*

Walt kept the gun fixed on her and rambled, "The old boy had more money than he knew what to do with, and I knew you'd get all of it. I knew that the day I proposed to you. I figured he'd die soon after the wedding because of all the stress, and he wasn't feeling too well. But the old guy just kept getting better."

Beth mumbled, "I never said that."

Walt shouted, "It doesn't matter who said it. Okay, it was Ralph, then. He said they were exhuming the body, and you would finally know the truth. Now you know, and look what's it's got you. Ten years later, and you just couldn't let it go. You had to dig him up. When did you first suspect?"

She wracked her brain, trying to figure out what he was talking about. Then she remembered a conversation with Ralph that had happened a few days before she and Walt left for the cruise, about an episode of *On the Horizon*.

She sucked in the air as she replayed the conversation in her mind. *Uncle Ralph said they were finally going to exhume the body and soon we would finally know the truth. He'd waited for months to see if the villain had poisoned the hero's father-in-law. Oh, Walt, what have you done?* She kept silent for fear that the madman in front of her would shoot.

Walt knew the truth about a fictional character in a soap opera? I don't get it. And because of that conversation, Walt left. Why would he care? Has he gone mad?

Walt shook the gun at her and shouted, "I said, when did you first suspect? Was it ten years ago? Was it right after it happened?"

This can't be happening. Because Walt overheard the conversation with Ralph. He faked his fatal accident. Oh, dear Lord. He…he's all but confessed to killing Father. Beth blinked as the pieces of the puzzle began falling into place. Her love for her deceased father rose up from someplace deep within her soul. "How could you? He gave you everything you ever asked for. How could you?"

"He gave me crumbs. I knew you'd be more generous." He sneered and stepped toward her.

Walt pointed the gun at Denny. "Get that satchel. I said, get it, *now*. And no funny stuff, or I'll kill her." He pointed the gun back at Beth.

Denny picked up the satchel he had dropped. He held it out to Walt. "Here's the money. Now you can go."

Walt motioned for Denny to place it on the floor between them. "Nobody tells me when it's time to go. I'll decide when I'm finished here." The gun was still on Denny.

Beth asked, "How?"

Walt turned the gun toward her. "What do you mean, how?"

"How did you kill Father?"

Walt laughed. "It was all so simple, in fact, it was you who killed him."

Beth gasped. "I did not kill my father. He died of a heart attack."

Walt's eyes narrowed. "That's exactly what I wanted everyone to think, and I got away with it for ten years. I put poison in the glass of milk you were warming up to take him before he went to sleep. You always took him a glass of warm milk at bedtime."

The same time, next door

Mary Lou shouted at Sandy, "Take this—you watch and record. I have to get over there before someone gets killed."

Sandy grabbed her arm. "Don't go! He'll kill you."

Mary Lou shook her off. "What else can I do? I can't just sit here. I'll call Bobby."

He answered on the first ring. "Do not do anything, Mary Lou. Don't let Beth and Denny go in the house. Help is coming. You can't do this on your own."

"It's too late. We're in trouble. Walt has a gun and is threatening Beth and Denny. I'm going over there."

Bobby stomped on the accelerator. "Stay where you are. I'm almost there. Where are they?"

"They're upstairs in the master bedroom. Sorry, Bobby. I'm going over there right now." Mary Lou walked out the door and crossed the lawn to enter Beth's house.

Bobby shouted, "No! Stop!"

Mary Lou pushed the door open and stepped in. "I'm here. I'm leaving my cell on. It's going in my pocket now." She dropped the phone in her shirt pocket.

Bobby screamed. "Mary Lou, don't! Mary Lou!"

The same time, at Beth's house

Beth's mind raced through the events of the night before her father had died. "Walt, you didn't kill Father."

"Yeah, I know, you think he died of a heart attack. He didn't. I poisoned him. Didn't you get the coroner's report?"

Beth shook her head. "There's no coroner's report. It's not necessary. I remember the night before Father died."

"Then you remember me being in the kitchen when you came to get the milk."

Beth held up her hand.

He shook the gun at her. "No sudden moves."

In a calm voice, Beth related her memories of that night. "Yes, I remember you were there. Then you went into the den to watch TV. I took the milk to Father. When I got to the top of the stairs, I tripped, and the entire glass of milk ended up on the carpet. I was going to get another glass, but when I peeked in, Father was already asleep."

Denny said, "You see, all of this is for nothing. There's been no murder."

Walt pointed the gun at Denny. "She's lying. I don't believe a word of it."

Beth took a step toward Walt. "It's the truth."

Mary Lou walked into the room, startling Walt. "Stop! Stop it, immediately! The police are on the way!"

The second Walt's attention focused on Mary Lou, Denny dove toward Walt. He got hold of Walt's hand holding the gun. A short but fierce battle ensued, both men dropping to the floor.

Seconds later, Denny jumped up, gun in hand. He pointed at Walt. "Get up."

Walt stood. He glared at Mary Lou. "Well, if it isn't our little troublemaker. I should have known you'd be snooping around."

Beth said, "It's over, Walt."

Walt cursed. "You liar. You made it up."

Denny racked a bullet into the chamber. "That's the last time you're going to talk to her like that."

Walt swore and lunged at Denny. Denny squeezed the trigger.

Light flashed. The bullet left the chamber.

Mary Lou stuck her hand out. "No-o-o." She leapt in front of Walt.

The explosion rocked the room.

Bobby Porter burst through the door, followed by three officers, all with guns drawn. He rushed toward Mary Lou on the floor, blood gushing from her chest.

He dropped to his knees. "Mary Lou. Get an ambulance!" He put his arm under her shoulders. Someone thrust a towel onto her chest. Bobby pressed it into the wound. "Mary Lou, can you hear me?"

The color had drained from her face. She forced a wobbly half smile. "I knew you'd come."

He leaned down and kissed her forehead. "Mary Lou, I love you. Don't go. Stay awake. Help is coming."

Mary Lou choked. "Greater love has no man..." Her voice weakened. "Than to lay his life down for... Good-bye, Bobby."

He felt her body go limp.

CPSIA information can be obtained
at www.ICGtesting.com
Printed in the USA
FSOW01n0037100215
5083FS